From Far And Wide

Telma Rocha

WordTree Publishing

Word Tree Publishing

This is a work of fiction. Names, characters, and incidents are products of the author's creative imagination or are used fictitiously and are not to be construed as real. Any resemblance to actual events, or persons, living or dead, is entirely coincidental.

First Edition

ISBN: 978-1-9990667-4-1

ISBN: 978-1-9990667-1-0 (ebook)

DEDICATION

To Terry,

For showing me the world through a unique perspective—
one I wouldn't have found on my own.

BOOKS BY TELMA ROCHA

The Angolan Girl

From Far And Wide

SUMMER

Present Day

CHAPTER 1

I'm Nowhere, I'm Everywhere

Adam

THEY CAN'T SEE, hear or touch me, but that doesn't mean I'm not real.

I'm nowhere.

I'm everywhere.

Standing over them as they restlessly fight sleep is how I spend my nights, how I find peace in this lost world. Only it's not the world that's lost, but rather…me. What am I still doing here? Misplaced, floating in this abyss. They need me. That's why I exist. My presence brings comfort, a sense of peace and familiarity to them; they are broken without me, and I must be the one to make them whole again. It can be only me who sets them free.

Sometimes throughout the day she stops, my mother does, and turns to where I stand. I hold my breath even though I can't breathe.

She lowers her gaze and walks away, and that's when I know my secret is still safe.

I don't always hang around aimlessly and watch them all day, sometimes I explore, learn new routes to undiscovered places. My most peaceful spot of all is on the lush, vibrant, Manitoulin Island, up high on the cliff of the Cup and Saucer Trail. This outlook overhang is one thousand, one hundred and fifty-five feet high, with a second cliff nestled a bit lower—also providing a resting stop for escape. The higher of the two outlooks is also the highest point on the island. Many tourists hike this two-kilometre trail each year and make their way to the ridges.

I stand here today on the edge of the peaked rock formation, arms outstretched wide to my sides, face held to the sky allowing the cool breeze a chance to penetrate my skin, only it never makes its way through; feeling is not a part of my senses, that ability died with me a long time ago—five years to be exact.

Beyond me there is nothing, but I see everything: water, trees, shrubs, true beauty to the eye. When I'm bored, I let myself fall off the cliff, spreading my arms out wide, like a free bird gliding, waiting to collide with the Earth: but that mishap never happens. Crashing seems impossible.

When I'm needed by them, I fly—this is how I get to each of them quickly. When they silently call for me, I'm always there, but they don't know it's me who comes to their rescue. They don't even have to speak my name for me to realize they need me. All they need to do is think of me, and I'm there: a flash lost in time.

With me close, they relax. It's as if I never left them to begin with, but I did leave, although leaving them wasn't my fault or choice. One minute someone is there, until they are gone, and that's how I came to no longer be.

Now, I sit in a small wooden chair in my mother's classroom at the school where she works, as she imagines me next to her and packs her things. It's the end of the school year, and I know she needs me more than ever, so here I sit, watching her grieve for me and for the life she once had—a life that's no more.

Dear Adam,

Why is it that when I'm deep in despair or even just lonely, all I have to do is think of you, and somehow, I'm instantly put at ease? It's as if you can hear me silently calling out your name while I wait for you to call back out to me, but you never do my son, you never do—waiting is something I've grown used to.

Love, Dad

CHAPTER 2

Far Away

Clairah

EVERYONE LOSES SOMEONE dear to them at some point in their life. Some lose a well-loved pet due to a speeding driver, some a parent due to old age, or a sibling due to a chronic disease. In my case, it's my son whom I lost. I think of him now, early this morning, as I pack the remainder of my belongings and take one last look around at my almost-empty, chilly classroom. This school has become my second home and the children, my students, are my extended family. Adam used to be part of my family until five years ago, when he lost his life. I don't often admit that he is no longer here, but today that realization punches me hard in the stomach, knocking my breath far away and allowing it to be seen through the chill in the air of a June morning.

Since my divorce from John three years ago, I gave myself to my job and classroom. Of course, I still have a family, but it's not the same one anymore, not since Adam died: that family, the one that I used to have, is now cut in half, literally. Defeat takes over, I don't have much energy for anything today, so I procrastinate and take much longer than I need and should, pulling my sweater around me tighter; I check the thermostat; twenty-one degrees Celsius, room temperature, so I shouldn't be this cold. Today's task should be quick and simple, pack my last remaining items and leave, but my legs are like jelly, making me afraid I'll collapse to the ground. School ended yesterday, but I couldn't bring myself to complete the packing then, needing one more day to say goodbye, so here I am again this morning. I should leave, this I know, but I'm afraid of myself—and of the loneliness that takes a hold of me and refuses to let go. My classroom fills my empty days and brings me some sense of purpose, without it, I'm lost, alone, and afraid. Summertime is the hardest time of year for me because it's when I lose not only my extended family, my students and my classroom, but I also lose my daughter. Ameleiah travels to Manitoulin Island to spend her summer with her father, my ex-husband, John. Ameleiah is thirteen-years-old, and she has a strong mind of her own, so even if I forbade her from going, she would disobey me and go anyway. She doesn't usually listen to what I have to say these days, often in her own world consisting of her phone and wireless earbuds. I blame John for everything that has happened to me, to us; I blamed him then, and still do today for leaving us when we needed him the most. And I blame him for Adam's death, but it wouldn't be fair of me to keep her from her father, the two are close, and have become even closer since Adam died. Adam's death tore me and Ameleiah apart, but it brought her and her father closer together, how is that fair to me? Why do I get the brunt of her sorrow now? I'm the innocent one here, aren't I?

My boxes are almost full, I have all my books, gifts from students, and student work I want to keep packed safely away and I'm ready to leave, but instead I sit. Sometimes Adam's presence is so strong, like now, and I swear I can feel him near, although I know this isn't possible.

Even though there is a strong sensation I ignore coming from my left, afraid to know what it is, I avoid looking in that direction.

A knock on the door interrupts my thoughts, "Miss Clairah, I didn't realize you were still here," says Jeremy, the school's old janitor, doing his daily runs. He always calls me Miss Clairah, instead of by my last name, Bennet, even though he's much older than I am.

I pull my sleeves down further to cover the shivers on my arms. "Jeremy, yes, I'm almost done; I'll lock up the classroom on my way out."

"Very well then, see you in the fall. Have a great summer." He walks away, hesitates and turns back around, "Take care of yourself Miss Clairah," he says, tipping his head.

A great summer, he said, but that's something I haven't had in five years. The cold sensation I felt a moment ago still lingers around me. I turn to look around at the empty classroom, pick up my boxes, walk to the door, and as my hand hovers over the light switch, I glance to where I sat moments ago. "Adam, is that you?" I ask into the empty room. Silence greets me.

I know I'm losing my mind. These sudden cold waves that sweep through a room—that's not Adam. Adam can't be here: he hasn't been here for five years. As my fingers finally connect with the light switch and the classroom darkens, I swear there's a silhouette at the desk to the left of where I sat only moments ago. I shake my head vigorously and make a mental note to book another appointment with my therapist; it's time to increase my dose of the daily anxiety pills I take. During the drive home, I flip through radio stations searching for a distraction from my own mind. Not wanting to hear music and not wanting to hear any news either, I shut it off and drive in silence, wrapped in my thoughts.

"Ameleiah, I'm home, sorry I'm late," I say, as I put my handbag down in the hallway of our three-bedroom, two-story, brown brick house. Our house used to be a home, but now it's no more than a lonely structure, and even when we're both here, it's still empty. Ameleiah doesn't talk much, at least not to me, but she has endless conversations on her phone with her friends and even her father, so it's only me who has the pleasure of receiving her silent treatment. I blame her father for leaving us. It was his choice, his doing, but she blames me, still, for his absence so this constant battle about who is right haunts us, like Adam's past.

"Ameleiah, we have to go if you want to catch the last ferry."

I peek into every room, searching for her, but I find each one empty. I walk outside to our backyard, and there she sits on her favourite blue-striped lounge chair with her earbuds in, so she can't hear me—my words lost in the wind. I often wonder if she has those white things stuck in her ears to avoid listing to me, or if she truly loves to listen to music that much and that loud.

"Ameleiah!" I say louder this time while tapping her on the shoulder.

She turns and pulls out her right earbud before responding, "Did you say something?"

"Are you packed and ready?"

"Yes."

I wait for more, but she offers nothing else. "Where are your bags?"

"In my room. I just have to put them in the trunk."

I hadn't noticed her bags amongst all the clothes tossed around in there and the unmade bed.

"You're late by the way." She rolls her eyes and peeks at her phone.

"I know, I'm sorry, I got tied up at the school."

"Really? How convenient is that!"

"What do you mean?" I ask tilting my head to the side. This is more conversation than we've had in a long time.

"There were no students there to keep you from coming home on time."

I ignore her last comment, knowing she's right. "Let's go, the last ferry leaves at seven thirty, and we still have a three-and-a-half-hour drive; you need to be there at least an hour beforehand."

"Yes, Mom, I know the drill, this isn't my first time taking the ferry you know. Or have you forgotten?" She rolls her eyes again. In the past,

I counted the number of times that my daughter rolled her eyes at me in a day, but that just dampened my mood even more, so now, I pretend she has something caught in her eye—lying to myself about my reality makes it a little easier to accept.

"Then what are you still doing sitting out here listing to music, or whatever else it is that you listen to with those things stuck inside your ears? What you're listing to shouldn't even classify as music with all the swearing."

She rolls her eyes for the third time during this brief conversation—but I'm not counting. And then she gets up.

"'Those things', as you put it, are called wireless earbuds." She stomps off towards her room, slamming the backyard door behind her.

It hasn't always been this difficult between the two of us, we used to be close, once upon a time when I had my entire family, alive, well, and under one roof. Even after Adam died, at first we were still close. She clung to me when she needed protection and reassurance about life, often questioning when she saw a still bird or any other animal, if it was dead or alive—she expected all still things to no longer be living. But when her father left us, his leaving drilled a wedge between us, and one so sharp that it's still splitting us in two, even years later. Not wanting to go back in the house and face her, I stroll around the side yard to the front and turn on the car to make sure there's enough gas as I forgot to check on my way home, my mind preoccupied on other things. I bring in the last box that was in the trunk and set it down in the foyer, not daring to go in any further, then head back out. I remain in the car, sitting and waiting for Ameleiah to bring her bags out so that I can begin my long and lonely summer.

My neighbour, Jim, pops his head out of his sliding door, "Morning dear," he yells to me, coffee in hand.

"Morning Jim," I respond, both of us leaving out the word 'Good'.

I try to push away thoughts that soon I'll be alone again, I'm always alone, fighting the inevitable—it's me against myself.

CHAPTER 3

The Least Broken of Them All

Adam

MY SISTER, AMELEIAH, is the least broken of them all. We were close, her and I. I'm younger than her by two years; I'm eleven, that is, if you can give a spirit an age as I was six years old when I died, and Mia—that's what I often called her—was eight. Each of my family members grieves in their own way: Mia turns bitter, distancing herself from our mother and hiding behind a veil when they're together. My mother wallows in her own self-pity, giving up on herself and the world. My father is probably the most normal—to the outside world, at least. But inside he, too, has deep struggles. He copes by keeping himself busy doing the things he loves most: working at the marina, fixing sailboats on the island, journaling. Since my death, my father's journal entries have become daily letters addressed to me. Dad has always wanted to be a writer, so he felt that journaling gave him some practice, a step towards this ultimate goal. Although he still loves sailboats, he hasn't sailed since my death—he now only fixes them. Solving other's problems, but not his own. He used to love to ride motorcycles, but that, too, is something he stopped doing years ago; right after my death he sold the motorcycle and I'll never forget that day because he truly loved his Yamaha. "It's a fun toy," he'd often say every time he got suited up in his safety gear to go for a ride.

My entire family has always loved the freedom the island offers; we used to spend our summers there together as a family every year. Mom used to love it then, she'd get all excited about a month before, and start packing way too early; she'd even pack things that we still needed for everyday life, only to find that she had to unpack them again. Dad used to say she was worse than us kids when it came to summer vacations. She was over the moon on the island, often taking off her shoes and socks to dip her toes in the water, no matter how bone-chillingly cold it was. That was always a special moment for her, dipping her toes was a mark that she had truly been there; this was her signature move. Like a cat rubs against a human to mark his or her territory, my mother connects with the water.

I watch my sister in her room gathering her bags, still listening to her earbuds so she doesn't have to listen to our mother complain or give her a hard time anymore. She walks straight through me, stops, turns, and continues on her way out to the car. I follow closely behind, maybe too close, only she doesn't know I'm here. Once we're at the car, she jams her bags into the trunk of the white Civic and slams it shut, hastily turns and crashes into our mother.

"Can you take those earbuds out for just a second?" asks Mom, rubbing the shoulder that Mia slammed into.

Mia rolls her eyes for the fourth time since our mother got home, hesitates, but pulls them both off. "There, are you happy now?" she says to our mother and stomps away, a frown covering her pimple-free, oval-shaped face.

Poor Mom brings her shoulders up to her ears, sighs, gets into the car, and slams the door. Mia opens the back driver-side door and places more bags in the backseat, the ones that didn't fit in the trunk, so I scoot in before she slams the door on my face. Not that it would matter anyway, I could just go in with the door closed, but sometimes even I forget what my abilities are. Neither of them speaks for the longest time, the silence is so thick it could choke someone to death, and even when they do speak the words are superficial, cold, forced.

"Are you sure you're not forgetting anything?" asks Mom.

"Nope, I got it all."

"Your phone charger?"

"Got it."

"Your anxiety medication?"

"Right here," says my sister, as she taps her purse next to her.

My mother decided about a year ago to also have Mia put on anxiety medication, to help her cope with life a little easier. She's not on a standing dose like Mom, just a PRN, which means that she takes it as needed when she feels a panic attack coming on.

"All right, I guess you've thought of everything and you don't need me." Mom looks straight ahead, hands gripping the steering wheel tight on ten and two.

Again, more silence. My throat tightens. Is it possible for a spirit to choke?

A few hundred kilometres away, on Manitoulin Island, my father sits on a rock, looking like one himself, stiff, unmoving; he's down by the marina where he works. He looks up after minutes of staring out across the water, then reaches into his back pocket for his small notebook and pulls out the pen he carries behind his ear; while a water snake slithers around the rocks, Dad composes his daily journal entry. My father's journals are mostly deeply personal letters addressed to me; he thinks I can't read them, but I can, and I do—always.

Dear Adam,

Guilt is dangerous, a self-inflicting feeling; it entices us to do things that we normally wouldn't do—forces us to go through each day plagued by horror—time standing still. It's been a few years since you've been gone but each new day brings on its own set of challenges, and relief still waits to surface in a world so thick with darkness that it has a hard time breaking through the barriers. One day my son, one day relief will come, that day is just not today. That day, the day you died, I should have listened to your mother—I shouldn't have been so stubborn.

Love, Dad

CHAPTER 4

Tobermory

Clairah

I WISH AMELEIAH WOULDN'T shut me out, but she does every day, this is her thing, it's what she's used to doing—it's how she copes. During the drive, I give her the space I think she needs and listen to the radio instead of trying to gain her attention. We left our small, cute town of Paris about an hour ago, so we still have another two-and-a-half-hour drive before we arrive in Tobermory. I love the simplicity and pretty town of Paris, the small hometown feels, the quaint downtown where the independent bookstore is, Green Heron Books, where I go to buy my books both new and used, the library that fills many readers' hearts and minds with stories. Stillwaters restaurant, overlooking the Grand River is magical in the summertime, it's situated in the core of downtown and up on the rooftop patio, the space is brightened with lights all around the tables and railing overlooking the Grand River. Paris is home to me; it always has been home. I used to love going for walks downtown through Lion's Park to see the Nith River, on the trails alongside the river that bend and turn to create a picturesque lazy susan landscape. Many cyclists can be found on any given day out riding, and dog lovers often bring their pets down for some exercise.

Standing on the bridge at the end of the path, you feel you are far away, up north somewhere remote, isolated, and certainly not in the little town of Paris. But these are not things that I enjoy anymore, so many memories linger there, memories I prefer to forget, try hard to keep out of my mind.

An old song of ours, John's and mine, plays on the radio, Purple Rain by Prince, and it takes my breath away, so I change the station with shaky hands—hardly able to turn the dial. Whenever that song came on the radio, the one we used to listen to while doing dishes and cleaning the house back when we were together, John would stop whatever it was he was doing and take me into his arms and twirl me around the kitchen, like school-aged lovers, if I concentrate hard enough, the softness of his hand around my waist is still so strong, so present.

Ameleiah's horrible rap music seeps through from her earbuds and contains more vulgar language than a normal vocabulary, I can hear the swearing clearly—that's how loud she has the volume turned up. I want to tell her to turn it down or she will destroy her hearing, and I open my mouth to speak, but decide there is no point in speaking words that no one will listen to. So instead, I keep flipping the stations until I come across a song that has no memory of Adam or John—I stop when the dial reaches a country song I don't know. Country music, that should do it, I decide. My family never listened to country music before, so it's a safe zone. For the remainder of the drive, I try to drown out the horrible lyrics blaring through my daughter's earbuds.

As we drive into the cute and touristy town of Tobermory, I give Ameleiah a nudge with my elbow so that she can take her earbuds out and listen to what I have to say. I hate having to constantly repeat myself to her, but a broken record hasn't got anything on me.

"What?" she says, as she pulls out one earbud, leaving the other in for security against me.

"Are you hungry?"

"Nope."

"Well I'm hungry, so do you mind if we stop for a burger? I rather not eat alone today."

"Yes, I mind. I have a ferry to catch."

"I know, but we have time still," I say, pointing to the display on the dashboard.

"Whatever," she says, putting the earbud back to avoid having to listen to me any longer.

She turns her head to look out her window, avoiding my gaze. Although I come here at least once, if not twice, a year to drop off Ameleiah, I can't help but remember the Tobermory from five years ago, when we were all here together for the last time. The town looks the same as it did then. The main square surrounding the docks is home to a few more stores than I remember, but otherwise it's the same tranquil harbour village located on the Bruce Peninsula that lives in my memory. Many adventurists visit Tobermory each year to experience its vastness in beauty and adventure. Tobermory is home to the Grotto, a small serene cave-like escape where many visitors dive into the cool green and blue waters in the summertime. It's also home to Flowerpot Island where you can visit the many well-preserved dive sites of shipwrecks; Fathom Five National Marine Park has twenty-two shipwrecks alone. The Bruce Trail footpath is where many hikers walk and run to become one with nature—sweating out their stress. Tobermory is known for being a freshwater scuba diving capital of the world. Located two hundred and fifty-four kilometres north of Toronto, Tobermory has three thousand, eight hundred and fifty residents living here year-round and covers and area of seven hundred and eighty-two square kilometres.

I find a place to park near one of the restaurants I know I used to like, Leeside Restaurant. Nothing fancy, but they make a juicy burger, or at least they used to. I'm not really hungry, I told my daughter I was as an excuse to extend the time I have left with her. I hardly eat these days, but I want to buy time with Ameleiah because each summer when she leaves me, I lose another piece of her, permanently. One more hour might be what I need to win Ameleiah over, to make her like me again; although I know this is wishful thinking.

I have lost so much weight in the last few years, and I can't put it back on as hard as I try. I was never big to begin with, I weighed one hundred and thirty pounds before the divorce, but since then, I lost twenty of them. Leaving my five foot four inch frame too slim and unhealthy with sunken eyes and brittle hair and nails. But who cares anyway, appearances don't mean anything—not to me anymore—not when there's no one to impress or dress up for.

We sit in deep silence again, my daughter and I, still in the car, and I don't know how to break the sour mood. I'm afraid to speak, afraid to say the wrong words to her, she's so sensitive around me these days so I tread lightly. Ameleiah keeps looking at her phone, she brings the screen to life for a few seconds at a time, checking in on the world, her Instagram account, her Snapchat app, anything to avoid me. How devastating it must be for her to not want to spend another dreadful minute with her own mother.

"Why do you keep looking at your phone?"

"I'm checking to see if it's time to leave."

She thinks I'm no fun anymore, maybe I'm not, but I could be if she let me into her world again; I used to be fun, before….

"Let's go." I finally say, having had enough of silence, and climb out of the car. We walk far apart to the restaurant I decided on, and to any stranger who watches us we, too, would be strangers to one another, unknown to each other; because she walks five feet behind me, pretending she doesn't know me.

Even when we arrive at the restaurant, the hostess says, "Table for one?" because Ameleiah won't stand close enough to me to suggest we are here together. I point to Ameleiah while correcting the hostess on the number of my party—my daughter frowns and retreats back even further towards the front door.

We're seated close to a window, and I take the seat that faces the outside so that I have a distraction, something to look at other than her frown. Within minutes of being seated, a young male waiter, looking to be no more than nineteen, approaches our table.

"What can I get you two lovely ladies to drink?" says the waiter, and he waits, ready to write down our orders; I ask for water with a lemon slice for myself and Ameleiah orders a Diet Coke. He says he'll return in a few moments with our drinks and to take our food orders, so I use this opportunity to convince my daughter to at least look through the menu that she's been ignoring.

"What are you eating?" I ask.

Without putting down her phone, she answers, "You dragged me here, and I'm here. But you can't force me to eat when I'm not even hungry. That decision should at least be mine."

I drop the subject of food, and when she refuses to even pick up the menu, I decide I'm not eating either. Two stubborn mules we are, her and I. Like mother, like daughter.

The waiter returns minutes later, "Here we are, one ice water with lemon and one Diet Coke," says the waiter, setting our drinks down in front of us. "Are you ready to order, or do you need a few more minutes to look through the menu?" He looks from me to my daughter, lingering a little too long on my daughter's face.

"We're not hungry after all," I say, closing the menu and pushing it towards him. "The drinks will be all for today."

I pay the insignificant bill of two dollars and fifty-five cents, and due to guilt for not having ordered food, I give the waiter an extra large tip of five dollars, more than the bill itself. His face brightens when he looks at the printed receipt from the debit machine. Well, at least I can make a stranger smile, if not my own daughter. As I sit at the table playing with the strap of my purse, I contemplate what to do next as we still have time to kill before Ameleiah needs to be on the ferry. "Okay, let's go," I decide to say on a whim, as I pick up my purse from the chair next to me, the strap dangling through my fingers.

"Finally," she says, loudly, and almost runs out the door, leaving me to walk through the restaurant alone, again.

We walk back to the car more than five feet apart from one another. Ameleiah's bags are still in there so we have to get them before she boards the boat. She is staying the entire summer on Manitoulin Island, so she does need quite a bit of stuff, but not as much as she's bringing. She has a full-sized suitcase, a smaller carry-on-sized suitcase, two backpacks, and a large purse. Certainly, this must be more than she needs for one summer, but who am I to argue over what a thirteen-year-old girl needs for eight weeks? I'm only her mother after all—to her, I don't know anything. I hand the carry-on bag to her, and I take the larger suitcase along with one of the backpacks. Although she brings the entire closet with her, I'm still confident she'll return at the end of summer with more than what I dropped her off with; she always does.

As we fumble with the luggage, her face softens and for the first time today, she begins a conversation I don't care to have. It's about a woman she met on her last visit to the island, Michelle. Michelle, apparently, is her father's new, younger, blond girlfriend, and Ameleiah met her last time she was there visiting on Victoria Day weekend back in May. When she returned home from that weekend away, Ameleiah had not stopped talking about Michelle the first few weeks back, saying things like, "Michelle is the prettiest," and, "Michelle and I went shopping." I had to force myself to listen; this was, after all, the only time my daughter really seemed to talk to me. Now she mentions how she's looking forward to going shopping with Michelle once again. That's all she says, but it's enough. And I already don't like this Michelle. And I know that's not fair as I haven't met the woman, but it's simply because my daughter likes her more than she likes me, her own mother, or though it seems. While my daughter trails behind me again, no longer speaking to me, we walk through the parking lot where cars and motorcycles wait to board the Chi-Cheemaun ferry. The ferry is already here, and so we walk up to the attendant booth to register.

"Name?" says the oversized male attendant wearing a long sleeve green plaid shirt; he barely fits inside the small booth. They really need to make these things bigger to accommodate everyone.

"Ameleiah Bennet." I announce for her, pointing to her to let him know she's the passenger and not me.

The man tells my daughter to proceed to where the others are waiting, barely being able to point due to the tight space in the booth. The ferry is a large, full service passenger and commercial vehicle ferry. There are many amenities on board, such as: gift shops, dining, and a licensed lounge for those interested in a glass of wine while enjoying the views of the passage. I'm sure Ameleiah will find herself a corner and sink onto a bench, sipping Diet Coke while listing to her vulgar rap music for the entire two-hour cruise.

My palms are sweaty, time is ticking by fast; I can't help myself, so I reach out and push back a strand of her loose hair. "Are you nervous, you know, considering…?"

She knocks my hand away. "Considering what, Mom? This isn't the first time I've ridden on this ferry alone."

"I know, but…"

"No, I'm not nervous," she says, as she stares out onto the water, gripping her bags tight. I can tell from the way her knuckles look hardened and red that she's antsy. Several rows of Harley Davidson motorcycles are lined up waiting to get on the boat, and this makes me think of him, my ex-husband. Pedestrians wait off to the side, where small children complain to their parents that the waiting is taking a long time. We're at the point where I can't go any further as I don't have a ticket, so I force myself to say goodbye here and now.

"Here, it's time," I say, handing her the bags I still have. She pulls the second backpack over her shoulder. "Have you texted your father to confirm he remembers you're arriving today?"

"Of course, he remembers. That's so typical of you, Mom, to assume he would forget me. Why would you think he wouldn't come for me?"

"I didn't mean that he…"

She interrupts me mid-point. "Sure, it's not what you meant…."

"It really isn't," I counter.

"I have to go Mom."

I take a deep breath and close my eyes for a second. "Okay, I know. Here take one in each hand," I say, pointing to the two suitcases in front of me. "This is a lot of luggage, I hope you can manage by yourself."

"I manage every year without you," she reminds me, and she's right, she does manage.

"Yes, you do. Well, be safe and call me when you arrive and are with your father, okay?"

"Yup," she says, as she walks away, a backpack slung over each shoulder, purse dangling from her elbow, and each hand holding onto a suitcase with wheels. She doesn't respond when I yell to her backside that I love her, and she doesn't turn to look at me either. I eagerly call out to her once more, her name shaky as it leaves my lips.

"What?" she says, with a raised and irritated voice, still not turning around.

I quickly think of something to say, something that won't annoy her, I search for different words other than the ones I want to say. "Do you have your meds?"

"Grrr," she grunts and stomps away, not answering my question.

I close my eyes and leave them shut for a few extra seconds, then I reach into my pocket for my phone and dial my ex-husband, John. We don't often communicate, only when necessary, if Ameleiah is sick, or when I drop her off at the ferry at the beginning of summers like now.

"Clair," he answers out of breath. "Is everything okay?

He must still have me listed as a contact as he knows it's me calling. He's the only one who calls me Clair, sometimes he shortens my name even more and calls me just C, or at least he used to—before…

"Hey John, everything is fine, I'm just calling to let you know Ameleiah is boarding the ferry now."

"Yup, she sent a text message about five minutes ago. I'll be heading out to get her in about an hour."

"What?" I adjust the phone so it's closer to my ear to make sure I'm hearing him correctly. "You mean…you haven't left yet?"

"No, not yet," he says, breathing a bit more evenly. He must have been running earlier.

"Don't you think that your cutting it a little too close?"

"Cutting what close?"

"Our daughter's pickup," I say a little loudly.

"Clair," he says, but I don't give him the opportunity to continue.

"I mean, Gore Bay is at least an hour from South Baymouth." I say, with even more annoyance in my voice.

"The ferry ride is two hours, so what's your point?"

I breathe away from the phone, so he can't hear the panic. "I'm only saying that if you hit traffic…" I can't continue because he interrupts me.

"I know a short cut; I'll get there in forty-five minutes. Relax."

"Don't you think it would have been wiser to just have left a bit earlier?"

"Really Clair, sometimes I think you call me just to give me a hard time." His voice is ice cold, his words clipped.

I consider my next words, "I don't mean to give you grief," I say honestly, regretting the last few words spoken. I head towards my car as we continue this heated discussion, this disagreement. "I just worry a lot about her is all, surely you can understand that?" I wait for him to respond but there's silence on the other end of the phone, so I continue. "I don't mean to give you a hard time, really I don't. Just be there and on time and call or text me when you have her." I hang up without saying goodbye and without giving him the opportunity to convince me that he was right, and that I overreacted—there's still plenty of time.

Speaking to John always makes my blood boil and brings my

anxiety full force to the surface. He's such a last minute type of person, never plans for anything and takes many chances. This used to be a major issue in our relationship when we were married, and it still is today in our dealings, and precisely what has brought us to this point. He took a chance with Adam then, too, and look where that got us. The past really has nothing to do with the situation at hand, but to me, it has everything to do with it.

I'm sitting in my car with my head resting against the steering wheel when a white bearded older man knocks on my driver-side window. I push the button on the car door to roll down the window an inch. "Can I help you sir?"

"Hey, Miss, you going to sit in the car all day?"

I pull my head back slightly caught off guard by his question. "I don't understand why you're asking me this."

The stranger lifts both arms into the air, pointing both of them toward the full parking lot. "Well, in case you haven't noticed, Miss, the parking lot is full, and parking is limited around here."

"Seriously? You want my parking spot? That's why you're knocking on my window?"

The man's eyes flinch. "What else would I be knocking on your window for?"

"You have some nerve!"

"Pardon me?" He leans into my window slightly as if he misheard what I said.

"It's not my problem the parking lot is full. Geez, you really do have some nerve, don't you?" I say, staring at him through the tiny opening in my window.

He backs up a bit, lifts both hands, palms facing me. "Take it easy lady, I don't want any trouble, just your spot, that's all I want, and I was just wondering if you were leaving soon is all."

"Well, no, I'm not leaving. In fact, I'm here for the night." I say, as the window rolls back up. After turning off the ignition, I grab my handbag and head back to the same restaurant Ameleiah and I were at earlier; I'm hungry, suddenly. Hunger runs through my veins like an addict yearns for their next high. The same young waiter as before serves me again and smiles when recognition sets in. He probably expects another large tip.

"You're back. That didn't take long. Do you need a menu this time, or are you sticking to lemon water again?" He winks at me, looks around the table and glances to the front door. Realizing I'm alone this time, his smile fades.

"Bring me a double gin and tonic, a cheeseburger and fries."

"A lady who knows what she wants," he says, then adds, "got it!" He walks away with my order committed to memory.

If only it were that easy to know what I really want. Do I know what I want? I thought I knew what I wanted, but these days, I'm not so sure anymore. After a few gin and tonics, and only eating half the burger and not touching the fries, I realize I'm in no shape to drive home. It's getting late now, and I've since received a text from my daughter telling me that she is with her father on the island. Wow, it's been at least a couple of hours already. I try to stand, but the restaurant spins so I clench a nearby table as I make my way out the door and walk to the nearest hotel and get a room for the night, purposely leaving my car in the public parking lot so that no one can have my spot. Luckily, there's a vacancy for tonight as there was a cancellation earlier, or I'd be sleeping in my car. After checking in, I walk to the nearby liquor store and buy a bottle of wine—a Niagara red—and I sit on the balcony overlooking the lake as I drink my sorrows away, the woodiness of the wine burning my throat as I swallow. I don't have an overnight bag with me since I didn't plan this little getaway, so when more than half the bottle is empty, I climb into bed, still fully clothed even though the sun has not yet fully set, and I dream of Adam all night.

After my daughter was born, we were happy, the three of us; my daughter and husband were all I needed, but as soon as I found out that there was another baby growing inside me, my heart filled with more joy than I ever thought possible. There was room in our life to spread more love.

I had just found out I was pregnant with Adam, and I was on my way home from the doctor's office, eager to tell my husband about our wonderful news. We had not really been planning to have another baby now, but I had gotten sick about two months before, carelessness on my part. After having had the flu, I fell out of routine and missed a few pills. After a few weeks, I grew suspicious, wondering why I was still nauseated every day, I no longer had the flu, so I made an appointment to go see my family doctor.

There I sat that afternoon at the doctor's office, waiting to find out the results of my blood test.

"Well Mrs. Bennet, I guess congratulations are in order," the doctor says, looking over his chart with his eyeglasses resting on the tip of his nose. "You don't have the flu anymore, but what you do have is another human growing inside you."

I grab hold of the rails of the bed I'm sitting on, afraid I'll fall over from hearing his words.

"Are you positive? How far along am I?" I ask.

"I'll send you for an ultrasound to be sure, but based on your last menstrual cycle, I'd say, eight weeks."

My eyes open up big. I am elated with this news and rush home.

"Eight weeks?" says John when I announce the unexpected news. He picks me up and swings me around a few times causing the room to spin, and again I run to the washroom. Once I was finished in the washroom, Ameleiah comes running towards us wanting to be a part of what she perceives as excitement. "Ameleiah, sweets, you are going to be a big sister." John reveals to her little scrunched up face. Ameleiah, oblivious to what her father has just said, frowns and walks away to go back to her dollhouse.

"John, you shouldn't have told her yet, she's too young to understand

what that even means. We should have planned it, bought her a doll first and explained it to her that way."

"If she didn't understand, what does it matter? Besides, girls are way temperamental. I hope this next one is a boy," he says, smiling from ear to ear as he rubs my still flat belly, and we dance around the kitchen.

CHAPTER 5

All Alone

Adam

I FOLLOW MY SISTER to the island to make sure she stays safe, and when the boat docks Dad is already there waiting, just like he promised Mom he would be. Chatter fills the truck as they drive and, already, Mia and Dad are having a great evening together—they even stop for ice cream before heading to Dad's place on Water Street in Gore Bay. Dad still lives in our tiny, old cottage, right by the water's edge and across the street from the marina where he works, so this is convenient. Dad has always loved sailboats, it's one of his things. That, along with writing and motorcycles. He's always had many hobbies, he used to say it's so that he doesn't get bored with any one thing. Mom used to love riding the motorcycle with Dad, the two of them used to scramble to find babysitters for Mia and me so they could go off on their own little riding adventures around the island. Mom doesn't have her license to ride, she was always a passenger; that's how she preferred it, back in the good days when she had a life she enjoyed.

Once Mia and Dad are back at his home, they stay up late chatting, and watching movies, so I leave them alone, I don't want to intrude on their time together.

Since Mia is safe and reunited with our father, the next morning I head back to Tobermory to spend the day with Mom; she needs me more than the others, at least my father and sister have each other. Mom, on the other hand, is all alone. By the time I get to her she is still in her room, sleeping—dead to the world. I watch her sleep through the morning, although not peacefully as she awakens often, tossing and turning. My poor mother. Her dreams haunt her each night, and her waking thoughts haunt her days; she has no escape from the terrible thoughts and sad memories. She has nowhere to run.

Seeing that she needs more time to rest, later in the morning I dash back to the island. Back at Dad's, Mia is already up and getting ready to go to a summer job that Dad lined up for her at a concession stand. Although she is under-age, she is employed because the owners know Dad and will pay Mia cash. The concession stand is across the street from Bridal Veil Falls, in the town of Kagawong. These luxurious falls are thirty-five feet high, and the water source flows from the Kagawong River to the North Channel of Lake Huron. Bridal Veil Falls is a popular tourist stop here on the island, and a fifteen-minute drive from Gore Bay so it's easy enough for Dad to get her there and pick up Mia most days, or whenever she has shifts. The falls are home to many water snakes that slither around swimmers' bare legs, the swimmers oblivious to their surroundings as they bathe in the cool waters. Today, Dad gets ready to drive Mia before he starts his day at his own job at the marina.

On their way to the truck, they see the one person that Dad doesn't like, his neighbour Henry Blake, and Dad lets out a disgruntled moan when he spots Henry but ignores him, nonetheless. Dad is a friendly fellow and gets along with everyone, except for this one neighbour. With Henry, there has always been tension and jealousy throughout the many years they have known each other. Henry used to be obsessed with Mom, in fact, they used to date before Dad came along, and that makes Dad uncomfortable—even now. The two men have always been at war with one another, it's a constant battle for who has the biggest sailboat, the faster motorcycle, the better and fancier cottage. Dad tried over the years, mostly in the beginning when they became neighbours, to be cordial, but Henry despises Dad so much that even when he sees him outside minding his own business, he will make rude remarks. He didn't even cut Dad any slack when I died, so that's how one knows the hatred that Henry has for Dad runs deep. What Dad doesn't understand, though, is that Henry had a hard upbringing; he grew up here on the island with parents who were less than supportive and always gave Henry a hard time. This upbringing of his contributed over the years to the man he eventually became. It's late morning and Henry is outside shining his motorcycle as Dad and Mia climb into the truck. There is no eye contact made, no pleasantries exchanged, and this is for the best because when words between the two are spoken they are often riddled with curse words that I shouldn't be hearing.

Mia shakes her head from side to side. "Let it go Dad, it's not worth getting into a fit over seeing him."

Dad ignores my sister, knowing all too well she is right, and turns on the ignition and pulls out of the driveway a little too quickly, presumably to get away from Henry's intense glare.

I ride along in the back to Bridal Veil Falls with them, listening to the chit chatter all the way. It's different between my father and sister than it is with her and my mother. Together, Dad and Mia laugh at Dad's silly jokes, they share stories with one another and sing along to music they both enjoy. Mia has not once put in her earbuds the entire time she has been here—it's Mom she tries to hide from, and since Mom isn't here, she doesn't need her earbuds to hide behind. Dad drops her off about forty-five minutes before her shift starts so, to kill time, she walks across the street to the falls, she takes off her new, still-clean white Vans and her ankle socks, and hikes up her jeans to her knees and stuffs the socks into her shoes. She walks down the grey steel staircase that leads to the falls carrying her shoes and socks, and places them at the foot of a tree next to a large rock where she sits, feet dangling into the clear water that runs over many smaller rocks. She sits in silence for the entire forty-five minutes, earbuds sticking out of her ears. There aren't many people here yet today as it's still early in the day, but within another hour, this place will be transformed as families come to get relief from the sun, photographers take advantage of the nature and beauty, and young couples in love come to have a romantic swim and kiss behind the falls—the straight veil of water that falls from above. There is one other waterfall on the island, High Falls, and it, too, is a part of the Niagara Escarpment and a well-known tourist attraction located off of Highway 6, eight kilometres north of Manitowaning. While its size doesn't compare to Bridal Veil Falls, its beauty still offers a relaxing picnic area for many visitors where they can enjoy the views of the falls from a distance. Only those who are extra adventurous take the risky hike over the rocky and slippery slopes to make it down for a closer view or to snap an up-close Instagram picture—unlike Bridal Veil Falls, that you can see up close and swim next to as the water cascades down your body.

Once Mia's short four-hour shift starts and she's settled in serving coffee and cold drinks to the many tourists, I explore like we used to when we were a family. There are so many sweet spots I love here on the island. Today I decide to head to Ten Mile Point, this is another lookout spot located halfway between the town of Sheguaindah and Manitowaning. This lookout point is home to the La Cloche Islands. Down at the water's shore resides a four hundred million-year-old rock formation that's considered to be a UNESCO Biosphere Reserve. Many hours pass as I admire the large rock formation and suddenly I realize I haven't 'felt' Mom all morning, and it's early afternoon. So, I do a quick mental check with her first, it's faster than flying, and discover she's still sleeping; she must have had a lot to drink the night before. Having had enough of the views that Ten Mile Point has to offer and feeling the need to go to Mom, I leave here and rush back to Tobermory, and as I'm travelling above the lake, a sudden bolt of energy punches me hard in my stomach. I almost land in the waves, but I manage to control myself before taking the plunge into the deep, wavy, waters; this has never happened to me before. A moment later, there's a pull by an unknown fierce force—something or someone wants me back on the island. I turn around and fly to Bridal Veil Falls first, as that's where Mia should be and that seems to be the source of the pull that energizes through me, but when I arrive she's no longer there. I try to reach out to her with my mind, but I'm met with darkness, unable to penetrate her thoughts, and in fact, I can't feel Dad either. With panic running through me, I scoot over to Gore Bay, and it only takes me seconds to get there. I search the marina for Dad and find he's on his phone. His eyes are bloodshot red, he is pacing, and runs his hands through his hair. What's going on? What did I miss in such a short time? Dad runs out the door, jumps in his truck and, with no seatbelt on, takes off at full speed, life in his own hands. I follow. We pass signs for Little Current, and I suddenly know what we're doing here as I have just been able to break through Dad's mind and read his thoughts; it took a little longer than normal, which is strange, his thoughts being all jumbled. Within a few minutes, I see signs to Little Current hospital parking lot, and my deepest fears surface—we are here because of my big sister.

I fly ahead, passing Dad even with him breaking the speed limit, and barge my way through the hospital searching until I find her. When I do, she is as white as a ghost—as white as me—and connected to machines with tubes in her nose and arm. I sit beside her and try to hold her hand, but I can't pick hers up as mine just runs straight through hers since I'm not solid. Within minutes, Dad is behind me, sobbing, pacing, and not knowing what to do as he aggressively runs his fingers through his already disheveled hair.

Someone in a white uniform strolls into the room, "Mr. Bennet, is there someone else you want us to call for you? Perhaps the child's mother?"

"No, I'll take care of it, thank you," he snaps at the nurse. Dad reaches into his pocket and pulls out his phone; he stares at it for a few minutes. I peek over his shoulder and it's Mom he is contemplating calling—her contact information fills the screen display. Mom, oh no, she can't be alone when she receives this news—this will surely kill her. I must go to her again, I should not have left her side; this will be her undoing. I fly as fast as I have ever flown from the island back to the mainland—willing Dad to wait before placing the call. When I reach Mom, I see her phone is ringing but it's on silent, so she can't hear it. I urge her to wake up, I plead with her to open her eyes. I wish so desperately that I could answer the phone for her, I know it's Dad calling, I can see his name on the display, and I can also feel him, and he is panicked on the other end wanting Mom to pick up. "Mom, please, I beg you, wake up, wake up, wake up," I say repeatedly to her sleeping body. Every so often the ringing stops and starts up again. Dad must hang up when it goes to voicemail and retries again. On the fourth attempt to reach her, Mom's eyes suddenly shoot open in alarm and she sits straight up in bed. She looks at the night table, sees Dad's name on the display and swipes aggressively to answer the call.

"John. What's wrong? I had a dream that…that Adam was here in my room trying to get my attention," she says into the phone while wiping her eyes of sleep. "It was so odd, it felt so real as if he was really here with me at my side."

"Clair, listen to me, you need to get here right away."

"Something is wrong isn't it?" Mom is up off the bed and looking out the window, squinting from the early afternoon sunshine and stares out onto the waves, phone still glued to her ear.

"Yes, there's something wrong. I'm sorry, but it's not good."

She drops the phone and it falls face down onto the grey carpet; she bends to pick it up. "Ameleiah?" she whispers into the phone.

"Yes, it's Ameleiah," says Dad with a low voice.

"Oh my God," cries Mom covering her mouth as she speaks.

"She was in a car accident on her way home from the concession stand. She had an early shift today to get acquainted and trained with the opening process and I was supposed to pick her up this afternoon, but she called to say she had a ride from another girl who lives nearby. They hit a deer while driving. She's in the emergency room, but in stable condition."

"Oh my God," Mom repeats again, drops the phone once more, and stares right at me.

"Mom, can you see me?"

Through the phone, Dad is screaming, "Clair, are you there, Clairah!" The phone is still on the floor, but Dad's shouts scream through the tiny speakers, nonetheless.

Mom runs to the washroom and bends over the toilet as the gin and tonic and burger make their way out. Once her stomach is emptied of the poison from the night before, she splashes cold water over her face, picks her phone up off the floor and turns it off while Dad continues to shout on the other end. She runs out of the hotel, not even checking out, and heads towards the ferry station. Mom is panting, she can't breathe properly and struggles to speak to the attendant on duty. "I need...passage…for the next boat, please. It's urgent."

The same man from yesterday, but with a flowered shirt this time, sits in the same crowded booth again. "Miss, you missed the eleven thirty morning ferry, so the next ferry is not until this afternoon at three forty."

"Shit, shit. Okay." She brings her hands to her face and wipes her eyes, then she reaches into her purse for a credit card but fumbles and the contents of her purse spill to the ground, coins rolling down the concrete. She's a mess trying to accumulate her belongings: something long, the size of my hand that's in a tube shape, a small comb, mints, several receipts, and a bottle of pills I've seen many times before—the label on the bottle reads Ativan, and I think it's used to treat sadness, but I'm not sure. I approach her and whisper into her ear, "Mom, calm yourself down. Breathe. Stay strong for Mia."

Within a second of me speaking these words into her ear, her breathing relaxes, and she manages to gather her items, minus the coins, and puts them all back in the purse, so I must have gotten through to her. A woman carrying a sleepy child on her hip approaches and asks her if she needs help. Mom calmly declines the offer for help, pays for her ticket, and walks away from the service station with her hands over her mouth. She goes to the dock and finds a quiet place off to the side to sit. She buries her face in her hands and cries for me and my sister while I sit beside her, my hands hovering over hers—it's the closest that I can get to holding her hand. I wish that I had the ability to transport her with me; if I could, we would be there within minutes. But I can't, so I stay and continue holding my hand over hers, although she can't feel me.

Back at the hospital, Dad goes to the gift shop, buys a small notebook and a pen and sits beside Mia's bed and writes in his journal.

Dear Adam,

Failure, that's a word I know all too well. I should win the Nobel prize for being the best at failing, if such a prize existed—but of course it doesn't. That would be too negative, too derogatory of society to impose such a dark, ominous prize on humanity. The world is full of failure—it exists in many forms. Some of us fail at school, some at jobs, others at cooking, I on the other hand am great at all these things—but what good does that do me without you by my side?

The things that are most important to me are what I fear at failing at the most. It doesn't matter that I know how to whip up the best cordon blue dish, when all I ever eat is microwave meals anyway, that is when I do eat at all. What I wouldn't give to trade being a failure to all the things

I excel at for just one more moment in time with you my son. Of all the things in my life that I could fail, you should not have been one of them. And now your sister lies here helpless, and I fear she, too, will be my next biggest failure. I already failed you that day, I can't fail her too.

Love, Dad

CHAPTER 6

Manitoulin Island

Clairah

IT'S BEEN FIVE years since I stepped foot on the island—five long and desperate years. I swore I would never go back; too many memories of him there, of many happy times that I'll no longer ever have. It's too painful to think about and so I avoid it. As much as I once considered the island my real home, it's five years later and a nightmare I must face. Is it not ironic that the one thing that's bringing me back there is the same thing that kept me from there to begin with? My children. I lost Adam to the island and that's the reason why I could never go back, and now Ameleiah is hurt, forcing me to return. How cruel is life mocking me this way? What have I done to deserve more misery, more pain?

I remember the horrific day as if it were only yesterday; it's been five years, but the memories live inside me—wildly and vividly. The sun was out, not a cloud in the sky—it was a hot day for the island;

forecasts called for a perfect family boating day, but they couldn't have been more wrong. That morning we set out on the sailboat as a family ready to enjoy the summer day. John and I had bought this sailboat together about a year after we got married—this was an upgrade for John, a 2004 MacGregor 26M, blue, fully equipped and ready to sail. The day we bought the boat, we had made the drive to Toronto Harbour to pick it up during a severe rainstorm: how ironic, when I think about that now.

The day onboard had started off well, blue skies, the sun warming up the earth, waves non-existent, but I was growing anxious after about two hours on the water. By early afternoon I had an uneasy feeling in the pit of my stomach, something urging me to go back to shore, to end the day trip early. We have been sailing for a couple of hours, and after listening to the nagging feeling as long as that, I start pleading with John to take us back, just in case.

"Really, why?" he asks, crinkling his cheeks up to his eyes because of the sun.

"I don't know why, it's just a feeling."

He tells me I'm being silly, uptight, and no fun. He encourages me to look to the sky for reassurance that the weather won't turn on us.

"Listen Clair, the sky never lies. Look!" he says as he points his hand towards the sky. "Just look up and you'll see. There's no way it's going to rain. I'd bet my life on it," he says as he brings both arms up and out in front of him pointing to the blue water surrounding us. "Just look at how calm the water is," he continues looking out across the blue lake that extends forever—small waves rolling onto the other.

Believing him and admitting, despite my rooted feeling, that I am being overprotective, I comply. "Okay, you're the captain, you know best," I say. I believe him and place my fate, and my children's, in his hands.

Those seven words that I spoke cost me dearly—they cost me my son's life. Despite my shaky hands and the butterflies swirling around in my stomach, we continued on our journey while John and Adam cast more lines into the deep lake, and Ameleiah and I went to prepare lunch down below in the galley. Lunch wasn't fancy, just peanut butter and jelly sandwiches served on whole wheat bread and cucumber slices on the side—cucumber slices sprinkled with sea salt were Adam's favourite.

As I cut the last cucumber slices to place on our plates, there is a sudden shift; I lose my balance, and I cut my finger on the knife. I reach for a napkin to wrap around the blood, to keep it from spilling onto the food, then glance out the porthole and, for a split second, I think I see clouds rolling in—but no, it can't be, it was sunny and clear a few minutes ago, and so I shake my head to wash away the thought. I must be imagining things. Continuing to doubt my vision, I reach for the light switch as it suddenly becomes too dark in the cabin to see well; my finger throbs under the wrapped tissue as I blindly search for the light switch. As I prepare the plates and sprinkle sea salt on the cucumber slices, Ameleiah pours our drinks; Crush Cream Soda for her and her brother. Suddenly, I'm shoved by…something, and I have to grip the counter in the galley for support and to prevent myself from being knocked over or pushed around. The drinks Ameleiah poured fly off the table and spill everywhere, walls and floor, leaving a pinkish stain on the surfaces that the liquid touches.

"Mom?" Ameleiah looks at me, wide-eyed. "What was that Mom?" she asks in a panicked voice, grabbing a white cloth to soak up the mess—the cloth immediately turns pink. I try to move forward to investigate and another force shoves me back in my place, preventing me from placing one foot in front of the other. The boat is rocking back and forth and much too fast.

"Mom, what's happening?"

"I'm not sure honey. Stay down here. I'm going up to check out the situation."

The boat continues to rock heavily, more than usual, and I stumble on my way up the stairs, hit my head in the companionway, then grab the railing for support and pull myself up. On deck, John scrambles to get the sails down as water gushes over the side, drowning everything in sight. The bright blue skies from before are dark, angry, rumbling—ready for war.

"Oh my God, John," I say in horror as I stand still, unable to force my feet to move forward. John's blue eyes meet my brown eyes, panic surging through his.

"Clairah, grab that side of the sail," he yells while pointing, but I remain frozen. "Clairah! Now!" I know the situation we are in is not good, but I can't bring myself to move; I'm stuck to the ground like chewed gum sticks to the bottom of shoes. John continues to work the sails and tries to bring the boat into a position so that the waves won't knock us over. Ameleiah is still downstairs, tucked away inside, safe for now.

I should have looked for Adam then, but I had assumed he was safe as he had been with his father where I had left them both when I went down to make lunch. But he was nowhere in sight and I, his mother, the one who was supposed to protect him, keep him safe, didn't even notice he wasn't there. Each minute that passed us by, the waves grew taller and plunged into the sailboat with more force than I had ever seen before. The wind picked up speed and momentum, and loose items blew off the deck and plummeted into the spiraling lake. It felt as if hours had passed since I was downstairs making lunch, but it was only minutes ago. We continued to desperately struggle with the sails as the wind continued taking over our efforts and left us feeling defeated.

"Mom, Dad, what's happening?" Ameleiah emerges from down below, standing in the companionway, rubbing her head. When she brings her hand away, it is stained with blood. "Where's Adam?"

Adam. Where is Adam? I can't see him; I can't hear him calling out for me. I glance from one end of the boat to the other, searching, but come up empty. I scream his name, "ADAM!" hoping he'll pop his head out from wherever he is hiding, surely afraid and wanting me.

"Ameleiah, go grab your brother, stay close to your mother," says John in a shaky voice, assuming that Adam was downstairs in the cabin with Ameleiah. The waves are so high they create a blanket—like a cocoon.

"But I don't know where he is! He's not downstairs," blares Ameleiah's voice.

That was the last thing that anyone spoke on the sailboat, other than the anguished screams that came next as we were carried away with the storm.

John had said that never in a million years did he think the weather would turn on us that day when I mentioned my ill feelings to him, only it did turn, and worse than John could have ever imagined. He'd said that he'd have bet his life on it, well…his life was spared during that bet. Waves taller than our sailboat had come crashing into us, wiping away everything in its path.

The boom sways violently towards me and knocks me over and I find myself being smacked in the face with cold water as I am swept underneath the lake, unable to let the breath escape that is caught in my throat. The boat has flipped over, the rudder points to the sky—we capsized. I sink deeper and deeper towards the bottom of the lake, losing the last bit of breath preserved in my lungs, then, realizing my fate, I use all my strength to swim back up to the surface. As my head breaks through the water, and I gasp out the breath that I had been holding, I am transported into the scene of a horror movie. There is no rating bad enough to describe the scene before me, this scene has nothing on the most horrific of movies. I look across the water to try to find my family, but all I see are our personal belongings floating next to me, around me, bobbing up and down with the waves. I am not a strong swimmer by any means, but I can swim enough to save myself so I swim as fast as I can around to the other side of the boat, yelling for my family—calling their names one by one in rapid fire succession. John is the first one I see, and he is holding onto something. No: someone. I squint to take a better look as the water blurs my vision, and another wave crashes over me, blinding me. When I come back up and break through the water's surface, I clear my eyes and see it is Ameleiah who is with John, those two are safe, but where is Adam? When John sees me, he swims to me, still holding onto our daughter, and asks me the same question I had just asked myself.

"Clair, where's Adam?"

"I don't know, I can't find him."

I am hyperventilating, unable to breathe again. With one arm flapping into the water and the other arm holding onto our screaming daughter, he says, "Clairah, you need to get a hold of yourself."

"Where is he?" I repeat in between sobs.

The three of us swim to the side of the boat where there is a place that we can hold on to for support—the mast, big enough for all three of us to grab.

"Hold on here," says John, taking my arm. "Keep one arm on Ameleiah at all times, don't let go of the boat or each other," he continues as he swims away in the opposite direction, into the waves, into the dangerous storm.

"Where are you going?" I yell.

"To find our son." As soon as he speaks the words he gets washed underwater.

It's just Ameleiah and I left in the cold water as rain pelts down on us, the wind so strong it pushes us up against the boat, bruising us in the process and crushing our bones.

"Mom are we going to die out here?" asks Ameleiah.

I place one hand on her face and turn her towards me. "Honey, no we are not going to die, we will be fine, but we need to stay calm and conserve our energy." Somehow, I find my strength to speak calmly to her. My daughter stares into my eyes and I see fear deep in them.

"Your father went to go find your brother. Where was he by the way? When did you see him last?"

"Mom," cries my daughter, "I think Adam was in the head. When I came up to the deck, the door to the head was closed—I remember now. He would have been in there when we capsized." Her face is covered with wet hair and she lets go of the mast long enough to wipe it off her face.

So, that was why I had not seen him on the deck. My world stops when I hear these words knowing all too well what that means—Adam wouldn't have had his life jacket on. It was the one time that we allowed him to take it off, for just the couple minutes it took for him to use the head. I became frozen, glued to the side of the boat, unable to rationalize my thoughts.

"Mom, did you hear what I said?" Her words are muffled.

"Mom!" repeats Ameleiah, louder this time, with trembling lips, forcing her voice to be heard over the wind just before another wave comes over our heads. I want to let go of the boat, let go of Ameleiah and allow myself to be taken away with the waves. If not for my daughter shaking next to me I would do exactly that, but for her I hold on despite the darkness and sinking feeling burning inside me.

During the entire trip, the children had both been wearing their life jackets, of this I was sure, but minutes before we capsized, Adam, who was only six at the time, must have taken his off to use the head. He had this thing where he needed to strip down naked to pee, and we didn't know that he was still in the head when we went overboard. We can only assume even today that's where he was. But even now, as I think about the events of the day, would it have made a difference if he had his life jacket off? If he was really in the head at the time, he'd have been trapped and not even a life jacket would have saved him from the walls closing in around him.

We are alone, stranded, holding on to an upside down sailboat. There are no other boats near us when we need them the most. Earlier on in the day when it was sunny and bright there had been many other families out sailing, enjoying their day, but they all left; they must have checked the forecast more often than John had. Now it's only us, the three of us stranded in the water, trying to stay afloat, and a sailboat floating with the hull pointing to the sky. The rain continues to pelt down on us as I keep my eyes open for John who tries desperately to find our son in the water, but every time he comes back to where Ameleiah and I are floating, he is empty handed. The last time John resurfaces from the water I tell him where Adam had been just before we flipped. The horrific look on John's face reveals to me that he, too, has the same darkest fear as I have—Adam had no life jacket on. While he is a good swimmer, much stronger than I am as he has been in lessons since he was three, he would have had a hard time surviving in these waves if he had managed to escape and not be trapped. John's expression darkens and he begins to desperately try to right the boat, but the effort is lost as the boat is too big. Ameleiah is still nearby me, close to my side, hanging on and I am the only parent here so I am the one who needs to comfort her, keep her calm; but Adam is gone and nowhere in sight and this makes it difficult for me to concentrate on her needs. The three of us begin to scream his name in desperate attempts to have him hear us and tell us he is all right. John tries to get to the head from underwater, but he can't, as every time a wave hits it pushes him further away from where he needs to be. Ameleiah's many tears pour down her face and add to the lake's depth. My daughter and I continue to scream my son's name, over and over while John dives continuously into the deep, dark waves several times to try to locate him, but it is a fast losing fight.

I am worried my entire family will die here this day in the water, and I wonder what death will feel like, what it will be *like. The water is colder than before, shivers cover my skin and I wonder if we'll die of hypothermia or drowning. I think about my parents, sitting on a beach in Costa Da Caparica in Portugal, their favourite spot. Surely, they must be having a better day than me—I'll never see them again.*

By this time, it's late evening and another half an hour has passed when a sizeable, bright light shines on me. I look up to see a large motorboat approaching from my left—it is the coastguard and help is on its way.

By the time the coastguard got to us, almost forty minutes later, I knew in my heart that I was less one child. Ameleiah was the first to be rescued, to be pulled out of the cold water and taken onto the rescue boat, into safety. I watched from the water as a man I didn't know wrapped a blanket around her trembling body. Once they were sure she was okay and that the bump on her head wasn't severe, they came for me next—ushering me onto their boat. I sat with a blanket of my own next to my daughter as she lay her head on my shoulder and wept for her little brother, her lips blue like the sky had been earlier that day. John refused to be rescued and was adamant about remaining in the water, searching hopelessly for our son. Eventually, hours after we capsized, the coast guard got John on board after he'd almost drowned due to another large wave that took his breath away and caused him to hit his head on the side of the boat and lose consciousness briefly: he had to be dragged out by two men. By that time, there was another rescue boat there, too, and they had immediately gone to John's aid. Yet another team of rescue workers had been dispatched, equipped with gear to search while the three of us mourned the terrible loss that we had just experienced and refused to believe was real. Ameleiah called out my name, but I ignored her. John, too, tried to speak to me once he came to, but I refused to answer him, I didn't make eye contact, and instead I waited patiently in my seat, wrapped in a blanket staring across the rippling water, waiting for a miracle that would never come. The guards had already begun to prepare us for the horrific news. "It's not looking good," they had said.

"If he was alive, we would have seen him swimming or floating somewhere." I push these words aside, afraid to believe them, refusing to believe them. The rain has stopped as suddenly as it had come, and the wind has died down, too. A helicopter circulates with a spotlight aimed into the water aiding in the search for my lost little boy. My son has many well equipped and qualified rescue divers searching for him, but his little lifeless body has yet to be found.

John comes to sit next to me, he tries to console me, he wraps his arms around my shoulders, but I can't stand his touch; it pierces my skin like a needle filled with poison, so I push him away. He doesn't give up and tries to touch me again, and instead of allowing my husband to soothe me, I smack him across the face with my dominant hand; he looks at me with wide, shocked eyes no longer blue, but red.

"Clair," he begins softly.

"Don't say my name. This is your fault. YOU!" I shout into his ear. "You did this." I scream into his alarmed face. "You killed our son."

"Clair.... How...could you say that?" he says, trying to grab hold of my arms, but I refuse to allow him to touch me. Tears pour down his face as he tries desperately to get me to look at him. As I glance a peek, the vein on his left side temple bulges. He tries again to pull me into his strong arms; I push him away.

"You didn't listen to me. You refused to listen and look at what you caused." I flail my arms and throw punches at John's chest. I tell him that he should have gotten off his high horse and listened to me and not have taken us out at all, and that because he didn't listen, I no longer have a son. Another man comes near to try to help calm me, and he leads me away, John stands staring at me while our daughter screams into the night.

"You killed our son."

I didn't know that those four words would have such a long-lasting effect on both of our lives, but they did as they became my anchor, my scapegoat.

This is the sad story about how I lost my Adam, and that day, that was the last time I stepped foot on Manitoulin Island.

For two years after Adam's death we tried to work on our marriage, but I was too full of resentment to really try, and to try at something means you must put in an effort, something I didn't do. Those four words that I accused John of that day on the rescue boat were all I could think of at first. They consumed me whole, and I grew to believe them wholeheartedly. Eventually, John grew tired of being blamed by me for Adam's death, and he kept telling me that I was acting like I was the only one who had lost a child that day, but I wasn't listening to his pleas. He claims that for years he had been following the marina reports and asked how he was to know that this storm would come out of nowhere. After being blamed for our son's death for so long, he'd had enough and left two years after Adam died. One morning, he packed and moved out of our Paris home and moved to the island full time; I never saw him again after that. Since then, Ameleiah has been spending her summers with her father, leaving me all alone for two months of the year and during the time of year that I need her most, when I don't have my students to fill my days. John has lived on the island all year round since he moved out there. There are only twelve thousand residents year-round, but in the summer months the number increases to closer to thirty thousand. I wonder if John prefers the winter to the summertime months, when he can be alone and hide.

I have been sitting on the edge of this dock for two hours while I wait for the time to board the ferry, thinking about the day Adam died, and the person I used to be. Time moves too slow for me while I sit here and wait as the world spins fast, out of control; but I'm afraid to move, so here I remain in this spinning nightmare that crawls over me.

I used to be different, I used to be fun. It's been five years since I have done the things I love. Years since I have been to the gym, painted a beautiful landscape, or even listened to music, other than the horrible rap music that constantly seeps through my daughter's earbuds. I don't even remember what it's like to enjoy something anymore, everything brings me pain; everything reminds me of my past. In my mind I see Adam attempting to do a push-up while I worked out, or I see him watching me mix colours on my palette, or a song he used to like will come on the radio. Life has a way of constantly reminding me of what I lost that day.

At two thirty in the afternoon, one hour and ten minutes before departure, as I make my way to my car I mostly keep my head down as

I walk, avoiding all civilization. A young couple trying to take a selfie but failing at it, asks me if I can take their picture for them, it looks like they are trying to get the ferry in the background but can't extend out their arms far enough to capture the image behind them. They ask me a second time to take their picture, as I didn't respond at first, but I ignore them again and keep walking, pretending I didn't hear their question not once but twice. I'm sure that the next person who walks by will be more generous with their time than I was with mine. When I arrive at my car, I get in but hesitate before turning it on. I look over to the passenger seat, expecting to see someone there, but it's empty. I start the engine and drive to the ferry to wait in line for boarding.

Once I'm on the ferry, I stay inside my car not bothering to leave. There's no point going to the lounge, I'm not interested in seeing all the happy families on vacation together when it's just me here, by myself. I don't mind being alone don't get me wrong, it's the thoughts I have in my head when I see others happy that sadden me. It's not jealousy, it's just self-pity. It's better this way, here inside my car, alone. It's safer for me and everyone else that will encounter my sour mood—I don't want to be responsible for spreading negativity, especially to other happy families on vacation. I happen to glance at my phone as it sits next to me on the empty seat and realize I had turned it off. Turning it back on now, John's name flashes across the display—he's calling me. Since my phone has been off, I hadn't heard the ringing. I ignore his call and turn the phone face down so that I don't have to look at the flashing light when he calls or texts. After about an hour, I decide I need to call him back since I don't know exactly where I'm heading once we dock. It's been too long since I visited the island, and what was once my second home has become a dark hole in my head. When I pick up my phone, I see there are five missed calls and all from John, along with several text messages from him as well.

John: Clair, call me back

John: Clair, you are freaking me out, why are you not answering my calls?

John: Dammit Clairah, I have enough to worry about here, are you seriously doing this now? Get a hold of yourself

John: Stop being so selfish

John: Pick up the damn phone

I should feel bad, I would feel bad if I could feel anything at all. I decide I should call, but only to check on Ameleiah, so I brace myself as I press redial on John's name that's on the display screen of my phone.

He answers on the first ring. "Clair, thank goodness, where are you?"

"My phone was off."

"I have been calling and texting you for hours."

"I know…I'm sorry…."

"Why the hell would you leave your phone off? You heard what I said earlier before we were disconnected—didn't you?"

"I heard you."

"Okay, so listen up: You need to get on the ferry first thing in the morning. Ameleiah is stable, but…"

"I'm already on the ferry," I say, interrupting him. "I'll be docking in about an hour."

"How is that possible? You were hours away from Tobermory when I called you, when we last spoke."

"That's not so."

"I don't understand then?"

"I was here still, in Tobermory."

"Why were you still there?"

"I stayed the night last night." I say, not offering information on the fact that I could not drive because I was tipsy.

"Okay, well good then. Do you remember how to get to Little Current hospital?"

I think about this for a few seconds before responding. "Yes, I think so. My GPS should find it."

"You know what, never mind, I'm coming to pick you up. You can leave your car parked at the restaurant. I'll be there to get you. I can't have you driving all this way by yourself, you will get lost, and it will stress me out even more."

"I won't get lost."

"Yes, you will."

"I said I won't," I reply with irritation in my voice.

"I'm not arguing anymore, besides, it'll be dark by the time you get here."

"So?" I counter, knowing all too well that the darkness in a foreign place will leave me feeling uneasy. But I want to pretend that I'm more tough now. I don't want to have to need John to pick me up, and I certainly don't want him to know that I really do need him.

"You'll get lost."

"I won't." I repeat, louder.

"Shit, Clair, why are you being difficult? I still remember who you are. Meet me at the restaurant; I'm calling there now to let them know your vehicle will stay there overnight."

"John, wait…"

He hangs up before I have an opportunity to dispute his plans. "Darn it," I say, annoyed, to myself. I turn the ringer on the phone back on so that I don't miss anymore important calls and realize that I'm low on battery. Darn, I don't even have a charger with me. I didn't plan on staying away from home this long, I was supposed to have been home yesterday already, and here I am on a ferry to Manitoulin Island to go see my hurt child, and I don't even have a bag with a change of clothes or a charger for my phone. I haven't washed my face, brushed my teeth, or showered since yesterday morning, and this is not how I imagined my first reunion with my ex-husband would be like. In fact, in three years I never imagined a reunion with him at all. I glance into the rear-view mirror and gasp at the image staring back at me. My long, straight brown hair is knotted, my face looks older than its forty years, and I have new lines under my eyes that I'm positive were not there yesterday. This is just wonderful; could things get any worse for me today? Before the phone's battery depletes even further, I make a quick call to my neighbour back home to let him know I'll be away for a while. I should also call John back to let him know my phone is down to ten percent battery and will be dead by the time I dock. I should also call my parents, but decide to wait until I've seen my daughter so I can accurately convey her situation—no need to worry them yet. Hesitantly, I press dial on John's number, hoping he doesn't answer and when I get my wish, I remind myself to be careful about the things you wish for. Instead of John's voice greeting me, on the other end of the phone is a woman who answers with a voice I don't recognize.

"Hey Clairah, I knew you'd be calling," says the unknown, high pitched chipper voice on the other end. Who is this woman? I want to ask but don't, and instead ask, "Where is John?"

"He stepped out; he'll be back in a couple minutes."

"Where did he go?"

"He went to the washroom, if you must know, but he left his phone here. I saw you calling, and so I picked it up."

No longer able to hold the question in, I ask, "Who the hell are you?"

"I'm Michelle, Michelle Boucher, I'm John's girlfriend. What do you want anyway? Do you have a message for him or not?"

The girlfriend, of course; this must be the same Michelle that Ameleiah told me about before, and kept going on about after her last visit with her dad.

"I need to speak to John."

"Of course you do."

"I'm sorry, but what does that mean?"

Instantly her voice changes and becomes more soft, supportive. "Hold on Clairah. Here he is, oh, and take care."

"Clair?" John says into the phone.

John is waiting for me to speak, but I can't find my voice.

"Clair," he repeats.

I can't take anymore and hang up. I check the battery life: eight percent. This phone is so old that the battery drains quickly. I wait for

John to call me back, but he doesn't, so when the phone's battery is at three percent, I send him a text message.

Clairah: Phone about to die. I have no charger with me, so if you call, I can't answer, but I'll be at the restaurant as planned. In case you forgot, my car is a Honda Civic—still the same one I had before

John: Did you hang up on me earlier?

Clairah: No—got disconnected, bad connection, I guess

John: Okay, I couldn't call you back right away as the nurse walked in and had some questions about Ameleiah

Clairah: No problem. Is she okay?

John: Yes, still stable, but she might need surgery for her leg; we're waiting for tests

Clairah: Okay, see you soon

I lay my head back and close my eyes and think of when the kids were little and we were a family. I remember our trip to Lisbon, Portugal together to visit my parents; Adam must have been three, and Ameleiah five-years-old then, and my parents were thrilled to see their grandkids. My parents had moved back to Portugal a couple years after we got married, they always longed to return to their roots there, and once I was married and they knew I was safe here with a husband and family of my own they decided to return to their homeland, the land of peace and tranquility as they call it. It was hard for me to let them go, but I didn't want to be selfish and make them stay here just for me. I should call them to tell them what's happened, it's not fair to keep them in the dark, so I pick up the phone and remember that it's about to die.

I'm sweating here inside the car, so I open the door a tad to allow some air through. I wonder if I'm sweating because of the heat or nerves. I remember past trips to the island, summers spent exploring. We used to love to find new little havens on the island. The kids loved Misery Bay Provincial Park, located on the south shoreline. It's a fifteen kilometre-long stretch of trails that welcomes many hikers each year. If you're not into hiking but more into nature, there's an information centre at the park, filled with books, pamphlets and other statistics on the many animals that inhabit the park. Ameleiah used to love to look through the pamphlets and put them back; Adam collected them all, even though he couldn't read. They both learned so much about this park during the time we spent there. The entire park sits on a flat foundation of alvar—a limestone plain that stretches as far as the park's beauty, but becomes flooded in the spring due to the high waters. If you hike through one of the trails, you end up at the beach area surrounded by rocky bottom—we used to do this often as Adam loved this beach area. We would walk out for a long time into the lake and not even feel sand beneath our feet, but rather the cool limestone—Adam used to say it was so cool to not feel sand but rather hard rock on the tips of his toes. This used to be one of my family's most favourite places on the island. We'd go often and pack a picnic, blankets, our hiking boots, swimsuits, and flip flops and hike to the beach where we would find a tree and sit under its shade eating peanut butter and jelly sandwiches, with cucumbers sprinkled with sea salt of course—Adam eating most of them. When the heat became too much on those extremely sunny days, we'd wade into the water, Adam always running to catch up to his bigger sister who would outrun him every time. Those were the happy days of my life, a long lifetime ago.

CHAPTER 7

Queen's Inn

Clairah

I MUST HAVE FALLEN asleep thinking of Misery Bay Provincial Park, because as I open my eyes, I see many people back in their vehicles. The ferry must have docked, and everyone is getting ready to drive off and begin their Manitoulin Island adventures. There is a little boy in the car next to me bouncing up and down in his seat, and I find myself wondering if he, too, likes cucumbers with sea salt. I turn my car's engine on, and after I drive off the ferry and make my way to the restaurant around the corner, I see him right away; he's leaning up against his blue F-150 pickup truck. He looks tanned and buff, he must have kept up with the gym all these years—unlike me, shit, why couldn't he be balding and unfit? That sight would be easier to deal with than this one. He looks better than I expect him to look, not that I have spent much time thinking about how my ex-husband looks now, but still. I had stolen a few glances at pictures on Ameleiah's phone over the last three years because curiosity is in us all, but they were mostly head shots or the photo was taken from a distance hiding his well-shaped physique, flat stomach, and broad shoulders, so I had not expected what stands before me now. He notices the Honda Civic right away and must know It's mine because his demeanor changes. He straightens up and squares his shoulders—probably preparing himself for a fight with me. It's always a fight when we talk these days. I don't like it, but that's the way it is between us, like a cold sharp wedge splitting us further apart each time we interact. I pull up next to his truck and he's quickly at my side opening my door—at least he is still a gentleman. He looks down on me for a few seconds before reaching out his arm. I place my hands in his and allow him to help me out of the car. He closes the door behind me and leans in and wraps both arms around me, swallowing me into him. This is the first time my husband—ex-husband—and I have had physical contact in almost five years. The first two years after Adam's death and before John moved out, he slept in the spare bedroom, ate mostly at work, and I only talked to him when absolutely necessary, so he might as well have already been living far away. My breathing quickens, and I pull away from him, afraid to have him notice my uneasiness. We still haven't spoken a word, but he breaks the silence.

"I'm sorry I had to give you the news about Ameleiah over the phone."

"I understand. You had no choice."

"It's good to see you Clair. You look good. You look the same."

Is this man mocking me? "I look horrible, I haven't even washed my face today," I say as I turn away, embarrassed about the way I must look to him. I don't give him the satisfaction of telling him that he looks good—no way, that information I keep to myself. If he's fishing for a compliment by telling me that I look good, well, he won't get one from me; he can ask his girlfriend for one, I'm sure she's throwing them out at him nonstop. I sigh and force myself to stop this nonsense. I remind myself that John is not like that, never has been like that and I doubt he is that way now. He must genuinely think I look the same if he has said as much. Worried about the silence between us I say, "Has there been any change in Ameleiah's situation?"

"She woke up before I left, so she's still stable. She broke her right leg, so she will definitely need surgery to repair the fracture, and she has a concussion, but other than that she'll be okay." His voice is soft as he speaks.

Relief washes over me as he says the word *okay*.

"How fast can we get to her?"

"Under an hour, I still drive fast," he says as he leads me to his truck, opens the passenger door for me and waits for me to climb in. He runs around the front to the driver's side, "Buckle up," he says, and smiles weakly.

The drive is excruciatingly long, even though it's only under an hour. My thoughts are racing the entire time, and I can't get Ameleiah off my mind. When I'm not thinking of her, the name Michelle fills my thoughts and it makes me sick to think of this stranger with my daughter. I want to ask John about her, but I bite my tongue, now is not the time or the place. I'll bring her up after I have seen Ameleiah, after I know she is safe.

"I noticed you don't have any bags with you," says John.

"No. I don't. I wasn't expecting to have to come here."

"Right, you decided last-minute to stay the night, isn't that what you said on the phone?"

"Yeah, I decided on a last-minute little getaway."

"That's no problem, we will figure something out."

We will figure something out—he had said *we*. "I know I'm not prepared but when you called, I panicked, I needed to get here right away. I'll figure something out, make a stop somewhere to get the essentials after I see Ameleiah." I emphasize the *I*.

"Don't worry about it, I'll take you wherever you need to go."

"That's fine, you don't need to concern yourself with me."

"Well, I'm not, I'm just being polite here, I mean, I'm not sure how you'll manage without me."

"Seriously, John have you forgotten you've been out of my life permanently for over three years? I'm sure I can manage without you," I say with a snippy tone.

"You don't even have a car here, remember?" He glances at me from the corner of his eye and raises an eyebrow.

Oh right, darn, why didn't I drive myself? "Sorry for the little rant—I forgot so… I suppose I'll need you to drive me after all."

"I'd already planned on it."

"Will your girlfriend mind?" Oh shit, I didn't mean to ask this question, it sort of slipped out on its own.

John ignores my question and keeps looking straight ahead at the empty road in front of us. To break the silence, I say, "My phone is dead, and I need to make some calls to see if I can book a room for a few nights in Little Current since it's close to the hospital. Can I use your phone for a minute?"

"You're not staying at a hotel in Little Current, not without a car. You can stay with me."

"That's absurd."

"Why is that so absurd to you? We were married for twelve years; we've stayed in the same house before. In fact…"

"Don't say another word." I silence him by placing my hand up in front of his face.

"Relax, I was only going to say that we slept in the same room," he says, looking at me again from the corner of his eye. "What did you think I'd say?"

I have no idea what I was afraid he'd say, so instead I reply with, "It's different now."

I can't stay at that house in Gore Bay, I just can't do it. The memories, the smells, the scenery; it will be too much for me, reminding me of Adam and the life we used to have together.

"How so?"

"Well, for starters, won't your girlfriend mind?" Darn, why do I keep bringing her up?

"You've mentioned Michelle more times than you've mentioned Ameleiah."

"No, I haven't."

"Yup, you have, but nobody's counting. So just relax. Besides, for the record, she's not my girlfriend, not really. We just started seeing each other a couple months ago, beginning of May. She's a nurse and works at the hospital, that's the only reason she was there today when you called."

She certainly thinks of herself as my ex-husband's girlfriend, but I don't tell him that's how she introduced herself to me.

"Girlfriend, no girlfriend, it makes no difference to me, really. Regardless, I don't know about staying with you. Won't that be uncomfortable?"

"Not for me. Listen, Clair, don't be stubborn, not now. Okay? Our daughter needs us and I don't want to cause her more stress by arguing all the time."

"I'm never stubborn."

"Right," he says, as he shakes his head. "Every inn will be full anyway, so I doubt you'll find a room, but you can try. Here," he says, passing me his phone, but when I don't take it from him he places it back down on the centre console.

"I'm sure I can find one room somewhere on this island."

"Yup, I know you're sure," he says as he smirks. "You're always so sure about everything, until you're not."

I have only been in the truck with him for forty minutes and already I want to throw my purse at him. I don't know why he has this affect on me, he makes me question my own motives and feelings and I don't like this loss of self-control that he has over me.

His phone is still sitting on the centre console, so I pick it up.

"What are you doing?" he asks.

"I'm calling around for a room."

"Yup, of course you are."

"What's that supposed to mean?"

"I see some things never change," he says, chuckling under his breath.

I google hotels near the hospital, and a few come up: Hawberry Hotel, Anchor Inn, and Bridgeway Motel. I decide to try Anchor Inn first, and a pleasant woman on the other end kindly tells me that they are full, so I make my way down the list and each hotel I call has no rooms available. I should have expected this, it's the end of June and the busiest time of the year for tourists. Wonderful, what will I do now? I'm determined to stay strong, (John would call this stubbornness, but it's strength), and so I stay strong and continue to try to find a place. I decide on a whim to call Queen's Inn in Gore Bay. This is not my first choice of place to stay, only because it's so close to John's cottage and owned by John's aunt, and I'm trying to keep some distance. The Queen's Inn is a historic bed and breakfast located across the road from the water on the north channel of Lake Huron. The Queen's Inn is where it all began back in 1998. It's where John and I first set eyes on each other: where we first fell in love. It's also where my possessive first ex-boyfriend, Henry, and I met years before I met John. I don't know what compels me to call the inn now, but I have this strong urge, a sense of closure looming over me.

I grew up coming to Manitoulin Island with my own parents, and the island has been like a second home to me for years, since I was little. My family and I used to stay at the Queen's Inn during our summer stay here. My parents used to say that the lushness of the island reminded them of some parts of their homeland. Through the years, as I grew older and finished high school and university, I started coming on my own with my girlfriends on long weekends, and it was at the inn where I first met John.

My best friend Tammy and I come to the island on a sort of retreat, to get away from it all after graduation—me from teacher's college, her from her business administration degree. We're staying in the Victoria room for the long weekend, this is the inn's grandest room, and the room my parents always stayed in when we came as a family. This is my first time staying in this luxurious suite. The inn contains eight rooms, each one carefully named after historical British royals. Being a teacher, I love history myself, so I find this fascinating.

It is early morning and, having just finished my breakfast of bacon and eggs, I'm sitting on the veranda of the inn on the middle floor overlooking the magnificent bay and marina. The veranda extends the length of the house, providing views of the water from many angles. I have my easel with me, and I am trying to capture the essence of the beauty in the views in my current painting when a man walks out onto the balcony. I'm startled by him, causing me to lose concentration and mess up on my colours.

"I'm so sorry Miss, I didn't mean to disturb you, I thought the balcony was empty. There is a board that's loose that Kelly asked me to fix up," says the gorgeous man before me while fumbling with his tool belt. I decide to ignore the belt and stare at his ocean blue eyes instead.

Kelly is the inn's owner, and John's aunt. John had been working for Kelly for a few years by then, doing some basic repairs and upkeeping around the inn as needed. John has always been handy at fixing things around the house, he can fix anything.

"It's not a problem, so go ahead and do what you need to do, just ignore me here," I say, as I try to hide behind my artwork from him due to embarrassment at having stared at him for so long. I try to hide my humiliation with my long brown hair by positioning it strategically so that he can't see the side of my face that's exposed to him.

He walks around the back of me, body heat emanating off of him. I try to ignore his presence and appear calm and collected, but my shaky hands betray me. He peeks over my shoulder to look at my work and nods his head a few times. "Hmm. Not bad, not bad at all. You could sell that here, you know, make some money. I know of a few markets around here owned by folks that would be happy to sell that on consignment for you. Folks around here are always looking for good artwork to buy from local artists."

"I'm not local, I'm here on vacation," I retort, rubbing the tip of my nose.

"That doesn't matter, they'll still take it I'm sure. The scenery is local."

"Well, that sounds lovely, but I don't sell my paintings—not to anyone! This painting goes home with me." I'm not sure why I am being so rude, but I am.

"What do you mean you don't sell the paintings? How do you make any money at it?" he asks, scrunching up his nose.

"I don't," I answer matter-of-factly, while putting some distance between me and the piece to take it all in, to really see it for the first time.

"Why the hell not?" He scrunches up his nose again and it forms tiny wrinkles around his eyes that make him look even cuter than he already is.

"Pardon me?" I ask, looking up with confusion on my face.

"Why don't you sell your paintings and make money off them?" he repeats, as if he could learn the reasons for my madness.

"I paint for me, and not for others."

"Well, isn't that the silliest thing I've ever heard," he says, shaking his head.

I stop trying to mix my colour and stare at him. "Excuse me?"

"I mean…then why do it at all? What other reason would there be for you to spend so much time out here painting, if not to sell for the money? A piece like that must take you a couple hours to finish at least, right?"

I exhale and my shoulders slump. At this moment I know that this man, though rather cute, doesn't understand me, or art, at all. "You know, you better get on with fixing that broken board, it won't fix itself." I say, pointing my paintbrush towards the railing, a drip of paint falling onto the deck. He has a good-looking body, but he sure doesn't know a thing about doing something for the love of it. Clearly.

"Pushy, and she doesn't like money," he says, as he pulls out his tools from his work belt and screws in a loose board.

I shake my head and re-examine my piece and decide I am happy with what I see. I had wanted to finish this piece today, but I find it hard to concentrate on the scenery before me as I focus on this man's backside. I've been biting my lips for so long that I fear they'll bleed. After a few minutes, he picks up his tools and places them all messily into his toolbox—I'd have organized them better. "Good luck with your not for profit business," he says, adding air quotes around not for profit.

I pretend to not hear him and keep my head down. He waits for a few seconds and walks back into the inn, leaving me to stare at my half-painted picture of the marina, still biting my lips. It had been going so well at first, and I was feeling this piece; the colours, the contoured shapes, the imagery was all coming together before he came along, and suddenly I have no desire at all to finish the piece. This man both irritates and excites me at the same time. Regretting not saying goodbye, I quickly pack up my things and head inside the house hoping to see him again, but by the time I get all my things together and secretly go looking for him, he is gone. I watch from the front door as he walks back to the marina with a hop in his steps, toolbox at his side. Instead of going back up to the veranda to finish my painting, I decide that I, too, need a walk down by the water. I need to cool off—my mind more than my body.

I set up my easle as close to the water's edge as I can and sit on a rock to think while faking interest at some fish pooling around together in the water; he stands a few feet away from me. So, he must be a boater then, I think jumping to conclusions. I've never been on a boat, and I rather think it would be a fun experience to be taken out on a boat. I'm not sure if he's noticed me right away or not, but I pretend again to not see him and stare into the water at the fish flapping around a rock. While I sit, he is constantly in and out of the building, now and then appearing with a clip-board in hand. I realize he must work here, as he'd started using his tools on one of the boats. Feeling ashamed for being here, for secretly watching him, I put away my paintbrushes in my bag hurriedly and unorganized;

turns out I didn't want him to catch me here after all. So I go back up to the Queen's Inn, smiling and thinking of him while my current piece remains unfinished.

Accidentally we meet again the next day, this time out by the dock. Since my friend, Tammy, is spending her afternoon doing yoga on the beach, I decided to hang around and paint by the water, too. I'm busy capturing the world on my canvas, so this time I don't have to pretend to be interested in fish. When I spot him working on the same sailboat as yesterday I drop my paintbrush, leaving a blue stain on the sand. I moan to myself and bend to pick it up, then stare at the ruined brush. I risk a quick glance his way and at first pretend not to see him again, forcing my eyes away from where he was when he looked my way...but suddenly our eyes lock. He must have become distracted because he smacks his head on the side of the large mast. I let a giggle escape but try to cover it up, placing my hand over my mouth. He pretends like he hasn't just smacked his head, but turns red and looks away from me. I sit on the bench, smiling at him while he sits back on his heels rubbing his head where he struck it. And then he speaks.

"You again. Are you seriously laughing at me? The woman who paints for free?"

"No, not really," I am laughing so hard that my stomach hurts, with no way to hide my amusement.

"It would appear to me that you are laughing at me."

"But I'm not," I say, still giggling, still holding my hand up to cover my mouth.

"Well then, the least you can do for distracting me to the point where I make an idiot of myself is to let me buy you a burger."

My eyes flicker as this catches me off guard. He registers my reaction by raising one eyebrow. "Oh, ahh… a burger?" I say stupidly, not able to find words.

"Yeah, a burger, you do eat them, don't you? Or is that placed on the same level as you not wanting to make money?"

"I eat, I definitely eat burgers." I look away at this point, feeling shy suddenly.

"Good, I'm glad you eat, so I'll take that as a yes then."

My heart beats fast and I am afraid to speak, unsure what or how the words will come out. "Okay, yes." I say, looking back over at him again, smiling large.

"I'm John." He holds out his hand to me.

"Clairah," I whisper, as if I am afraid to tell him my name, afraid it means more than just a casual greeting.

"Clair," he says, "nice to meet you."

"No, not Clair," I correct, "Clairah."

"I like Clair better. To me you're Clair."

No one had ever called me Clair before, and I wasn't sure why I said yes to his dinner invitation, but I was captivated by his blue eyes and his energy pulled me in, so I did say yes. That afternoon, and many more times afterwards. We ended up having lunch together that afternoon at the restaurant by the marina. While we sat outside enjoying the warm air, we talked for hours. We met again for lunch the following afternoon, and dinner that same night as well when John was done work. That second night after dinner, our third date, John suggested we take a walk by the water, and we did. We both knew that the end of the weekend was approaching, and we were both feeling apprehensive about it as the chatter between us diminished. We sat on a rock down by the water, the same rock where I had sat and painted when he bumped his head; we talked for hours about our lives, our upbringings and our futures, what we wanted and what we hoped for. We discovered that night that we had many of the same goals, and while I was telling him about growing up in Portugal and moving to Canada as a young girl, he reached out and took my hand in his and brought it up to his lips and kissed it gently. There was no sound on all of the island but our breathing, and then he leaned into me and pushed back a strand of my hair that had fallen out of place. He placed his soft lips over mine. It wasn't the first time I had been kissed by a boy, but it might as well have been because it shook my universe.

That weekend turned out to be a weekend of many firsts for me: first time jumping into the lake with my clothes on; first time going on a hike to visit the Cup and Saucer trail; first time falling in love. By the end of the weekend, when I was supposed to leave, I already had a connection to John, one so strong that my heart ached at the thought of leaving him.

As we said our goodbyes towards the end of my stay, I asked him why he looked like he had just lost his most precious best friend in the world, and he told me he felt like he was about to.

Then he says, "I've fallen for you, hard."

I hold in a smile, not wanting to show my joy too much. "Why did you go falling for me?"

"Kind of hard not to." He reaches out to push back a loose strand of my hair and tucks it behind my ear.

"Well, you knew I had to leave, you shouldn't have fallen for me knowing we'd have to part." I say, although I, too, feel the same.

"Clair," he has continued to call me Clair the entire weekend, "we can't control or choose who we fall in love with." He takes another step forward.

I lean into him. "I think we can."

"I think your wrong. It's the universe that decides, not us. It's the cosmos that bring souls together, and they've brought you to me." He whispers into my ear, holding my face in his hands, our foreheads touching.

"Clair…hey Clair, you're off in some other land," says John, as the thoughts of the weekend we met fade away to nothing. *Please don't ask me what I'm thinking about.* I don't want him to know that I was thinking of him, of our first encounter, our first dinner, our first kiss. Oh, that first kiss was so sweet-tasting, if I lick my lips I can still feel the touch of his on mine—it's been five years since I thought about that kiss. Frustrated at myself, I shake my head as if to empty it of the memories that linger. "Sorry, I got distracted thinking of Ameleiah," I lie.

After calling all the inns on my list, including the Queen's Inn, I still don't have a room. I shouldn't have expected to find one empty this time of year—it's almost impossible.

"Well, have you found a room, or are they all full?" he says, breaking the silence.

I look over to John. He's still in deep concentration on the road before him, doesn't take his eyes off what is in front of him, which is nothing but empty space. I breathe in deeply before speaking. "I might have to stay with you, the inns are all full, every last one." I look down into my lap and stare at my fidgeting hands while I confess this.

"What? They're all full? Really?" He shakes his head from side to side. "Wow, imagine that. I wouldn't have guessed something like that could happen, not here, not this time of year," he says with a smirk on his face. I take another deep long breath and say nothing else while I continue to look down at my hands in my lap.

CHAPTER 8

A Spirit Floating Through Air

Adam

IF I WASN'T a spirit floating through air and aware of the unknown, this would be the big moment of clarity. The moment I start to believe in another life, in undiscovered universes. But I do already believe, and I know what awaits the living soul.

I never thought this day would happen, but I dreamed of it: my parents being together again. And, yes, although I no longer have a physical body, I do still dream. Mom handles herself with grace, she is trying to hold in tears—really trying, I can tell as her eyes well up and become red and glossy.

When they pull into the hospital in Dad's truck, she fidgets with the bottom of her top, rubs the fabric through her fingers; she does this when she is nervous. Dad pulls into the parking lot and carefully maneuvers the truck into the first spot he sees, barely able to fit into the tight space. He runs to Mom's side, opens her door, and offers her his hand. He is still the gentleman I remember from when I was little. Mom hesitates at first, but lets the blouse slip through her fingers and places her shaky hand in his, and together they walk into the hospital to see my sister. I can read thoughts, and this is sometimes both a blessing and a curse, depending on the thoughts I hear and to whom they belong; sometimes I wash them away, pretending not to hear anything, but today I know that Dad is hoping that Michelle is not around. He doesn't want Mom to run into her. Together, and with hands still linked, they walk in through the emergency section as that is where Mia still is. She is now awake, sitting up, and there's a team of nurses around her, preparing her for surgery. When my mother sees my sister, her eyes instantly fill with concern, she runs to her side, holds her hand, and kisses her forehead.

"You have no idea the scare you gave me and how worried I was," says Mom.

"I'm okay Mom; you don't have to worry. Besides, Dad was here."

At the sound of my sister's voice, my mother breaks down crying and lays her head on Mia's shoulder. Dad is right there to console her and rubs her shoulders for her. This is what she should have allowed Dad to do for her when I died, but instead she pushed him away and blamed him.

"We're taking her into the surgery preparation area now, so you two must leave," says one of the nurses. "You can sit and wait in the waiting room, right over there." The same nurse points to an empty corner with four chairs and a small table next to a large dirty window covered with tiny fingerprints. "We'll come get you when she is out of surgery and in recovery."

Dad places his palm on Mom's back and leads her out of the room at the request of one of the nurses as the other nurses prepare Mia for surgery.

"Let's go get a coffee," says Dad, as he ushers Mom down the hall.

Mom stops in the middle of the hall. "No. I can't leave her."

"We'll return before they bring her back. The surgery is an hour or so, and she'll be in recovery for about half an hour, we have time for coffee."

"What if they need us and we're not here?"

"They'll call my phone; we won't be far. I promise."

Mom's legs shake and she stumbles backwards, grabbing onto the wall for support. Dad reacts quickly and places his arm around her back to steady her.

"You all right?" He looks her up and down, "Clair, how long has it been since you ate?"

She considers his question. "Yesterday, I think," she says, still gripping the wall for support.

"That's it, let's go, we have to get some food into you, or you'll be the next one lying in a hospital bed."

"I'm fine really."

"Yes, I know you are. You're as fine as there are vacant rooms available. I get it. Now let's go." Dad grabs Mom's arm and drags her down the hall, not allowing her to get away.

My parents make their way out of the emergency department, Mom no longer resisting.

"I don't want to go far," she pleads.

"We're only going up a block, a couple minutes away so we can be back here in under five minutes if the hospital calls. I promise you that." Dad heads west, towards Meredith Street, and hangs a left, then turns right onto Worthington Street, and right onto Water Street.

When Mom realizes where they are, there's a glimmer in her eye. Dad brings Mom to one of her favourite coffee shops that she used to love, Loco Beanz Coffee House. My parents used to bring us kids here often when we vacationed as a family on this part of the island. Dad heads straight to the familiar table they used to sit at before, "The one with the prettiest vantage point," Mom used to always say to him then.

"All the tables have the same view," Dad would reply.

"To you they do, but that's because you don't look at things through an artist's eye, like me."

"You're an artist?" Dad would tease, and Mom would pretend to punch him in the arm. Those are the memories of the coffee shop that Mom remembers now.

Dad is hoping to make Mom more comfortable, more relaxed, and that's the reason he brings her here, where it's familiar. He sits Mom down, gets her order from her, and goes to the counter to place it while she waits back at the table. In the back pocket of his jeans, his phone vibrates, it's still on silent from when he was in the hospital. He answers it on the first vibration, "Hey is everything okay?"

"Yes, Ameleiah is fine. I'm on my break and came up to see you, but you were gone. I thought you would be waiting for her in the waiting room," says Michelle on the other end.

"I'm with Clair."

There's a few seconds of silence. "Why?" she finally asks, annoyance seeping through her voice.

Dad's eyebrows join as he responds. "I'm getting her some food while we wait for the surgery to be over."

"But why are YOU out with her?"

"What do you mean, why?"

"Geez John, must I spell it out for you? I mean, is it necessary? She's a grown woman, surely she can get her own food. You didn't have to accompany her."

Dad's already joined eyebrows knit together even more at her comment. "She doesn't have a car here, I picked her up at the ferry. Besides, why is that such a problem for you?"

Michelle ignores Dad's last question and instead asks one of her own. "So, does this mean you will be spending all of your time with her now?"

"Michelle, I'm not sure what you're implying here, but yes, for the time being I'll be spending time with her. She is the mother of my child, who happens to be in surgery from a car accident, or have you forgotten that important part?"

Dad raises his voice, several people look at him and this gets Mom's attention too, so she looks to where he stands in the lineup at the counter—their eyes lock and he turns to face the other way, phone still in hand. I continue to listen in on the conversation.

Aware that others are staring, Dad lowers his voice. "Listen, I have to go," says Dad into the phone, he presses the end call button and places it in his back pocket, head shaking.

"Is everything okay?" asks Mom.

Dad returns to the table with two large coffees and two sandwiches in hand. He places the items on the table and runs his fingers through his hair.

"Everything is fine; it was Michelle, just checking in."

"Yes, I figured it was her. I could hear some of the conversation. She's not happy that you're with me, is she?"

Dad doesn't answer Mom and instead says, "Lets eat, you need to get some protein into you." He passes her a sandwich, ham with swiss cheese, and unwraps his own and takes his first bite without even looking at Mom. "I hope you like the sandwich; this was all they had left."

They eat their sandwiches in silence, not even looking at each other. When they finish, Dad wipes his mouth with a napkin and asks, "So how have you been Clair, I mean, really been over the last few years?"

Mom takes a sip of the coffee, lets the warm liquid linger in her mouth before swallowing. "Wonderful actually, keeping busy with my students during the school year, and when Ameleiah is here with you in the summers, I hike lots, paint like crazy, hit the gym most days." She stops to take another sip. "You know what it's like, just trying to immerse myself into all the usual stuff that I love to do."

Dad's eyebrows raise. "Really?"

"Yeah."

"That's great," says Dad, as he brings his eyebrows together, not believing Mom.

She must sense his hesitation because she goes on about exercising. "I started this new exercise program called CrossFit, have you heard of it?" Dad shakes his head indicating he hasn't. "It's a multifunctional full-training program that encompasses cardio, gymnastics, weightlifting, high-intensity training." Mom has never done CrossFit before; in fact, she doesn't go to the gym, or paint, or hike. At all. She only knows about CrossFit as she had looked it up once for her therapist as part of her therapy homework assignment.

Dad scratches his forehead, "Sounds intense."

"It is," says Mom not looking Dad in the eye and fidgeting with the hem of her top underneath the table.

"And you've been painting?"

"Of course, why wouldn't I be?"

"Sounds like you have a good life there. I'm happy that you're well. Really, I am."

Mom tugs at her hair and gathers it all in her hand, bringing it to the side of her shoulder, and changes the subject. "John I…I'm sorry that I blamed you before, but I don't blame you anymore, you know, about…."

Dad clears his throat, "I don't think this is the time to talk about that." He stares into space.

After a few more minutes of silence, and when they are both finished their coffee, Mom says it's time to leave, she wants to make sure they are back at the hospital when Mia is taken to the recovery room.

When they get back, they pass Michelle standing over a desk, writing something. Michelle looks up from her paperwork and her cold eyes lock with Mom. Mom doesn't know what Michelle looks like, so she smiles at the stranger, but Michelle returns a hard stare, confusing Mom. Beside Mom, Dad stiffens; this is the encounter he was hoping to avoid.

"You're back," says Michelle eagerly and dropping the pen on the desk.

"Shit," mutters Dad loud enough for all to hear.

Mom's glance shifts from Dad to Michelle as realization of who this woman is sets in.

"Michelle, this is Clairah, Ameleiah's mother."

At the mention of Michelle's name, Mom's smile fades and her expression hardens, but she is polite and holds out her hand to Michelle, nonetheless.

Michelle pulls back. "Please forgive me, but I don't typically shake hands here in the hospital, you know, germs and all," says Michelle, stretching out her lips into a full smile, revealing perfect white teeth.

Mom pulls her hand back. "Oh, of course," says Mom as she puts her hand inside her pocket, not knowing what else to do with it, embarrassed.

Michelle walks around the desk to where my parents are and places both of her hands on Dad's arm. "Can I speak to you for a minute?" says Michelle to Dad, lifting her hand into his.

Mom's eyes shoot to her hand on Dad's arm.

"Can we talk later? I want to go back to my daughter's room. I'll call you later tonight," says Dad as he walks away leaving Michelle behind, her hand slowly slipping off Dad with each step he takes.

"Well, I guess your girlfriend doesn't like me."

"Why? Because she wouldn't shake your hand? It's not that at all, she's just obsessed with germs and cleanliness, I think working in a hospital has done that to her."

"She didn't seem concerned about touching you, knowing you just came in from outside," questioned Mom, then immediately regretted what she said, afraid she would come across as the jealous ex-wife.

Dad considers this remark. "You're a stranger to her, she doesn't know you, but she knows me."

"Then I guess that's it," says Mom, unconvinced and feeling uncomfortable about meeting Dad's new, younger, girlfriend, with her long flowing blond locks, for the first time when Mom herself has not showered or brushed her teeth in two days. She suddenly brings her hands to her head and runs her fingers through her unruly hair—a failed attempt to tame it.

My parents find Mia's nurse and she tells them that only one parent is allowed in the recovery room. Dad encourages Mom to go and so she runs down the hall and a nurse tells her to slow down, like a parent would tell a child to settle. Mia is still asleep when Mom enters, but she pulls up a chair next to my sister and lays her head down on the side of the bed and waits for her to awaken.

One hour later, after Mia is awake but still groggy, the nurses return her to her room where Dad sits waiting patiently staring out the window. The doctor arrives to speak to my parents and so they step out into the hallway.

"Mr. and Mrs. Bennet, I'm Doctor Cole, your daughter's surgeon. The surgery went well."

Mom and Dad both let out a breath at the same time. "Your daughter suffered a displaced open fracture, so we had to operate to set the bone fragments into place. We had to insert an external fixator."

"What is that?" asks Mom, not taking her eyes off the doctor.

"It acts like a stabilizer; it contains metal pins to keep the bones in their proper position. She will be in a cast for about twelve weeks before we can look at removing the external fixator, but she should heal fine otherwise with some follow-up therapy. She has some bruising along her ribs, and she suffered a mild concussion so that will need to be monitored for a few days. Other than that, she is a lucky girl: you can never know these days what the result of a car accident is—it could have been worse, much worse. The girl that was driving only suffered a broken arm herself."

"How long will she need to stay in hospital for?" asks Dad.

"A couple of nights at most, we want to monitor the concussion."

"Thank you, Doctor," says Mom, holding out her hand. Dr. Cole takes Mom's hand in his and shakes it firmly. "My pleasure," he says. Mom thinks how odd that a doctor didn't mind shaking a stranger's hand.

"Can we visit with her now?" asks Dad.

"Certainly, just don't overdo it with too much conversation," says Dr. Cole before he turns and leaves to tend to his next patient.

My parents sit on either side of my sister for the remainder of the day, watching her doze in and out. They also stay into most of the evening as I, too, watch standing by the window, enjoying the view of my family together again and talking to one another when Mia finally wakes up. After a few minutes of chatter, Mia yawns again, and shortly after her nurse comes in to say that visiting hours will soon be over, and that Mia needs rest. Mom's breathing quickens, and I know why, this is the moment she has been dreading, the moment when they must go back to Dad's house together, alone, the house that used to once be our family cottage.

Dear Adam,

Fear. It flows through us all in a captivating wave as if we welcome it, cherish it, want it. It must, otherwise how could it be so present in our everyday lives, take over our sanity, rule our worlds. Fear shows itself in our reflection; each time we look in the mirror we are faced with yet again more fear. They say that if you fear you have something to lose, but what, my son, do I have to lose now that I have lost you? I should be fearless, like a warrior set out to battle on the fields, like a ship about to set sail in the high winds, and like a turtle placed in a race. Yet fear is something that I live with each minute of each waking day and by night, my fear is converted to thoughts plaguing my sanity. Although I've lost you my son, I still have your sister to consume my fear into. Sometimes I wish I had nothing to lose in life because if that were the case, I'd never fear again. When will this fear end and make this bitter, cold, and unassuming ways disappear into the unknown, into another world—one without fear, or without me? Please, tell me this Adam.

Love, Dad

CHAPTER 9

An Extra Hardened Rock

Clairah

"CLAIR," SAYS A voice into my ear. The same voice must be tugging at my arm, as I feel my sleeve being pulled away from my skin.

"Hmm," I say sleepily, looking around the white, stale room, remembering where I am.

"We should go, it's getting late, she needs her sleep." John continues to tug my arm.

I'm lying with my head on the side of Ameleiah's bed, I have been for the last few minutes and John is right, it's getting late. Feeling the affects of the day for the first time weighing down on me like an extra hardened rock, I fell asleep briefly.

I try avoiding John as he stares at me, fearing I'm hideous. "I could use a hot shower, some new clothes. Do you think there are any stores open at this time?"

John lifts his eyebrows. “Have you forgotten where we are? This is Manitoulin Island not Toronto,” John says smiling at me. “You won’t find anything open this time of night here.”

“Right,” I say, running my fingers through my hair to make it look better by patting down fly-aways.

“I can give you a shirt to sleep in and an extra toothbrush, and tomorrow we can go to the store by the house before heading up here again.” John now refers to the cottage as a house. As he should, since it’s his fulltime home.

“Before we leave, I need to talk to the nurse on duty. I want to make sure Ameleiah will be comfortable through the night, then we can go.” I walk out the door, heading towards the nurse’s station.

Once I’m convinced by two different nurses that my daughter will be well taken care of, John and I leave her, alone. I’m not sure why I suddenly feel as if I’m about to throw up, but my stomach feels queasy, unsettled. I excuse myself and stop at a public washroom in the emergency department on the way to the parking lot, afraid that I might lose the sandwich and coffee I had earlier. After locking the door behind me, I gather my shoulder length, unwashed hair into a ponytail and lean over the toilet, waiting, but the sandwich doesn’t resurface—I freeze, staring into the toilet bowl. After a few minutes, there’s a knock on the door.

“Clairah, are you all right? You’ve been in there for a long time,” says John from the other side of the door; I’m startled back to reality when his voice seeps in.

“I’ll be out in a minute; you can wait in the truck.”

“I’m not going anywhere; I’ll wait right here. Take the time you need.”

I wish the nausea would subside, but it doesn’t. I search my purse for a plastic bag, anything that I can use in case I get sick in the truck, but my purse contains no such safeguard. I splash water over my face and pat my hair down again. As I look into the mirror, I’m horrified by the woman staring back at me. This is a woman I don’t know, a woman who looks lost, frightened, and broken—when did I lose myself? Several times I hear the knob of the door being turned as others check to make sure that the room is really occupied. Another few minutes go by, and I know I can't stay in here hiding forever. I must face this; I must be able to hold it together and walk back into that memory-filled cottage. It's either that or I sleep here at the hospital, but I also know that John won't let me do that, he'll carry me screaming if he must, that's the kind of man he is. Besides, I really could use that hot shower, it will do me good, it will relax me and make me feel more like myself, so I take one last deep breath, still looking at my reflection in the mirror, then I open the bathroom door. Right in my view is John, sitting in a chair, hunched over with his face in his hands. At hearing the sound of the door opening, he looks up at me, sighs and stands.

"I'm sorry for making you wait. I needed a few minutes to collect myself. I thought I might be sick, but I'm better now. We can go now."

John tilts his head to the side and walks towards me. He doesn't respond with words, but offers me his hand—I slip mine into his and we walk to the truck in silence.

In the truck I lay my head back, close my eyes and try to focus on nothing but my breathing. I don't fall asleep, but I remain in deep concentration, eyes closed the entire drive. Before long, I hear John's voice. "Clair, wake up, we're here." He must have thought I'd fallen asleep.

When I open my eyes for the first time since leaving the hospital, a wave of panic hits me. We are sitting in the driveway of the cottage I used to know so well and loved once, back when I was happy, back when I was still me. Being here is too much for me, and as much as I try to choke back my tears, they still come flowing like a fast river.

Memories of the children running around the front yard flash before me. Ameleiah doing summersaults—she learned how to do them here. Adam squirting his water gun at his sister while she practiced her summersaults, saying that he was doing this to keep her cool, even though she hated it and yelled at him to stop getting her wet. Memories of the two of them walking side by side in front of John and I as we headed down to the beach for an afternoon of family time. Memories of John carrying a sleeping Adam in his arms later that same afternoon, as he was tired from a day out in the sun. Memories of John and I sitting on the front step drinking a glass of cabernet sauvignon—our favourite red wine. Happy memory after happy memory flash before me; then these memories fade and newer, darker ones emerge. Memories of having to come back here the same day Adam died, less one child—the house now empty, even though there were still three of us inside. Memories of the pain, the torture, the emptiness I felt walking back through the front door without him—his scent lingering in the air, taunting me in each room I stepped into. Memories of the stone-cold silence amongst us all lasting for days. Memories of Adam's memorial service that we decided to have here on the island, even though we didn't have his body to bury—it was never found. It was left lost in the lake.

I bring my hands up to my face to conceal the hurt that John will see by looking at me. But he knows me, and he doesn't have to see me to know that I'm in pain.

He reaches out to touch my shoulder; from between my fingers I see his hand hover, so I shrink back and knock it away. "Do you want to talk about it?" asks John with a frown on his face.

"There's nothing to talk about."

"Back at the café, you said you were sorry for blaming me, and I shut you down when you tried to talk, so if talking helps, I'm here to listen."

I wipe my nose with the back of my hand. "No, you were right, I shouldn't have brought it up, this is not the time or the place," I say, as I open my door and step out into the cool night. My feet are shaky as I climb the steps of the front porch and so I grab the old, rusted steel railing for support. John walks behind me, close enough to catch me if I fall—he must have noticed my unsteadiness.

John opens the front door. "You know where everything is, nothing much has changed since you were here last." He pauses for a moment. "In fact, it's all still the same."

He's right. As my eyes scan the rooms, the cottage looks identical to how I left it five years ago. The same pictures of the kids still hang on the light grey walls, the old furniture we bought together is exactly how I remember it, and the kitchen is organized the way I used to place things on the counters. I open the old oak cabinets and inside things are arranged the same way I used to; the peanut butter jar is still in the same location as always. I have always wanted to change these cabinets but we never got around to it. For a split second it's as if I haven't left, as if I haven't been away for five years. It's as if this is yet another summer holiday spent together, the four of us, after a fun day out on the water. But I have been away, and this isn't a holiday. And although nothing has changed, everything has changed.

The cottage consists of three bedrooms; the master, and the two for the kids, each had their own room. I'm afraid to look into Adam's room; afraid I might find it still the same way I left it. I never have asked John what he did with Adam's things. I didn't want to know; it was easier to not think about it and ignore. But as I open his door cautiously, I walk into a brand new bedroom—the rest of the cottage was left untouched, but this room has been transformed. John has painted, replaced all the furniture, and hung paintings of landscapes that I painted years ago. I had no idea John even had these paintings anymore—I had forgotten about my own work, my own creations. The room looks warm, inviting, and unlike that of a little boy's. I'm glad that he at least redid this one room. I don't know if I would have been able to stay in this house otherwise, as this is the room I'm meant to sleep in tonight. If the room had not been transformed, I would have preferred to sleep on the couch, afraid of being shocked to death through the night by memories.

Back in my home in Paris, I have kept Adam's room the same, untouched—afraid to wash away the last memories of him if I redid his room. So, there, the same light blue paint is plastered on the walls, Thomas the Tank Engine posters hanging on them—a reminder, a stab to my heart every time I walk in there. His desk still holds all his notebooks from the previous year at school from when he brought them home at the end of his senior kindergarten year, including the unreturned library book that the school's library eventually called to tell me we didn't have to pay for. "It's on the house," the librarian had said, afraid to cause more grief to my already grieving heart. As if a pardoned library book would make it all okay, make it all go away.

There's a gentle knock a few minutes later and John enters the bedroom and hands me a bundle of clothes. "Here are a couple t-shirts of mine that you can sleep in, and a butterfly pajama bottom that belongs to Ameleiah, I don't think she will mind you borrowing it. My pajama bottoms will fall right off you, given your size compared to mine," he points to me then himself.

I reach out and take the clothes from him, our hands touching as I take the items from him.

"I don't really want to go through her clothes, so I brought you my t-shirts. It's all right if the tops are big. Her pajama bottoms just happened to be on her bed, so I grabbed them. I hope they fit, they should fit, the two of you are not much different in size."

"This is great, thank you."

"There's an extra toothbrush in the main bathroom, it's brand new, still in the package," says John, as he looks at me and waits for a reply. When I don't offer one, he continues, "I've left it on the counter for you so it's easy to find." He pauses again, giving me an opportunity to speak, and continues, "Well, let me know if you need anything else. Towels are on the usual closet shelf; you remember where that is right?"

I nod so that he knows I understand—when, really, I'm afraid that I remember way too much—and walk past him to the bathroom carrying the bundle of clothes in my hand and leaving John in Adam's room, alone. Once in the bathroom, I lock the door behind me, turn the water on in the shower, and when the steam is hot and thick, I step in, sit on the bathtub floor and let the hot water fall all over me as I cry like a baby would cry for their mother, only my own mother is far away in Portugal right now. I make a mental note to call my parents to let them know about the accident as I still haven't done that. I need to let them know that my daughter is okay.

I haven't put in the tub stopper, as I wanted to shower, not bathe, so I eventually grab onto the sides of the tub and pull myself up, grab the shampoo and lather it through my tangled hair. I must take about an hour in the shower, and I do feel better after I'm clean, hair washed, teeth brushed; I take my dirty clothes to the laundry room and run a cycle. I want to wake up early the next morning and go for a walk to the store and buy some new clothes; I don't want to put these soiled items back on. I look around for John, but he is nowhere to be found. He must be in his room, wanting to give me space. I step outside and sit on the front step as I wait for the wash cycle to finish. I know how to use these machines as they are the same ones I used to wash the children's clothes when they were little. Once the wash cycle is done, I remove the clean clothes from the washing machine and place them in the dryer, turn it on and tiptoe past John's room to Adam's room and climb into bed.

I wake up bright and early—in time to see the spectacular sunrise warming the Earth. Dragging myself out of bed, I get dressed in my freshly washed clothes and walk outside and sit on the front step, reflecting on the beauty of the island. Soon afterwards the sun fully rises, and the sky promises to be a glorious day, no clouds in the sky. There are a few more sailboats out on the water than I remembered there being the day before, and more boats at the dock today, and I wonder why those owners are not out on the water sailing like the others. Perhaps there's a storm coming in later, so they stay put rather than risk venturing out and being caught in choppy water, like we were. I shake that thought away and replace it with a new thought, the way my therapist taught me to do when my mind wanders to unhealthy memories. Then I remember how early in the morning it still is and that's probably why the boats aren't out yet. I force myself to think of the serenity and eye catching views of the island instead of boats out sailing. John's cottage is directly across from the marina, affording views worth capturing on a canvas—like I used to. Directly in front of the house's large yard is a quiet road, and on the other side, the sparkling water. The house is on the same street as the Queen's Inn, only a few doors down about a kilometre apart, so both locations share the same spectacular views. The water is narrow on this part of the island as it's a water way and on the other side of the water is a cliff. Its lush, tall, green trees, shrubs and bushes line the other side of the shore creating a blanket of nature over the glistening water. There is a lookout from up above that cliff where you can see out for miles and miles and become mesmerized and one with nature. There's a pathway that runs along the marina and leads to a restaurant in a round building with brown wooden panels, white stripes running across, and a red roof. I have a good view of the restaurant and its balcony from where I am. A man wearing a white uniform and chef's hat is on the balcony already this early in the morning. He must be the cook, judging by his uniform; he's leaning over the railing, camera in hand, facing the water and taking pictures of the sailboats that are docked. He is obviously taking a moment to enjoy the little things in life, and this makes me smile; I used to do the same. I go back inside to check the time, the clock on the stove reading eight thirty-nine now: wow, I've been sitting outside for a couple of hours already. Remembering that the stores open at nine, I head back out and walk along the pathway past the restaurant and turn right and away from the water and head up the first street. I pass a cute Free Little Library, it's light green in colour, and it has a sign reading: Seed, Recipe and Community Exchange, Charter Number 13249. On the same block of wood as that sign off to the left is another sign that reads: Take a Book, Return a Book. I stop and open it to check if there's anything of interest that I might want to read, and I pull out Emma Donoghue's *Room*. I recently watched the movie but haven't read the book yet, but it's on my To Read list. There are other titles that look interesting that I haven't heard of: *Sleeping Beauty* by Judith Michael, and *Detour* by James Siegel. I decide I'll read these two next, and I remember that I'm only here long enough for Ameleiah to recover so most likely won't have time to read even one full book during my stay. Careful to not damage the books, I put them back inside the Little Free Library where I found them and close the door to protect the precious words inside. I keep walking past the Little Free Library and turn left when I get to the next street. I continue for a few more blocks on Meredith Street, passing by a coffee shop—another Loco Beanz Coffee House, a smaller one than the one in Little Current. I stop and order a large latte to go. I arrive at the general store before finishing my coffee so, not wanting to waste coffee, I sit on a bench outside the store and watch families laughing as they happily walk past me discussing their day. Husbands and wives holding hands as their children run on ahead, like mine used to. I look away, pretending not to notice their happiness spread across their faces. Taking my last sip, I dump the paper cup into a nearby garbage can, take a deep breath, and walk into the store. I need to brace myself for familiar faces, locals from my past here shopping, people who will try to talk to me and ask questions about my life, questions I don't want to answer. It's not that I'm antisocial or rude; I just want to be left alone today…and most days, actually. A lifetime ago, I was the one who would stop to talk to everyone, strangers even, and ask them how their day was, what they had planned for the afternoon, offer suggestions on what they could do. But now my life is different and I often find myself lost for words, unable to carry a conversation. I keep my head down and swing my hair forward hoping not to be recognized, but my efforts are for nothing.

"Well, look who it is. If it's not Clairah herself, here in the flesh," says Harold, the store's owner. "I barely recognized you when you first walked in. Had to look twice to make sure it was really you."

Oh, here we go. I breathe, and answer, "It's been a long time Harold, how are you?" I say, forcing a smile.

"I have been well. You? How is that lovely daughter of yours?"

"Well, Ameleiah is the reason I'm here."

"Come and tell me all about it. As you can see, you are my only customer this morning so come keep an old man company for a few minutes…like old times."

And that's how I spend my next hour. As I'm leaving the store, I have two bags full of clothes, a new toothbrush to replace the extra one John gave me, pajamas, flip flops, and a new charger for my phone. I say goodbye to Harold after promising to not stay away for as long this time, and walk back to the cottage: John's home. This time, instead of walking along the pathway by the water, I walk on the sidewalk across the street from the path and stop in front of the Queen's Inn. How I loved this place, and even still do. It's so magical with its grand front porch, balcony on the second level and cream coloured siding. Kelly still does a fantastic job keeping the place looking spectacular and inviting. There are three steps that run the length of the entire porch, and on each one is a pot of flowers. On the porch itself there are more pots of flowers and a wooden bench on either side of the grand front door. The driveway is gravel, just like I remembered the last time I was here. There are no cars in the driveway, all the guests must be out, so I decide it's safe for me to sit for a minute and enjoy the views, like old times when John and I used to sit here doing nothing but admiring each other.

I begin to think about that one particular evening that I left Manitoulin after the first weekend we spent together, after we met, and how devastating it was to leave him. That was the same evening that John had told me he had fallen for me. John didn't want me to go, but I had to, my life was back in Paris, not here on the island. The island was a vacation spot, not my permanent home. He begged me to stay longer, and I teased him that he would forget all about me before I even crossed the lake back to Tobermory. That evening, he drove me to South Baymouth even though my friend Tammy had admitted about being upset and feeling abandoned that she had to drive by herself. But I wanted to spend the last hour of my time on the island with the man I had met only a few days ago, a man who had already claimed my heart.

My girlfriend eventually was okay with driving on her own, leaving me with John, knowing all too well I wanted more time alone with him.

"You're a fool if you think I'll ever forget you," he says.

As we drive to South Baymouth for me to catch the evening ferry back to the mainland, back to Tobermory, John's free hand, the one not on the steering wheel, is over mine the entire time. I have only known him for four days and I feel my heart tearing apart in two at the thought of leaving him. He squeezes my hand in his, revealing so much with that one gesture. His car has a manual transmission, so he needs his right hand to shift gears, but he keeps my hand securely under his, wrapped around the gear shifter. Every so often he steals a glance my way, and I pretend to be looking out the window so that he doesn't know I was staring at him too.

"What are you thinking about?" he asks.

"How I'm going to miss our morning walks along the beach, our nightly drive to get ice cream, and our little dances on the street."

"We can do all that again you know, as soon as you come back to me."

I take note of his choice of words and squeeze his knee with my other hand, my right hand, as he has his hand tightly wrapped around my left. When we get to the boat launch, he becomes quiet and won't look me in the eye. I reach out to take his face in my hand and make him turn to me and I see he has tears in his eyes; I wipe the tears away for him.

"I'll call you, we'll talk for hours and it will feel as if I'm still here with you."

"Nothing will be the same unless you really are here."

The announcement is made to have all passengers with no vehicles board.

"John, I have to go."

"I know, I just keep wishing that you could stay."

"I'll come back to see you, I promised you that and I intend on keeping my promise. I will come back."

"When?"

"On the next long weekend."

I have my first teaching job lined up, and so I need to get back in time to prepare myself for it both physically and mentally. The next long weekend is Thanksgiving weekend, and Thanksgiving is early this year so I will be seeing him again in two months, but that feels like it is a lifetime away. As I kiss him goodbye his left cheek is warm, soft against mine. I feel his arms wrap tight around me, not wanting to let go. I force myself free from him and walk away, leaving him with his hands in his pockets, head hung low, standing alone.

I'm still sitting on the front steps of the Queen's Inn reminiscing when an unknown car pulling up the driveway brings me back to now, and as I look up I see it's Kelly, the inn's owner and John's aunt—I would recognize her anywhere. Embarrassed to be sitting here, I quickly stand before she gets out, and speed away not looking back. I can't go through more questioning, especially with a family member of John's. When I return to John's cottage, I find him outside working on his truck, polishing it to a shine. A man stands a few feet from him, with his back to me and arms flailing—his voice carries with the wind and vulgar words escape his mouth. John ignores the man as he continues to use rags to wipe his truck down to a shiny finish. As I approach closer, I recognize the man standing next to John; it's Henry, his neighbour, long-time rival, and my ex-boyfriend. Henry's head whips around urgently when he hears my voice.

CHAPTER 10

The Silence Surrounding Them Speaks Volumes

Clairah

"CLAIRAH, WOW, IS that really you? It's been how long, two, maybe three years?" Henry says in an enthusiastic voice and sparkle in his eye—his arms resting on the sides of his legs and no longer aggressively moving about in mid air. My glance shifts naturally to John, he rolls his eyes like a bored teenager would do.

"It's actually been five years, Henry, not just two or three, and it's nice to see you too."

"Five years, wow, you look younger with each year."

At that comment John clears his throat, interrupting Henry. "Don't you have something to do, man? We have a family situation here and we don't need you hanging around." John stares into Henry's eyes.

Henry takes a step closer to John, fists balled at his sides; the two are barely inches apart. The air between them, thick with their hatred for each other only just manages to cut through.

The silence surrounding them speaks volumes. I thought they had gotten over their feud from years ago, but I must have been wrong. The hostility between these two men began back when John and I first met.

Henry Blake, a long-time resident of the island himself, had, on more than one occasion, tried to get me to go out with him and I refused him so many times. I first met Henry four years before I met John. I was at the island on vacation with my parents then, and we were having dinner together, the three of us—as I'm an only child—at the restaurant by the marina that John and I frequented often with the kids. I noticed Henry looking at me often, but trying to be inconspicuous about it, probably because my parents were there. I was never attracted to Henry, so when he finally cornered me and asked me out that day during dinner, when I had excused myself to use the washroom, I declined. But he was persistent and didn't give up for a long time. Not even until after John and I met and got together. That same week when he cornered me at the restaurant with my parents, Henry asked me out three more times, and each time I told him the same thing—I wasn't interested. This continued into the following summer when I finally agreed to go out for dinner with him out of pity—I was feeling bad that he liked me. We ended up spending some time together, and I got to know him a little, and the more I learned about him the less I wanted to be with him romantically. I didn't consider him boyfriend material, but in his mind, our time together formed a different story.

During the first few years of my relationship with John, Henry would make comments to John about how I chose the wrong man, how Henry would be a better provider for me than John. On many occasions the two men ended up sprawled over the front lawn, proving to one another who was stronger. They were young then, barely adults in their early twenties, inexperienced and both raging with jealousy and testosterone. I had thought that all these years later they would have gotten over this rage, but I was wrong. It seems that both men still have something to prove to one another. John has never gotten over the jealousy and Henry has not gotten over rejection.

Frightened that one of them is going to hit the other, I step in between them and face John. "I'm going to shower and change. I'll be ready to leave for the hospital in less than thirty minutes, but first I need to eat, I'm starving. Is there food in the house?" I ask, temping him to come inside with me.

Still looking at Henry with deep set eyes, he says over my shoulder, "Yeah, I'll come in and make you some breakfast while you get ready. I'm done here anyway."

Henry makes a snorting sound but steps back and with a monotone voice, says, "Until next time." He comes in front of me, face to face, his expression softens. "Clairah," when he says my name, I turn my head to face him too, "it was nice to see you, really. You look good."

John takes a step towards him, but I put out my arms to his chest to stop him. *Don't*, I mouth to him so Henry doesn't hear, as he's already walking away. From behind my back, I hear footsteps retreating, and John and I remain alone, my arm still out on his chest. "John, let it go," I say again into his ear next to his bulging vein.

Without a word he turns, and stomps back into the house, slamming the wooden door behind him, and from the front window I see him walk towards the kitchen and open the fridge to make me breakfast. I reach into my pocket and touch the bottle of Ativan waiting to be consumed. I better take one before going to see my daughter and running into Michelle. I try not to take the pills often, despite my therapist telling me that if I had diabetes I'd take insulin without hesitation, but to me it just doesn't seem like a good comparison.

CHAPTER 11

A Much-Needed Break

Adam

MY MOTHER LOVES to cook, or at least she used to. Come to think of it, I haven't seen her cook in years, other than opening pre-made frozen packages of food full of preservatives and tossing them into the microwave—that hardly constitutes as cooking. She taught my father how to cook over the years and he, too, became good at preparing mouth-watering meals. Mom used to love it when Dad cooked for her, she said it made her feel special, so Dad, being the romantic type that he was then, would often prepare the weekend meals, giving Mom a much-needed break. Breakfast was his specialty: homemade buttermilk waffles or pancakes with fresh fruit and whipped cream dolloped over the top. This was Mom's number one favourite, although I haven't seen her eat that in a while. Now instead for breakfast most days she has toast with peanut butter, or cold cereal. Dad remembers this about Mom, and so after he storms off back into the house, he heads straight for the kitchen, pulls out flour, eggs, milk and other ingredients required for waffles and gets to work while Mom remains outside sitting on the front step alone, watching Dad from the front window.

Soon, Mom walks inside and gasps when she inhales the scent that lingers in the air of the freshly made waffles and squeezed orange juice. Dad's busy wiping down the flour-covered counters and doesn't acknowledge her standing in awe before him. So, Mom walks away, stomach growling, to grab a quick shower and change out of the clothes she wore to the island and into the new items she purchased earlier today. It's nothing fancy, a pair of stretchy black leggings and a silky long-sleeve top. She walks into Mia's room, picks out some of her pinkish makeup and applies it to her cheeks and eyes. She rummages through her drawers and finds a straightener and plugs it in. After running the straightener through her hair a few times, she takes one last look in the mirror and with a nod of her head walks out the bedroom and into the kitchen where Dad sits at the table, arms crossed and waiting.

When Mom approaches, Dad is looking down, but he glances towards her and his eyes flicker, but Mom doesn't notice this as she stares at the seat across from Dad.

"Thanks for breakfast; you didn't have to go through all this though."

"It was no bother, I had to eat too," says Dad, picking up his fork with one hand and the maple syrup with the other. "Sit and eat before it gets cold," he gestures toward the chair and Mom hesitantly takes a seat while smoothing down her already straight hair.

"You look different today." Dad looks at Mom intently.

"Better, I hope? More like myself?"

"You look good."

"I was at a disadvantage when you saw me yesterday. It's amazing what a shower, a new outfit and little mascara and blush can do for someone." Mom has lowered her gaze and is picking at her food, moving pieces of cut-up waffles from one side of her plate to the other.

"You appear calm today."

"Calm?" asks Mom for confirmation on what he means.

"Yeah, calm," is all Dad offers for a reply. Mom doesn't say anything else after this, because she's busy contemplating the meaning of what looking calm is. She's wondering if she was way too flustered and out of control yesterday and decides she probably was.

They sit across the table from one another; I'm stuck in the middle as their mediator, only I can't guide them into further conversation. Mom hardly eats, despite this being her most desired breakfast, and Dad notices as he keeps looking at her still full plate.

"Do you not like the food?" he finally asks. "I can make you something else."

"No, this is great, really. I guess I'm just not as hungry today as I thought I was."

"Well, we're not leaving here until you eat. You're wasting away to nothing. Hurry up and get a full waffle into you so we can get going," says Dad, as he takes his plate and utensils to the sink, rinses them off and places them in the dishwasher. Mom continues to battle with the waffle on her plate as if deciding which way to place the couch in an empty room. I'm not sure which I prefer, silence or arguing. Mom manages to force down a few bites, and when Dad leaves the room she immediately tosses the remainder of the food into the trashcan, and covers the evidence with a napkin, like a stubborn child would do, not that I've ever done that myself—I don't think.

In the truck on the way to the hospital, Dad's hands are firm as they grip the wheel. "Did you have to be so charming to him?"

"First, I'm calm, now I'm charming? You really like the 'C' words these days don't you."

Dad raises an eyebrow at her, "I'm being serious Clairah." He's calling her Clairah instead of Clair. He only does this when he's upset, usually.

"Charming to whom anyway. Henry?"

"Yes, of course, Henry. Who else?"

"I said 'it was nice to see you too'. That's hardly being charming. I was being polite, how is that putting on the charm? And even if I had tried to charm him away this morning, what is it to you?"

Dad grips the steering wheel even tighter; his knuckles are bulging and red. I fear he will rip the steering wheel right off. They drive the rest of the way in silence, each lost in their own memories; the memories I can all too well see them daydreaming about. They are both so much in one of their stubborn moods that they aren't even taking a minute to look up and admire the beauty that surrounds them. Everywhere you look is a new, inviting lake blanketed by nature. Lake after lake and rows of lush trees make up the grand landscape that both my parents are oblivious to at this moment. Occasionally we pass groups of motorcyclists, travelling through the paradise of what this island has to offer. The group of motorcyclists ahead of us surely have the best view, not being obstructed by a windshield. There are five bikes in total in this group, some of them single riders and a couple have passengers on the back. The passengers on the backs of the bikes bob their heads up and down and side to side—helmets moving to the movement as they take in the mesmerizing magic around them.

Dear Adam,

Regret, we all have it, experience it, live it. Each of us battles with things that we wish we had done better in life, said more of, and abstained from, but the reality is that we often don't learn from our regret and continue to make the same mistakes over and over, until one day we stop, look around and regret the mistakes we have made yet again—a vicious circle—the circle of life and creator of all havoc. The things we regret in life are lessons learned, or they should be if we would only stop, pay attention, and listen. I have so many regrets my son, but the most painful one of all is of that day, I regret not checking the forecast more often, not listing to your mother, not inspecting the head to look for you. I regret so many things for so many reasons, but most of all, I regret failing you.

Love, Dad

CHAPTER 12

There's Colour in Your Cheeks

Clairah

"AMELEIAH, YOU LOOK so much better today. There's colour in your cheeks," I say, as I try to push back strands of hair off her pretty face.

"Mom, please don't fuss over me, I'm fine," says Ameleiah knocking my hand away.

"I'm sorry; I can't help it at times."

"Where's Dad?" She looks around for her father, scanning the room with wide eyes.

"He dropped me off at the front entrance and went to find a parking spot. The emergency room must be full today; there were no parking spots available."

"But he's coming right?"

"Of course he's coming."

"Okay, as long as he'll be here soon, I want him here."

"Why wouldn't he be here? Besides, I'm here for now, I can get you anything you need or help with whatever it is that you need help with."

"It's fine, I'd prefer to wait for Dad."

"I see."

She raises her eyebrows and looks me in the eye. "I was worried he wasn't coming because you're here, so that's why I asked."

I take a deep breath, "Ameleiah, we've been civil with one another. I even stayed at the cottage last night."

Her jaw drops and her eyes open wider. "It's not a cottage anymore, Dad lives there year-round, it's his house, and it's rude of you to still call it a cottage."

My head jerks slightly at her remark. "I apologize, I stayed at the house."

"Why did you stay there? I mean, you could've gotten a hotel nearby instead. Why stay at Dad's?" Her voice increases a notch. "Was he upset by you being there?"

"No, of course not. Your father offered, rather insisted I stay there."

"Seriously?"

"Yes, seriously. I tried to stay in a hotel; I really did. There wasn't a vacant room anywhere nearby, I had no choice really," I say, making sure she understands that this was by force and not by choice. "Is it that big of a deal to you that I stayed there?"

She shrugs and smiles as John enters. "Hey, there's my girl," interrupts John before Ameleiah has the opportunity to answer my last question.

"Daddy!" she says as she leaps forward in her bed and hugs her father for a long time, leaving me alone to watch the warm and welcome exchange that I didn't receive.

I step away from the bed, giving them space. "I think I'll go check in with the doctor."

Too consumed in their embrace, neither of them hears nor sees me leave the room. Once out in the hall, I let the tears fall freely as I stand with my back to the wall and face in my hands. My eyes are closed, so

I don't notice Michelle approaching until it's too late—until her high pitched voice pierces my eardrums.

"Clairah, was it? Is everything all right with Ameleiah?" she asks, most likely noticing my red blotchy face that I suspect I have.

"Everything is fine Michelle."

"Good because I know it can't be Ameleiah causing you sorrow, I checked in on her just a few minutes ago and she's well."

"Are you her nurse?"

"No, I work in the emergency room only, but I check in on her regularly, you know, for John's sake. She's a lovely young girl, so friendly and polite. She reminds me so much of my John." She won't meet my eyes, but I can see her trying to steal a glance at me from the corner of hers. "We had a nice chat filled with many laughs this afternoon."

Her John. Is this woman for real? "Listen, I appreciate your concern, but I'd rather be alone right now, so please leave."

"I'm only trying to offer my support," she says with a grin.

"Well, this is an important time for family, and you're not family so...."

Michelle shifts from one leg to the other. "Wow, a little jealous, are we?"

"Hey, there you are," says John, with his eyebrows knitted together as he notices Michelle. "You left so suddenly; we didn't even realize you were gone."

Neither Michelle nor I say a word, and so John presses further, "Ameleiah says she's tired from the medication and wants a nap so it's a good time to go pick up your car." He waits for a reply, a gesture, anything; but I remain frozen, so he repeats, "Clair, your car?"

"Yes, my car," is all I manage for a reply.

"Did I miss something here before I walked out?" asks John, looking from me to Michelle and back at me again, searching my face for... for something, but I don't know what he's looking for. "No. Let's go get my car, I just need a minute, and then we can go."

Michelle readjusts her scrub top over her waist before speaking.

"John, I'm off in half an hour, if you wait, I could ride along with you. You know, so that you don't have to make the drive back all alone." Michelle has a hopeful grin on her face.

"We don't have half an hour to wait," says John, shaking his head.

"Why? What difference is half hour?"

"We need to leave while Ameleiah rests, I want to be back by the time she wakes up. It's almost two hours there and back."

"I see, well all right, how about we get together for dinner later?"

"I'm not sure, we'll see."

"Come on John, why the hesitation?"

"Michelle, my daughter's in the hospital, be a little patient and understanding, will you?"

Michelle's face turns a bright red and her eyes enlarge at hearing his rejection. Before she can rebuke, John walks away, annoyed, flapping his arms, and I hurry along behind him, eager to leave Michelle's presence. From behind me I can still feel her looking at me and sending me negative thoughts, bad energy. I pick up my pace to increase the distance between us—to shield myself from her darkness. "I need to use the restroom before we leave." I call out to John as he is now a few feet away, and I'm unsure if he even heard me.

He turns around to speak, "I'll get the truck and wait for you out front."

I'm back in the same washroom I was in last night—I'm spending way more time than needed in this washroom. I guess Ameleiah doesn't use waterproof mascara; I wipe off the smudges around the bottom of my eyes that was caused from crying earlier and reapply lip gloss. I rub my shoulders to relax my aching muscles from sleeping the wrong way. Why do I allow Michelle to get under my skin? That woman makes me feel like I need to try harder at everything, she makes me feel less than I am. Satisfied that I've done all I can with the lip gloss to try to save my face, I leave the washroom and find John's truck parked at the entrance, waiting for me.

The drive is long and sombre; John doesn't say a word the entire drive, but that's okay, because I don't say anything either. We are like two school-aged children, refusing to break the silence, waiting for the other to go first. When we pull up next to my car, I get out and slam the door. I don't know why Michelle has made me feel like a burning ball of fire today, but I do. I turn my head to look at John once I'm in my car, but he doesn't look back, instead, his head is facing forward, eyes glued to nothing ahead, truck still turned on but not moving. I google the address for the hospital on my now-charged phone and punch it into my car's GPS. As I put the car into drive, John startles me with a knock on my window. I push the button on the door to roll it down.

He leans his head in as far as he can. "Follow me so you don't get lost." He walks away and climbs back into his truck, not giving me a chance to respond.

"I don't need your help," I yell after him, but he's already inside the truck. My phone beeps, a text message, so I look at the screen.

John: Yes, you do. Follow me

So, he did hear me after all. I smack the steering wheel with the palm of my hand in frustration, then I reach out and press stop on the GPS route that has already been calculated for me and I do what John wants me to do, I follow him while he smiles through the side mirror—he likes getting his way.

We spend the rest of the afternoon and early evening at the hospital, and by five o'clock, my stomach growls. John and I have our own vehicles here, so I'm not at his mercy and can leave when I want, no longer dependent upon him—but I'm not sure where I'm supposed to go, so I spend some time today making calls, trying to get a room somewhere, anywhere, but of course, they're all still booked. I don't want to impose on him anymore by assuming I'm going back to his place. Nothing has changed from yesterday, though I suspect John will insist I go back with him, but after the encounter with Michelle this afternoon and with Henry this morning, I'm questioning if it's a good idea and if he even wants me there. As I brew over my misery and try to think of a solution to my predicament, John approaches and tells me that he thinks we should leave to get food. I look up at him from where I sit, startled. He is so complicated at times; earlier today he acted like he didn't want to be around me and now he asks me to dinner. I accept the dinner offer, if that's what it is, and so we decide to meet back at the house as John says he will cook. Luckily, there are no further encounters with Michelle this evening—I'm grateful for that as I don't know how I'd explain dinner tonight with John since he turned her down earlier today.

When I pull up to the street where John's cottage—house—is, it's Henry I see first. He's on his side of the property working on his motorboat that's parked in his driveway. He smiles when he sees me get out of my car. I ignore him at first, not wanting to draw any attention to myself—I've arrived before John; he said he was stopping at the market for some fresh vegetables. But I decide I'm being rude, so I walk over to Henry, curious as to what he is doing with the boat as it wasn't here earlier this morning.

"I pulled her out of the water this morning. I'm fixing her up a bit, replacing the carpet, making her new again, and then I'm selling her to buy something bigger. She'll be a beauty when I'm finished with her," he says, admiring his hard work. "So, what's the deal?" He asks tilting his chin up.

"Deal?" I raise an eyebrow.

"With you and John. You two back together or something?" He asks swinging a polishing cloth.

"Oh, no it's nothing like that." I lower my head, "I guess you haven't heard?"

He stops wiping the already polished spot on the boat, "Heard what?"

"It's Ameleiah, she…"

"What's wrong with Ameleiah? I saw her just the other day. She seemed fine to me."

"She was in a car accident yesterday, but she's okay. She'll be out of the hospital soon, but in a cast, she broke her leg."

He puts the rag down, "Clairah, I'm so sorry, I didn't know." He reaches out to touch my face, but I pull back not wanting the contact. "Are you staying with John then, here at the house?"

Even Henry calls it a house and not a cottage anymore.

"Yes, I am but only because I don't have a choice, all inns and hotels are booked, it's the season after all," I say raising my arms, accepting defeat.

"That must be odd for you, having to stay with your ex-husband after all this time."

I swallow hard and hope he doesn't notice. "We're managing fine."

"You know, I have a spare room you could use," he offers raising his eyebrows.

I'm taken aback by his offer and step back a bit. "Thanks, but…"

"Clairah, relax, I'm only teasing you. I know you'd never stay at my place, even though I do have a spare bedroom, two in fact," he says raising, only one eyebrow this time.

My back is towards the road, so I don't notice John's truck pull up the driveway until I hear him call my name. "Clairah!"

I turn around to face John, not wanting him to come any closer. "I have to go," I say and walk away from Henry before John approaches.

"Perhaps we can have coffee sometime, like tomorrow?" yells Henry after me.

I heard Henry, but I just wave at him from behind without answering.

"I'll call you," he says again as I cross the lawn to John's property.

"What were you two talking about?" asks John.

"Nothing."

"It didn't look like nothing to me."

I shrug my shoulders as I walk past him and into the house, turn around and look him straight in the eye. "Even if it was something, it isn't anything to you anymore."

CHAPTER 13

An Hour of Silence

Clairah

JOHN IGNORES ME for a long time after I brush him off, but I don't care—it really is none of his business what Henry and I were discussing. I don't know why he cares so much and wish he'd concentrate on other things besides me. After about an hour of silence, John prepares our dinner while I do the dishes that are piling up in the sink from cooking. The smell fills my senses; it's a sweet smell with a hint of curry and makes my stomach growl. I offer to help with the rest of the dinner preparations when the dishes are done, but he says he has it all under control. This is the most he has spoken and the first thing he has said to me since the encounter outside when we got home. Fine, he wants to be this way, well two can play at this game. I get he is upset because Henry was talking to me, but he should not take it out on me. The feud between them was so long ago, and as far as I'm concerned, it's between those two and not me. When dinner is ready,

John makes a quick announcement that he's opening a bottle of wine and doesn't wait for me to tell him if I even want a glass as he is already pouring two glasses of red. With a stern look, he picks both drinks up and hands me a glass as if I had agreed to the drink. I really want the drink, don't get me wrong, but it would have been nice to have a say and not have him assume for me. I take the drink from him, and he sets his down on the table next to mine, but still doesn't speak. We sit down to eat the beef curry dish fifteen minutes later; silence fills the room, save for the sound of chewing and utensils clinking against the plates.

Since John cooked, I offer to do the cleanup, he agrees and leaves the room after taking a last bite of the beef curry stir fry and walks away, shoulders slumped forward, still carrying his glass of wine —this is his second refill. He heads towards the front foyer and I hear the door slam behind him. To keep myself busy, I pack the leftover food, clean up the new dishes from dinner, wipe the stove down, and sit at the table and roughly mess around with a few different sketches of ideas I have had recently for a new painting. Earlier this morning, I bought a small sketching notepad and pencil, just in case. It has been years since I have painted anything, but being here on this island again has awakened something within me…a little, at least. After two minutes, I put the sketchpad and pencil down on the table and go back into the kitchen, looking for something else to do—suddenly sketching doesn't interest me anymore. John has been gone a couple hours, and I need to continue to keep my mind occupied, so I consider going back to the hospital, but I don't want to be the overbearing mother my daughter says I am. Even though the counters are spotless, I grab the same cloth I used earlier and wipe away the pre-existing cleanliness. Deep into thought while wiping off the already sparkling kitchen counters, I don't hear the car pull up. At first, I think it's John coming back from wherever he went earlier, but then there is a heavy knock, and this I'm not expecting. Peeking out the window, there is a red Toyota Corolla parked outside. I don't know to whom the car belongs, so I open the door a crack to see who it is; before me stands Michelle, smile from ear to ear, holding a casserole and a bottle of red wine.

Her smile brightens even more when I open the door and she sees me. "You again," she says, showing her white teeth.

"Hello Michelle," I say, trying to force a smile of my own.

"I'm here for John," she says with no greeting.

"John is not here."

"I totally know that, he's at my place. I left him there."

"I don't understand, if you know he's not here, why are you here?"

"I was supposed to be off this evening from work and we were together at my place, but I got called in for an emergency and so I decided to stop here and drop this casserole and wine off for him. Needless to say, he had enough of it already earlier at my place. Anyway, I made this dish for John earlier today."

"If you got called into work for an emergency, don't you think you should have gone straight there? Also," I press on, "if John was with you, why not leave the casserole and wine for him to bring home then?"

She forces out a cough. "The stop is on my way, and besides, you know men. He would forget it and it would go to waste. Anyway, I must run, the sooner I get there, the sooner I can get back to John."

"Well don't let me keep you," I say, taking the casserole and wine from her and attempt to shut the door.

She extends out her foot to stop the door from closing. "By the way, I think John is staying the night at my house, at least he looked extremely comfortable when I left him, so don't expect him back tonight or possibly even tomorrow." She lowers her voice as if she's afraid to have anyone else hear her and says, "I think it might be getting a bit crowded here for him. No offence to you, though." With a wink of her right eye she turns on her heel, and I slam the door behind her, wishing it could have hit her.

My heart beats so fast, many questions race through my mind; I don't understand why. Michelle is the woman he's seeing, he owes me nothing, and we have been divorced for years now—three to be exact, and separated for two years prior. Still, I pace the room for a few minutes before deciding to go next door to see Henry—I don't want to be alone tonight. It's best to have company than to brew in silence, even Henry's company is better than no company at all. As I walk to his house, I see three deer on the side street foraging for their supper. The island is littered with them. They stand on the side of the road, watching me as I make my way to Henry's front door. The evening's warmth penetrates my skin. There's a mixture of red, orange, and pink in the sky as the sun sets over the land behind the house, and I get a glimpse of the fire ball as it peeks in between the trees. The waterfront street where John and Henry live is home to the vibrant sunrises across the water, but the sunsets can only be viewed from the backyards.

I hesitate as the gap between me and Henry's front door diminishes. Am I sending the wrong message by coming here? What message am I sending anyway, does there even have to be a message of any kind? Can two old friends not just have coffee after years of not seeing each other and leave it at that? I decide seeing him can do no harm, especially considering the mood I'm in tonight, so I knock.

Moments later, the door opens before me. "Clairah! What a pleasant surprise. It's so great to see you," he says looking me over and frowns. "Is everything okay?"

"Everything's fine."

He softens his stiff shoulders some. "Then why do you look so sad?" he says as he reaches out his arm and lifts my chin.

"If the offer still stands, maybe we can have that coffee now?"

Henry tilts his head to the side, "I'd like nothing more. Do you want to stay in or go out?" He opens his door slightly, inviting me in and allowing me to peek inside.

I think about his question before responding. "Let's go out. It's a nice night for a walk." Not to mention safer being out in public.

His face changes slightly, and I wonder if he knows that I notice the disappointment wash across the contoured lines. "Done, let me grab my wallet," he says as he hurries off and returns thirty seconds later, wallet in hand and smile back on his face.

Since it's late evening, there are not many places open to go for coffee, the island being small, so the only option is Rocky Raccoon. This restaurant is a short five minute walk from Henry's house and located on the water's edge. The moment I suggest going out for coffee, I regret speaking the words, so I'm hoping that we don't stay out late. Being here with another man, late evening, is unlike me, out of character for me. Not to mention that the look that came across Henry's face when he asked me if I'd prefer to stay in or go out was definitely disappointment, at best. When we arrive at the restaurant, Henry opens the door for me, and I walk in secretly hoping that there's no one here I recognize. I don't want any rumours circulating. The hostess tells us that we can take any table we want, and so Henry chooses a secluded one near the window so that we can have a pretty view of the water—I was hoping for a less romantic setting. The waiter approaches to take our orders and we inform him we are only here for coffee—he returns minutes later with two steaming cups in hand. I like my coffee black, so I begin to drink the minute it's set down in front of me. I drink my coffee fast and while it's still steaming, burning my tongue in the process for not being patient enough. I finish my cup even before the waiter returns with cream and sugar for Henry. When Henry's done nursing the coffee he's been holding in his hands for way too long, he suggests we sit at the docks, but I come up with an excuse that I'm tired, although he doesn't believe me; he raises his eyebrows questioningly. I also catch a glimpse of him rolling his eyes when he thinks I'm not watching. Henry leaves enough money on the table to cover the coffees and as we walk out, he places his arm around my back, guiding me.

"Come on Clairah, live a little. Sit with me; it will do you good to get some air."

"I really must go, I'm sorry." My hands shake violently despite the warm evening.

"There's nothing I can do to convince you to stay out and sit with me a while?"

"No, really, I must go. I'm sorry, I shouldn't have come to your house at all, I was upset."

"What had you so upset?"

"Michelle came by earlier; she gets under my skin."

"Ahh, yes Michelle, you're not alone in that feeling." He looks me up and down then says, "Fine, I'll walk you home." He offers me his arm, and to not be rude I link mine through his.

It's late now; the sun has fully set so I accept his offer to walk me home as I'm frightened of what I might run into at night while alone on this dark and secluded island. I don't like the dark and I don't like animals creeping up on me, so that thought is enough to allow Henry to escort me back. Besides, we are both heading in the same direction so even if I didn't want him to walk me home, I'd have no way out of it. As we approach the cottage/house—I must remember to not call it a cottage anymore, this annoys my daughter for some reason—I don't expect John to be sitting on the front steps. His squared shoulders, tight lips, and narrowed jaw reveal his emotions, anger seeping through with each breath he takes. His stare is hard and cold as I make my way to the house, my arm wrapped around Henry's. The moment Henry notices him, he stretches himself out to appear taller and pumps out his chest. John stands, does the same, lets out a groan, then returns to the house and slams the front door for the second time this evening—the sound of the door slamming rings in my ears.

"Well, wasn't that pleasant?" says Henry, with a smirk on his face. Is he truly enjoying this as if we are barely adults once again?

I take a deep breath and say goodbye as I, too, walk through the door, shutting it a little hard myself. The poor door has been through a lot today.

The next few days pass by much the same way as the first few did. I worry that I have given Henry the wrong idea by going out for coffee with him. He's coming to the house daily and has somehow gotten my phone number, I have no idea how, and is calling and texting often as well. I'm busy, spending my days at the hospital and my evenings cleaning up around the house and trying to force myself to become excited to work on my sketches, to pay him any attention. I hope my silence aimed towards him speaks volumes. John and I have barely spoken since the night of the door slamming—it's easier this way, to hide behind the silence. Ameleiah is recovering well, and the next day we bring her home from the hospital.

Ameleiah complains about everything and everyone, except her father, day and night for the first twenty-four hours after arriving home. She has a hard time getting around on crutches at first, but she is persistent, and by the time she is home two days she's covering much more ground and doing things on her own. I consume myself with taking care of her as much as I can without being a nuisance and risk her calling me overprotective. During the day, John resumes his work at the marina, and I cook breakfast, lunch, and dinner for Ameleiah; of course, I also make enough for John, too. At first, my daughter tells me that she prefers her Dad's cooking, but I don't let this deter me, so I go on a Google search for new and improved ways to make chicken tacos, burritos and anything else Mexican, her favourite food.

"What's this supposed to be? Is this a taco or a small, fried burrito? It doesn't look like either." She says one day, after I spent hours fussing over this new authentic Mexican recipe I got online for chicken tacos, which do look more like spring rolls than the tacos that we are used to eating. I don't allow her sarcasm to get to me though, so instead I just sit in front of her and enjoy the meal I prepared. Sometimes John joins us for supper, other times it's only the two of us. I suspect these are the evenings he eats with Michelle, and this is fine by me as it gives me more time with my daughter, alone. On these days, when it's the two of us, Ameleiah has no choice but to rely on me for certain things, including helping her get dressed. This small change in our routine feels as if we have moved mountains between us.

CHAPTER 14

The State I'm In

Adam

THE WORSE PART of being in the state I'm in is the knowing. I know why Dad is upset, I know why Mom went out for coffee with Henry, and I know why Mia is so hard on Mom. I have all this information locked inside my tiny head and I can't do anything with it—I can't share it with anyone. Dad purposely works later than he needs most nights instead of being at home, and when he's not working he's with Michelle. She calls him every day she's off work; she brings him food to eat at lunch and offers to cook him dinner.

Dad is busy working on a small twenty-six-foot sailboat, fixing the outboard motor, oblivious to the family of deer watching him when Michelle approaches. "Hey what brings you by?"

"I came to see you," says Michelle. She keeps tugging at the top of her white see-through blouse—I'm not sure why she keeps doing this. "Can we have lunch today?" she asks smiling.

"I can't, I'm on a deadline here, things are crazy today. I'm going to run home and grab a quick sandwich and get back to it."

Michelle's smile turns to a frown. "How about tonight? I can make you that pasta with chicken you like."

"I can't tonight; sorry, I'm having dinner with my daughter."

"You mean your daughter and Clairah."

Dad's nose scrunches up, "Yeah, my daughter and Clairah, she's Ameleiah's mother, remember? And she is staying with us for the time being, so yeah, Clairah too, I suppose. Unless she already has plans, that is. I have no idea what she's up to these days."

Michelle pulls the top of her blouse down even more so that more and more of her skin is showing. "Tomorrow night then. It's settled, and I'm not taking no for an answer." She waits for a reply before continuing and when Dad doesn't reply, she presses on. "I'm off then, so come by after work tomorrow, we can open a bottle of wine, relax…" she says, as she softly rubs her hand down his arm.

"Sure, why not." Dad doesn't look at her as he answers.

"Perfect, it's a date!" Her smile returns.

While she walks out of the marina, two other men's heads move with her and follow her as she traverses through the room, their gaze lingering as she passes them. The men are probably wondering why her top is so low, but they don't say anything about it, they just stare.

During the last few days, Henry has remained persistent, so Mom finally replied to one of his many text messages. Later at night, Mom asks Dad if he will be around for dinner the next day to keep Ameleiah company, as it's Friday and she has agreed to go to dinner with Henry, but she omits this small detail at first.

"Why are you not around tomorrow?"

Mom lowers her head before responding, "I have dinner plans."

Dad clenches his fists so tight his knuckles turn bright red. "Yeah, I'll be around for Ameleiah," he says as he storms out through the front door, slamming it for the third time this week. Mom assumes that Dad is running off to Michelle's house, but that's not where he goes, he thinks about it, but last minute decides to go to Rocky Raccoon for a drink. I don't think this is a good idea, something tells me that Dad should stay away from that place, but I can't tell him my thoughts. I can't see into the future, as the future is constantly changing, so this is not a premonition, but rather, a feeling of sorts. Something feels unnerving, unsettling. The bay that's usually rather calm, due to the land around it, is strangely dark and choppy tonight. Two sailboats look like they will break free from their tightly formed knots and sail away due to the heavy wind, even though their sails are not raised. Every sound is amplified as if the Earth's volume is set high, each movement is exaggerated, shifting like a video on slow motion. I want Dad to turn around and go home, I want this so badly, but we can't always get what we want.

The restaurant is full tonight. Laughter from a large family with small children emanates from a booth near the front, their happy sounds fill the air. When the hostess greets Dad, he requests a table near the back, creating distance between himself and the loud booth—happiness is something he tries to avoid when he's in a bitter mood. He orders a beer and a plate of chicken curry as he has not eaten yet and skipped lunch. He never did make it up to the house to get that sandwich due to his heavy workload—he hadn't lied to Michelle about that. He's in deep thought staring out across the water, so he doesn't notice Henry standing tall over him, beer tightly gripped in his hand.

"Hey man," says Henry, staring at Dad who doesn't respond as he keeps looking down at his own beer. "I was sitting over there," he continues, as he points to his table, "and noticed you sitting here, alone." Henry's voice carries, he's much louder than usual, and much louder than he needs to be given their proximity.

Dad grips his beer bottle with both hands tighter and avoids looking up. With a sharp voice he says, "What do you want Henry?"

"You don't have to be so rude man, you know, the history we have is just that, history. I don't hold it against you anymore. Also, I wanted to thank you."

"Thank me? For what?" says Dad, looking up at him this time. "And keep your voice down. You're practically screaming, you want the entire restaurant to hear you or something?"

"I wanted to thank you for agreeing to get off work early tomorrow to stay with Ameleiah so that your sexy wife and I, oh I'm sorry, I mean ex-wife and I can go to dinner—together," he adds casually. "She texted a few minutes ago to let me know it's a date," he says and winks.

If Dad were to grip the beer bottle any tighter, it would shatter in his hands. It takes Dad less than ten seconds to register Henry's words and then he pushes the chair back and launches himself forward. In one swift move he knocks Henry down flat on his back. The beer Henry holds flies across the room, almost landing on the table of the couple sitting closest to them.

This catches Henry off guard, but he manages to gain control quickly and throws a punch with his left arm, that must be his non-dominant hand as he misses and tries again and misses a second time. Dad is on top, so he has the upper hand and swings his right arm forward and his fist connects with the side of Henry's face. The happy family with children that were being loud with laughter earlier are screaming in horror at the fight before them. The couple who almost got a beer bottle smashed into them move to get out of the way. Dad and Henry continue to struggle, each trying to get punches to land on each other's faces, when two men dressed in chef uniforms grab Dad and roughly pull him off Henry. A third man grabs Henry and lifts him to his feet.

"You two better get it together," says one of the men holding Dad. "This is a family restaurant, in case you haven't noticed." Dad and Henry remain held apart by the men, fury in both sets of eyes. "Any more trouble from you two, and I'm calling the police. I don't care who you two are." Both Dad and Henry are escorted outside and told to not return today. The fight doesn't end here though. Once outside, Henry lunges for Dad and catches him off guard this time as Dad's back is to him. Dad loses his balance and almost flips over the wooden railing.

Henry's hands fly to his head. "What the fuck was that for in there?"

Catching his balance just in time before toppling over, Dad says, "You don't think I know what you're doing?"

Henry raises his eyebrows questioningly. "Not at all, so why don't you enlighten me?"

"Well that's a lie." Dad holds himself back from lunging at Henry again.

Henry takes a step back. "I was being friendly, letting you know I was over the feud from years ago, and I was also thanking you, just before you lunged at me and punched me. There's a restaurant full of witnesses that heard me thanking you and saw you attack me first." Henry shrugs his shoulders.

I want to tell Dad to walk away and that it's not worth it, but I can't be the parent, I must leave that choice for him to make on his own accord.

Dad takes a step towards Henry, closing the gap between them; their faces are inches apart—expression hard on his face. "You make me sick." He says these words slow, deliberate, accentuating each one with a pause in between. "You stay the fuck away from my family. If you come onto my property again, I'll have you arrested." Dad spits, blood comes out from his mouth, then continues, "That's a promise."

Henry raises his hands, palms facing the sky. "On what grounds? You were the one who attacked me first. As far as I'm concerned, it should be me warning you to stay off my property. I should be calling the police on you." Henry turns to leave but stops and looks back across his shoulder. "By the way, Clairah and I have a date tomorrow night, so I'll be there to pick her up as planned." He winks at Dad and takes a breath and continues, "And besides, she is no longer your family. She hasn't been a part of your family for three years. You were the one who screwed that up, not me. You're the one who left her alone—you're the one who created a void big enough for her to need me again."

Dad's face is fiery red, his breathing is heavy, laboured. He looks directly into Henry's eyes, then, instead of pushing him, his right fist connects with the wood causing him to curse repeatedly. He pushes Henry's shoulder with his left hand, and says, "You lay a finger on her, I'll kill you."

"Another threat, that's two now, you should keep them coming, you're giving me more ammunition. More reason for me to call the police."

Dad shakes his head back and forth. "You're not worth it." Dad walks away, leaving Henry standing in front of the restaurant, smiling.

"Shit," says Dad, as he waves his right hand up and down, trying to shake off the pain from punching the wall. His knuckles are cut, and blood spills from the opening onto the newly stained wood on the staircase of the restaurant. When he gets back home he doesn't go inside, instead, he jumps into his truck, pulls his keys out of his back pocket and drives the three blocks to Michelle's house. When he arrives, he considers leaving again, but turns off the ignition. He hesitates at the front door for about five minutes before knocking. He knows he shouldn't be here. He knows he should not be leading her on. He has intended to end things with her for a long time, but if he is being honest with himself, he does get lonely at times and she fills the void. "Just for tonight," he tells himself. "One more night to help me get through this." Following a deep breath, he brings his hand up and rings the doorbell. As soon as the chimes ring, he regrets it.

"John, what a wonderful surprise! Come in." Michelle moves off to the side to allow Dad enough space to enter.

"Hey Michelle, I know I said I was busy tonight, but…." *But what?* he wonders.

Michelle brings her index finger to Dad's lips. "Don't say another word. You don't have to explain or make excuses. I'm so happy you're here." She leans in and kisses him lightly on the lips. "Are you hungry? Have you eaten?" She glances down at his bloody hand. "John, what on Earth happened?"

Dad ignores her last question and instead thinks about whether he is hungry. He imagines the chicken curry that he ordered that he didn't have a chance to eat—the plate probably still sitting in the kitchen at the restaurant, ready to be thrown out. "What a waste," he says aloud.

"What's a waste?"

Realizing he spoke out loud Dad says, "Nothing."

"Well, have you eaten or not?"

"Yeah, I've eaten," he lies.

"In that case, let's not waste time." Michelle takes his arm and leads him into her bedroom, Dad trails behind. Michelle thinks that the way to get Dad to be closer to her is to constantly get him into her bed. This in fact does the opposite as it reminds him that the time he spends with Michelle is strictly physical and emotionless. Michelle has the same white see-through top from earlier pulled up over her head, revealing her flashy pink bra that looks to be too small as it makes her boobs bunch up and squish together. She drops the top on the floor before they enter the bedroom.

Later at night, the two of them lay in bed, naked but under the covers, so that's good for me. I don't need to see them with no clothes on—seeing Michelle without a top earlier was enough for me. Michelle wonders about Dad's hand but is afraid to ask again. This is a small town and she has heard the rumors flying around that Henry still has a thing for Mom. Michelle worries that the bloody hand is a result of a fight over Mom and she couldn't be more accurate, only she doesn't know how right she is. Afraid to know the truth, she leaves the question unasked.

Dear Adam,

Jealousy is like a volcanic mountain; you never know when it will erupt and swallow your world whole. I've never really been a jealous person, not really, not until your sister was born. The day we brought her home from the hospital, was the first day I ever felt jealousy stab me in the centre of my core. I was, you see, secondary now. If she needed a diaper change, your mother was there ready, if she needed to be fed, your mother's breasts were always plump and full, if she was tired, your mother would go nap with her. I was quietly waiting on the sidelines, hoping to be needed, waiting for that one meaningless job that I'd be given so that I could feel a sense of accomplishment, a sense of contribution towards something, towards her. I was better at being on the sidelines waiting, than on centre stage, so this was all right with me, and I didn't complain—ever. My time would arrive soon, that special moment that would allow me to be the superstar, but until then, I'll hide away and wait for my turn.

Love, Dad

CHAPTER 15

Looking for Something or Someone

Clairah

AMELEIAH APPEARS PREOCCUPIED tonight, pacing from one room of the house to the other looking for something or someone. She stops in the kitchen while I'm making an herbal green tea before turning in for the night. "Where's Dad?"

I shrug my shoulders before answering her. "Out, I suppose. He's probably at Michelle's house."

I look at Ameleiah and she wears a perplexed look, then says, "That's strange, he left earlier without saying anything to me, not even goodnight."

I pour a teaspoon of honey into my mug and stir. "That's rather odd."

"Did you say something to upset him? This is his house you know. If anyone has the right to be here, it's him." She stands before me, arms crossed over her chest.

I know she's angry with me and doesn't intend to be mean. She's hurting inside and taking it out on me, but still her words cut right through my fractured heart. I can handle this, though, I can take it.

I ignore her last question and comment. "Do you want me to help you with anything before I turn in for the night?"

"No, I'm fine."

"Would you like a cup of tea?"

"No."

I put the honey and package of tea back in the cupboard. "Are you going to bed soon?"

"No. I'm just going to sit here and wait up for Dad. He should be back soon."

"Okay honey, you know where I am if you need help getting around or need anything. If you do, come get me, okay?"

"I won't need your help," she says looking away from me.

"Okay then, goodnight." I wait for a reply, but there's none.

After I've gone to bed and fallen asleep, I'm woken up startled by a scream. At first, I'm not sure where I am, and it takes me a couple seconds to become orientated. Once I do, I realize the screaming I hear is Ameleiah, and so I yank the covers off me and run to her room where I find her covers and pillow on the floor next to her bed. "What's wrong?" I say as she sits up in bed with fear in her eyes and locked with the wall.

"I had a nightmare again, about… him." She still won't look at me and continues to stare at the wall.

She refuses to refer to her brother by his name. She always refers to Adam as 'him'.

I approach her bed slowly, giving her an opportunity to tell me to not come close, but she doesn't say anything. "How bad was it? Do you want to tell me about it?"

She brings her hand up to her face to cover the tears; I sit on the edge of her bed, rub her leg and push back the stray hairs from her face and tuck them behind her ear.

At first, she doesn't speak but eventually she opens up. "It was the same as always. The day he died, we were on the boat and…"

I continue to stroke her hair, waiting for her to tell me to stop. "I know honey. It still hurts, even after all these years. I, too, still have the same recurring nightmare, reliving that same afternoon on the boat."

There is another sob, then, "Mom."

"Yes honey?"

"I miss him."

"I know you do, I do too. It's okay to miss your brother honey. I know how you feel. I really do," I say, stroking my daughter's face and running my fingers through her hair like I used to when she was a little girl. A tear travels down her cheek as she lets herself fall lifelessly into my arms, and together we lie in her bed for the rest of the night, blanket and pillow still on the floor.

That night Ameleiah is not the only one who has a nightmare about Adam.

I wake up in the morning to a strange room and empty bed. I'm perplexed, as I'm not sure where I am at first and suddenly I remember last night, and my heart skips a beat as Ameleiah is not here. I take a sniff of the air and the pleasant scent of bacon fills my nostrils, and I pull the covers that I had eventually picked up off the floor through the night off and walk into the kitchen. Ameleiah is holding herself up with one arm over the crutch and flipping strips of bacon on the stove with the other. "Oh, morning Mom. I didn't hear you get up."

The table is set for three. Orange juice fills the three tall glasses on the table alongside the steaming pot of coffee, and a vase with fresh cut flowers from the small garden finishes off the inviting table decor. There's a bowl filled with scrambled eggs, and apples with oat crumbles next to it.

I reached down to smell the flowers, their scent sweet and inviting. "Did you do this all yourself or did your Dad help you?"

"I did it. Dad must still be sleeping; I haven't seen him yet this morning."

"Sleeping? I don't think so. Your father doesn't like to sleep in, or has he developed a new habit?"

She considers this. "No, you're right, he's still the first one up at the crack of dawn, I just assumed he was sleeping but maybe he left for work early, I haven't checked if his truck is here."

The truck being in the driveway doesn't confirm whether he's at work as he lives so close to the marina and sometimes walks. However, I can't resist the urge to peek, so I glance out the window, and where his truck is usually parked is a deer instead, looking into our living room window straight at me.

"Should we check his room, wake him if he's asleep? He was out late last night so he might be extra tired today. He wasn't home when I went to bed," she says.

"He's not sleeping. His truck is gone."

"Oh. Well, I guess it's just the two of us," she says, smiling at me for the first time in years.

I try to force a smile back, but my lips won't move despite the pressure I put on them.

Then she yells, "Dad!"

I turn my head at the sound of Ameleiah calling her father, and John is suddenly in the kitchen, hand bandaged up.

He has a frown, but the moment he sees Ameleiah his expression softens. "Hey kiddo. How are you doing?" he asks, kissing her forehead.

Ameleiah points towards the table and says, "I'm great. I made breakfast for us, all of us."

"You made the breakfast? How did you manage on your own?"

"Dad, I have a broken leg, but I'm not completely crippled."

John avoids looking at me and takes a seat at the kitchen table, busying himself with food and conversation with Ameleiah. "Sorry I wasn't around last night. I went to see Michelle, we were watching a movie, it got late, and we fell asleep."

"It's okay Dad, you don't have to explain yourself to me. You're an adult, I get it. Adults need sleepovers too," says my daughter, as if she were much older than she is.

With a flushed face he glances my way, and I force a fake, weak smile. After breakfast, John showers and gets ready for work, telling Ameleiah to text him after I leave tonight. I had already told Ameleiah yesterday that Henry and I were having dinner together, so it must not come as a surprise to her when he says this.

"Don't worry about me, I'm okay here on my own."

John disputes this fact, but I convince him this time to give our daughter space.

When evening arrives, I'm a bundle of nerves. I know it's only dinner, but it feels like a date, a real date this time, not just coffee. I haven't been on a date since John and I were together. I'm questioning my wardrobe, my hair, my nails…oh gosh my nails are short, chipped and the cuticles are overgrown. I remind myself to clench my fist during dinner, to hide their horrible state. I don't have any appropriate clothes to wear either, as I only bought a few key things. I should cancel, this is silly. Who am I to go on a date and with a man that both John and I have history with? I stare at myself in the mirror, but I don't recognize the woman staring back as this woman is about twelve pounds thinner, and at a height of five feet four inches, weighing one-hundred-and-ten pounds is considered severely underweight, unhealthy even. I bring my face a little closer to the mirror, magnifying my image—there are dark circles under my eyes, and new tiny lines, that I swear weren't there at the beginning of summer only a couple weeks ago, forming at the sides of my temples. I lift my arms and wiggle them in the air: pipe cleaners are what I see in the mirror.

My daughter's voice startles me. "Mom, what are you doing?"

I didn't realize she was behind me, watching me. "How long have you been standing there?"

"Long enough to know that you've been staring at yourself for a long time. What's the matter Mom? Why are you wiggling your arms around?"

My first thought is to tell her I'm okay, to be the parent and not have her worry about me, but I remind myself of last night, and the breakfast she prepared this morning was her way of saying that she is sorry for the way she acted, sorry for the things she said. This has been a breakthrough moment in our relationship, and I'm scared to death of screwing it up with her again. So, I decide on the truth, treating her more like I'd speak to a girlfriend. "I don't know if I should go to dinner tonight." I tell her about my lack of wardrobe, my unruly hair, my disgusting nails, my pipe cleaners for arms—she laughs at me and we are both standing side by side staring into the mirror.

Ameleiah brings her hands to her hips. "How much time do we have before Henry picks you up?"

"Henry's supposed to be here at seven."

She looks at her watch—five. "I can't fix the lack of muscle tone in your arms in that short amount of time, but that's plenty of time for everything else," she says with a smile.

"Plenty of time for what?"

"To make you look beautiful again."

"Ameleiah, I appreciate you trying to help me..."

"Mom," she interrupts, "trust me okay?" She asks so little of me, so I do.

By six forty-five, I'm wearing a baby blue and white flowery, knee length, peek-a-boo- shoulder dress that's pinched at the waist, pink polished toenails and fingers, and my hair is shiny and straight, thanks to Ameleiah's revolutionary flat iron. She sits me on the toilet next and applies a light layer of tinted moisturiser to even out my skin tone and remove all the red blotches and puffiness under my eyes. She lines my upper eye lids with black liner and sweeps a pinkish colour of eye-shadow over my lids and covers my lashes with thick black mascara and dabs some highlighter on the inside of my eyes, lightening up my face. She takes the same pinkish colour she used on my eyes and mixes in a deeper pink shade and blends it together, reminding me of how I mix my colours for my paintings, then sweeps the new colour over my cheek bones. Just below the pink blush, she uses an even darker shade, browner in tone, and sweeps underneath the jaw line. "For the finishing touch," as she puts it, she covers my lips in a soft caramel-like coloured gloss.

We even share the same shoe size, almost; I'm size seven-and-a-half, she's an eight, but I manage to borrow a pair of open toe sandals that I stuff with a liner to keep from slipping. The shoes are the same baby blue as the dress.

"I don't know about the shoes honey. I'm afraid it's over the top."

"You must wear the shoes Mom, it makes the dress stand out," she says, convincing me.

"You really are okay with me going out to dinner with Henry?" My daughter doesn't know the story, the history we share.

"I don't love the idea, only because it's Henry and he can be a bit rude to Dad at times, but hey, Dad has a girlfriend, and you need to do something for yourself for a change."

"Thank you for understanding."

"Oh, wait here," she says as she hurries off to the living room, leaving me looking at my reflection in the mirror—at the transformation she created. When she returns, she has a tiny handbag in her hand. "Here, use this, it matches the shoes and dress." It's no wonder she has so much luggage when she visits her Dad, she brings all her belongings with her—everything she owns.

I can't help but think about the comment that Ameleiah made about Henry being rude to John, it's odd how she says he's rude; I have found him to be a real gentleman so far. Ameleiah must feel this way because she's protecting her father, there can't be any other reason.

"You know Mom, even though Dad has a girlfriend, he's still jealous."

I turn away from my reflection to face her. "Jealous of what?" I ask honestly.

"Of you and Henry, of course."

I nod, "That's not so, your father holds ill feelings towards Henry because of a fight they had years ago, over me, nonetheless. But your father no longer thinks of me that way, he hasn't thought of me in that way in many years. Trust me when I say he's not jealous of me and Henry."

"Right, well you know best. Afterall, you're the parent," she says waving me off as the doorbell rings. "I'll get it, that way you can make a grand entrance." She leaves me standing in the washroom, staring into the mirror. A woman I remember from years ago stares back.

Henry is in the doorway when I approach and looks me up and down a few times. "Wow, you look fabulous," he says, as I stand before him trying to hide my hands in the folds of the dress. It's a bad habit I have now, to hide my nails when they're not polished. It has been forever since I polished my nails, and so even though they are brightly polished now, I'm still not used to showing them off, like I used to.

"Thank you. I'm ready, just let me get my sweater."

Ameleiah has retreated to her room, probably avoiding an encounter with Henry.

"Let's go," I say, holding the bag in one arm and the sweater in the other as Henry places his hand on my back, leading me to his truck.

"Where are we going?" I ask, as he closes my side of the door for me.

"To the Manitoulin Island Country Club, it's less than a ten-minute drive. I made reservations. I hope that's okay with you?"

"Sounds perfect." I say with another forced smile.

When we arrive, Henry walks to my side and opens the truck door for me while taking my hand in his. I accept gracefully. As we walk up the pathway to the door, his arm rests on my lower back, but this time it's a little too low for my liking as his fingers are spread wide, allowing him to reach even a little lower. He gives the hostess his name for the reservation, and as she leads us to our table there are many eyes on us. I'm not used to this type of attention anymore, so I lower my head. Once we're seated, the waitress comes to get our drink orders and I ask for a six-ounce glass of red wine, a merlot this time. Henry orders a nine ounce of the same. While we wait for the drinks, Henry compliments me often. I try to come across as grateful, but not too forward, so for lack of a better reply, I say, "Thank you, it's all my daughter's doing."

We haven't decided on dinner yet, so I pick up my menu to browse through. Deciding on a steak dinner, I set the menu down and notice Henry is staring at me again—or rather, still.

"Is there something wrong?" I ask, grabbing the napkin off the table to keep my hands busy.

He clears his throat before speaking. "Nothing at all. What could possibly be wrong with this picture?" At hearing his words, I shift my focus to the right of me, onto the older couple sitting next to us. They look to be in their sixties judging by their grey hairs and wrinkles; I wonder if theirs is a new relationship or one that has been put through the test of time.

After what feels like forever, our meals arrive. Dinner is just as awkward as having the pre-dinner drink. I don't know what to talk about with a man, and all he wants to talk about is me and my appearance. He continues to constantly compliment me, which most women would love, but his advances make me want to leave at once and not return. I keep one hand on the fork and the other, when not needed to cut up the steak, safely tucked away under the table playing with the hem of the dress. Guilt plagues me, but why? I'm not used to the dating scene and I remember how awkward it all is—trying to have a meal with someone you hardly know: only I do know Henry, and this is what begins to worry me. I want the night to be over, and when the waitress brings the bill, I try to hide my excitement. I offer to pay for half the bill, but Henry refuses to accept my offer and hurriedly pulls out his Visa, slapping it on the table next to the bill.

"It's still early, would you like to have another drink maybe at the bar this time, or go for a drive, or perhaps a walk even? It's a nice night."

"Thank you for the offer and for dinner, it was most lovely, but I really do need to get back, I told Ameleiah I wouldn't be out late; she'll be waiting up for me."

"She's a big girl, I'm sure she'll be fine."

"She's recently been in an accident," I remind him.

"All right, I'll just have to take you out again another night. But next time you're all mine for the night, so don't make any other plans."

His last comment leaves me with butterflies in my stomach, and I remain quiet on the drive back to John's house. Once we're in the driveway, I attempt to unbuckle my seatbelt, and while I'm slightly bent towards the driver's seat fussing with the notch, Henry moves in closer, bringing his lips inches from mine and slowly closing the gap. I back away in a sudden panic and hit my head on the hand rest above the door. Ignoring his advances, I unbuckle the seatbelt and grab my handbag and sweater and rush into the house—Henry doesn't follow me.

"I'm back," I announce, flustered, as I walk in the door. John is in the living room on his iPad, surely surfing the net. He's focussed on the screen but glances towards me, and the flutter in his eye doesn't go unnoticed. I peek over his arms to see what he's looking up: motorcycles. He loves motorcycles and had always had them the years we were together, but now, come to think of it, I haven't seen one the entire time I've been here.

I lift my foot so I can reach my shoe and take it off, my feet are sore from wearing these kitten heels. "Are you thinking of getting a new one?" I ask, pointing to the screen.

"Hmm?" he says, not listening to me.

"A new bike? Are you buying a new bike?"

He glances my way, "Oh, maybe, I've been considering it lately."

"I remember the trips we used to take through the island, me riding on the back and loving life. That feels like a lifetime ago now."

"Yeah, it sure was long ago."

After I pull off the second shoe, I sit beside him and rub my right foot, trying to ease the throbbing; with my other hand, I take his hand in mine. "What happened to your hand, John?"

John ignores my question, puts down the iPad and instead asks, "Would you like a glass of wine?"

I have already had a glass at dinner but decide I better accept; I better try since he is. "Sure, that would be lovely. But just one glass."

CHAPTER 16

A Glass of Wine

Clairah

AFTER JOHN GETS up I sit nervously, trying to hide my hands under my legs as he pours us each a glass of wine.

"Is cabernet sauvignon all right?" John holds the glass in front of me.

"It's perfect."

When I reach to take the glass, my hand shakes violently, and so I use the other one to hold the glass steady. I'm not sure why I'm so nervous today—this used to be a natural pastime for us, sitting together drinking wine. We used to often enjoy sitting outside the Queen's Inn when we were first dating with a glass in hand, watching the stars sparkle in the night and listing to each other's stories. On some of those nights we would chat away endlessly, but on other nights we just sat beside each other, shoulders touching, listening to the hypnotic sound of silence—the beauty of this island. There isn't a whole lot to do here, the island being scarce, but there's plenty to enjoy if you're into serenity: nature walks, hikes, landscapes that stretch for miles, waterfalls that glisten, and lakes and winding roads that never end. We are only down the road from where some of these memories live, but it feels as if we are miles away. Although the memories have never faded. I remember sometimes we'd sit on the veranda of the Queen's Inn into the early morning, rather than in the evening, watching the warm glistening sunshine wash over the island, erasing all its troubles from the day before.

John looks at the still shaky glass in my hands and looks away, probably pretending he didn't notice my nerves to save me embarrassment. "So, tell me how dinner was tonight with…." He hesitates to finish. "With him?"

"His name's Henry. You know his name, so why don't you use it?"

"Yeah, I know his name all right, but I wish I didn't. That's one name I wish I could forget."

"John, I don't want to argue…"

"I'm not bringing him up to argue. You're free to go out with whom you like—I can't stop you. I get that it's not my business anymore; it's just that it's easier when you're not here. Having you back in Paris and dating is one thing, I don't see or hear about it, out of sight out of mind, but here, right before my eyes, well it's awkward, despite the number of years we have been apart and not to mention, with him no less.

I lower my head and stare into my glass. "I'm sorry, I didn't realize that it's awkward for you."

"Don't apologize." He opens his mouth to speak again but stops himself. There's an awkward moment between us, neither of us knowing what to say next, so John clears his throat and breaks the silence, "But I just want to say one more thing about him. Be careful as he… Henry is still Henry, and I know you think he's charming and all, but you don't know him the way I do. I'm the one who's been here for the last few years, living next to him."

The wine in my glass swishes from side to side; I bend forward to set the glass down on the coffee table. "John, we had coffee together once and dinner once, that's it. He hasn't proposed marriage or anything like that," I say, as I pick the glass back up because I'm indecisive, and take a sip of the wine, allowing the dry and boldness of the flavour to soak into my taste buds.

"I'm only telling you to be careful. Just promise me you won't fall for him. Anyone else is fine, just not him. Please."

His words ring in my ears. "I don't think we can control who we fall for, you know that better than anyone, you yourself said that to me once, do you remember?"

He runs his fingers through his hair, "Yeah, I remember saying that to you."

I sit the glass down beside me this time, on the side table because I can see the liquid inside swishing higher and higher the more I drink; I can't seem to keep the glass steady. "John," I begin, but stop.

"Yeah?"

I lower my gaze, afraid to meet his eyes. "I tried to tell you something when we were at Loco Beanz coffee, but you shut me down."

"Yeah, I know." He stands and his hands are in his pockets.

"I tried to tell you that I'm sorry for blaming you all these years, you know, about Adam."

John clears his throat and takes a big gulp of wine. "Can we not talk about Adam tonight? I just can't do it, not yet, at least not tonight."

"Why?"

"It's too soon."

"It's been five years John."

"Yeah, I know, and it feels as if it happened only yesterday."

Needing something to keep my hands busy with, I pick up my wine again. "It feels like that for me, too, I think it always will." I'm gripping my wine glass so tight, if it were not made of thick glass, it would shatter in my hands.

Quietly, Ameleiah enters the room. "Hey Mom, you're back. Can I hang out at Nena's house tonight? Maybe watch a movie at her place?"

"I'm not sure I can drive honey, I've already had a couple glasses of wine, and so has your father."

"Oh, it's fine, her Mom offered to come get me and she said I could stay the night. Would that be okay then?"

"I don't know still," I say, trying to think up another excuse to not be left alone with John tonight.

"Ameleiah, I don't know either, you still can't move around on your own," says John in my defense.

"Dad, I'm doing fine, I can even cook now. Remember I made breakfast?"

"Yeah, you sure did."

"So, come on then, say yes. I need to get out of this house. Please, Daddy?" She gives her father the eyes that he most certainly can't say no to.

"Fine, but as long as it's okay with your mother also."

"It's okay with me," I say, not wanting to be the overprotective, overbearing parent.

"Thanks a million. Oh, Mrs. Cameron is here, see you in the morning," she says, running out the door blowing a kiss to each of us.

Nena Cameron and her parents live up the road, three kilometres away. Nena and Ameleiah have been friends since they were toddlers. I'm not comfortable with the idea of her leaving, as this means that John and I will be alone and I worry things might get ugly, but I suppose if we don't discuss Adam or Henry things will be just fine—keep the conversation superficial, I remind myself. I take a full gulp from my glass; it's easier to just drink the wine than to try and not spill it, and when John notices my empty glass, he insists on pouring us another and suggests we play a card game, Crazy Eights.

"Really, you want to play Crazy Eights right now. You do know I'll still win, right?" I tease, knowing full well that John is a much better player than me, but for some reason I used to always win against him. It has been years since we've played a card game together, so I'm curious if he will do the same thing he used to do before—let me win purposely.

"Well, maybe I've been practicing for the last five years, and I'll win this time."

As usual and as expected, I win three of the four rounds.

"I guess I haven't been practicing enough," he says collecting the cards.

I let a smile form. "I know you're allowing me to win still, just like you used to before."

"Not true. I suck, you won fair and square," he says as he winks at me. "Another glass?"

My head is foggy, I can't think straight, and the furniture looks like it's moving around the room—or maybe it's the room that's spinning around the furniture, either way, I remain seated even though I need to desperately use the washroom.

"I don't think I can have another. I've had two glasses here already plus the one at dinner. I might fall over soon if I have any more to drink." Our eyes lock for a moment.

"I won't let you fall, that is, if you allow me to help you," he says, as he turns away from me, pours himself another full glass and walks out the front door leaving it wide open behind him—an open invitation.

His words, "If you allow me to help you," cut through my heart. I remain inside the house, alone, watching him from the front window. He's standing at the edge of the driveway facing the waterfront, waiting—the front door still wide open, inviting the evening breeze in. For a split second, I consider following him out, but decide I best leave things the way they are and not shake the pot anymore, at least not tonight—tonight we have made progress. After a few moments, watching from inside the house, John leaves and walks down towards the water. Instead of joining him, I pour myself a tall glass of cold water, and when he's out of view, I walk out the front door myself, despite my wobbly legs, and sit outside on the front step under the stars, glass in hand steady this time. After about an hour, John is still not back from his walk. His car remains in the driveway, so I know for sure that he's most likely at the water still, where he loves to sit and think of new hobbies to get himself involved in. When my water glass is empty my mind is clearer, and I pull out my phone and call up the Chi-Cheemaun website; I book my passage back to Tobermory for the following day. It's time I leave the island and return to my own life in Paris. Once I make sure that the confirmation has been sent to my email, I put my phone on silent and walk back into the house and remove the makeup that my daughter carefully painted on my face, slip into my pajamas and lie in bed, eyes wide open. Sleep eludes me, so I check the time on my phone, it's well after midnight and I hear footsteps out in the hall—John has returned and the last thing I hear before sleep finally takes me is his bedroom door shutting gently.

CHAPTER 17

Nothing Happened

Clairah

"I DON'T UNDERSTAND WHAT happened between last night and this morning?" asks John early the next day as he watches me pack my bag and paces the room, hands on his head.

I look around for missing items, and confident I have packed everything, close my bag—making it final. "Nothing happened, it's just that Ameleiah is doing much better now. I have no need to stay here any longer. I need to get back and take care of things at home. The grass will need to be cut, the gardens weeded, the trash taken out. You know about all the usual responsibilities that come with home ownership."

"Yeah, I suppose you're right," he says, as he scratches his head. "I just didn't expect you to leave today that's all, especially after…."

Waiting patiently for him to say more, I hold my breath, then let out the trapped air when I realize he's not saying anything more, so setting my bag down next to the bed I prompt him, "Especially after what?" I'm looking directly into his eyes, wondering if he will say, 'After last night'. I silently beg him to say those words, to say more, but those words remain unspoken.

"Nothing," he says instead. "Does Ameleiah know you're leaving today?"

"Yes, I've already texted her, she's on her way back now."

"What time is the crossing?"

"I'm booked for the late afternoon crossing, three fifteen, but as usual I have to be there an hour before. I'll need to leave here by one thirty at the latest."

There's a wrinkle on his forehead that appears to be more prominent today than it was yesterday. "Well, at least let me take you and Ameleiah out to lunch before you go. We can go down to the restaurant by the marina, sit outside by the dock. I think she'd like that."

"That's okay, you don't have to do that. I don't want to make this a big deal or anything. I had to leave eventually."

"It's no big deal at all. Besides, I'm thinking of Ameleiah."

"You're right, she would like it. Okay, in that case, one last early lunch would be lovely."

"Great! I'll call to make sure they save a table for us. I think I hear Ameleiah coming in."

"Mom?"

"I'm in the spare room," I yell out to her. I almost said Adam's room. As I walk towards the door, Ameleiah appears at the entrance, a frown on her pretty face.

"What's going on?" she points to her phone. Your text said to come right over because you're leaving today? Did you and Dad have another fight? What did you do this time?" There's that same accusation again, another slap on my face.

"No, honey, we didn't fight at all. In fact, we had a really nice time together last night." I glance towards John to see his expression, but he turns his face away from me.

"Then why are you leaving so suddenly?" Her voice is weak now, pleading. "I don't get it Mom. What are you playing at?"

I take a step towards her. "Ameleiah, I'm not playing around. This is not my home, remember? This is your father's home. I didn't even come prepared with any clothes, or a toothbrush for that matter. I stayed at Tobermory the night I drove you there, and the following morning I took the ferry here right after your Dad called to tell me about your accident. I came in the same two-day-old clothes, unwashed hair and all. The few items I do have with me, I purchased once I got here."

"Okay, but that still doesn't explain why you're leaving so suddenly." A tear escapes her eye, but she wipes it with her sleeve, as if afraid to show me her true feelings. "What difference would another day or two make?"

I reach out and put my hands on her face. "Exactly, what difference would it make?" She considers my question and narrows her eyebrows. "Do you want to come back with me now? You know you can if you want to. You don't have to stay here any longer if you don't feel comfortable."

She responds right away, "No, I want to stay here with Dad for the rest of the summer as planned. I already don't get to see much of him during the school year."

"That's fine honey, I understand. You belong here with him, I don't and that's why I have to go."

Her tears are running down her face full force, and she can't wipe them away fast enough, so she gives in and embraces me, like she has not done since she was a little girl. Without saying a word, John leaves the room to give us privacy.

Lunchtime approaches too soon and I'm not even hungry yet, but John has insisted and so I go along. The restaurant we have lunch at is small on the inside, but the outdoor patio contains an additional nine tables. The outdoor space is more commonly used than the indoor dining room, especially when the weather is dry. In all the years I've been coming to the island, I've never eaten inside this restaurant. The restaurant isn't fancy but offers a relaxed atmosphere, with great views and a mouth-watering burger. Today, however, I decide on the fish and chips—something different. I haven't even left Gore Bay yet and I already miss this place. Last night there was a slight shift in my relationship with John; not a gigantic shift but a shift nonetheless. For the first time in years I had the urge to go to him last night, wrap my arms around him, comfort him, it took everything I had, all my strength to not follow him out last night. That would have been a tremendous mistake, we had been drinking, and we were not in our clear frames of mind: words would have been said that we could not have erased, and things would have surely happened that we would have come to regret. It's been so long since we were last together, and what we had once is buried deep. Unlike Adam. I need to move on with my life, figure out what that life is for me, and how I want to live it. I need to fix myself, not complicate things by staying here longer than needed and throwing myself into my ex's bed. When the waitress comes around for the final rounds asking if we'd like anything else, I tell her that we're ready to leave and to bring the bill. I want to get out of here as fast as possible; suddenly I feel as if the island is suffocating me, preventing me from seeing clearly. I have never wanted to be somewhere so badly in my life and yet wanting to leave it so quickly. The waitress places the bill in the centre of the table and John picks it up before I do and places his Visa down on it to prevent it from blowing away as the wind has picked up a bit. The one and only bag that I borrowed from John is packed and in my trunk already, I'm not planning to go back to the house after lunch other than to pick up my car as we walked here. I won't step foot inside the house anymore for fear that I might decide to stay longer —I don't trust myself. No, I won't do that. I'll simply walk straight towards my car, say goodbye, and drive away, leaving all the memories behind. When we approach the driveway, the silence is thick as the three of us prepare for the final goodbye. I kiss my daughter on the forehead, and she wraps her arms around my waist, then backs away to allow her

Dad to come closer. As we stand beside my car, John places a hand on my shoulder.

"Take care of yourself Clair."

"I will, and you take care of yourself, too, and our daughter." I reach for the car door handle, his arm slides off my shoulder, prickling my skin, and before I can open the door John places his hand over mine. "You need to let me go," I say, pulling mine out from under his firm, larger hand. He doesn't fight me and removes his hand completely, allowing me to get into my car, releasing me.

Once I'm inside, he leans inside the window. "Drive safe," says John, and kicks the front of my tire, surely checking to make sure it contains enough air—his overprotectiveness towards me showing.

"I will." I look to Ameleiah and wink before turning on the ignition.

"I love you Mom."

I lean out the window so that she can hear me more clearly. "You know I love you to the moon and back," I say to my daughter. As I roll up the window of my car and drive away, my family fades in the rear-view mirror.

The weather is overcast, and a little cooler with the lack of sun shining down. I turn off the air conditioner and roll the front windows down to feel the freeze blowing in, it feels exhilarating. My hair flies over my eyes obstructing my view and I quickly reach for my purse and feel around the bottom for a clip without taking my eyes off the road. There's a family of deer up ahead on the side of the road, and when I see them I slow down a bit and stop the car on the side to watch them. They look happy and free, wandering about the afternoon like the four of us used to. There aren't many cars out on the road today. I open the door and step out, leaning against my car, waiting for nothing. The only other vehicle that passes me is a motorcycle equipped with saddle bags. I check the time on my phone. There's a text from Ameleiah, but I don't reply to her, and although it's still early, I decide I should get going. Being late is a trait I avoid at all costs. I used to bite my tongue when John would make us late for appointments or dinner dates with friends—I'd remind myself that not everyone is as punctual as I am and I'd not say anything to avoid an argument, so, for this reason, and others, I don't want to miss this ferry today under any circumstance. Waving goodbye to the family of deer that ignores me, I get back in my car and drive away down the long barren road surrounded by small lakes everywhere. Manitoulin is the largest freshwater lake island in the world. It's home to breathtaking views, the place for serenity, and it's where people come to gain a sense of peacefulness—I hope to take some of that back with me now. The island itself contains one-hundred-and-eight freshwater lakes, and some of these lakes have their own islands on them, so as I drive there's lake after lake after lake—it's an explosion of water all around me. I glance towards each body of water, fighting to push away the thoughts of John and the kids burning in my head, pushing away what I once longed for, desired, craved and instead focus on the ripples the birds create in the water by dipping their beaks. It's not that I want to forget: forgetting is both a pleasure and a curse; it allows us the freedom to pretend something never was, but it also blocks our deep emotions and ability to forgive and heal. This is the advice that my therapist always reminds me of. She says that, rather than forgetting, one must face things head on, like a nail being hit by a hammer, being pushed in deeper until it's definite—irreversible. It's good advice, and I wish I were stronger so that I could incorporate it into my own life.

CHAPTER 18

Crashing in the Process

Adam

AFTER MOM LEAVES, Dad and Mia remain frozen on the driveway watching Mom drive away, hoping she turns the car around. When Mom makes up her mind to do something, she does it with full force and full speed ahead, sometimes crashing in the process. Dad is different, Dad takes his time, contemplates things, ponders. Dad has his arm around Mia's shoulder, she leans on her crutches for support. "Well kiddo, looks like it's just you and me again. What do you want to do for the rest of the day?"

Mia lets out a yawn that had been trying to escape. "Dad, I'm tired, I didn't get much sleep last night, would it be okay if I had a nap? Perhaps maybe later this evening we can go sit out by the water together, do some fishing like the old days?"

"You feeling okay?"

"Yeah, just tired."

"Sure kiddo. Go ahead then."

Mia leaves Dad, walks into the house, leans her crutches up against the wall and climbs into bed with her clothes on. Tears run from her face onto the pillow as she texts Mom, telling her that she hopes she has a good trip back home and that she will talk to her soon. She stares at the phone for a few minutes waiting for a reply, but one doesn't come as Mom is driving. When she realizes this, she puts her phone down on her nightstand, and closes her eyes and pretends to be asleep when Dad peeks into the room a few minutes later to check on her.

It used to be Mia and me; we called ourselves The Two Musketeers. Mom would constantly correct us saying, "You can't be the two Musketeers; the Musketeers consist of three, not two."

"We're starting our own group," Mia would say in our defence. She was always there for me whenever I needed her. She would cover for me when I was in trouble for forgetting to pick-up after myself in the washroom, do my homework for me when I got lazy, and stick up for me at school when older kids called me names and stole my lunch—which happened a lot. She was my protector, my biggest fan, my hero. She was the person who saw me cry the most, even including our parents. She was the one I told everything to when I was upset, and she was the one who always comforted me when sorrow would drag me down. I sit on the edge of her bed, watching her pretend to sleep so that she can avoid questions from our father. I want to reach out to wipe her tears away, but I can't feel. I want to tell her to not worry, and that it will be fine, but my voice has no sound, so, instead I climb in under the covers with her and she shifts and moves over suddenly, as if she's making room for me—but that's impossible as she doesn't know I'm here.

Eventually Mia's breathing deepens and she falls asleep next to me, so I take this opportunity to check on Dad, to see how he's making out. I find him outside sitting on the front step staring at a tree, a can of beer in his hand. He's supposed to be at work, but he's not. I try not to read his thoughts, they are private and I don't want to intrude on his private time, but he's blasting them out for the world to read, not able to control himself or his emotions. He receives a text message, and I look down onto his phone. It's from Michelle.

Michelle: Dinner tonight?

John: Nope, I can't

Michelle: How about a drink afterwards then?

John: Can't do that either

After responding to the last text, he sets his phone to silent, turns it over so that he can't see the display and become distracted by further texts. He leans his head back on the brick wall and closes his eyes, remembering the day that he and Mom bought this house together.

They were young, only married six months, but they knew this was where they wanted to spend their summer holidays. This is where they wanted to teach their future children to swim, this is where they wanted their kids to learn how to ride bikes and learn how to hike, explore the world around them—teach them about nature. This is where Mia and I learned all these things. The house was Dad's idea, as he found it first and presented Mom with the suggestion. He'd known that she wouldn't be thrilled with the décor, but with the suggestion of the purchase came promises of redecorating.

Years later, the kitchen cupboards are still the original dark wood panelling, the front porch is barely big enough for one, let alone two chairs, and the gardens are no more than a few evergreen shrubs. But this little cottage on Water Street was their summer escape from the daily lives they lived in Paris, and it brought them both many years of joy, laughter, and love, until it brought Mom much deep, anguished pain.

Dad's wishing that he didn't let Mom go today; he wasn't ready, as there is still so much that has not been said that should no longer remain silent, but he understands why she felt the need to leave suddenly. And as much as he doesn't want to admit the reason, it was time for her to go back, time for him to move on; having her here has been rather disruptive to his sanity and peacefulness.

Mia is still in her room; she has not so much as opened her eyes in a long time. I return to her, lie back down beside her, reach out my arm to touch her and leave it hovering above her face, like a hovercraft waiting to land. She stirs suddenly as if she can feel me, turns, and looks directly at the empty space that is my face. Our moment is interrupted by the sudden loud noise outside her open window, she throws the blankets over the bed and hops over to check what the commotion is outside. My curiosity gets the best of me, so I follow her, but I already know what the fuss is about, I don't need to see it to know, I'm all-knowing all the time—most of the time. From the window, we stare at Dad and Henry standing an inch apart. Dad's face is bright red, and I can tell he is breathing heavy due to the rapid rise and fall of his chest. Mia rushes out the door with her limited speed, crutches under her armpits, ready to intervene.

Dear Adam,

I'm not really a procrastinator, despite what your mother and everyone else thinks of me. I'm a man full of ideas, and I just worry about committing to one thought in case a better one surfaces—so instead of acting right away, I wait. Sometimes this waiting comes across as me being lazy and makes me late for commitments, but that's in no way a true representation of my character, or of the real me.

Sometimes life just gets in the way and causes too much turmoil, derailing us from what is really important, and before you know it, a year passes, then two, then three, by that time, we've temporarily forgotten about the original idea; because we've moved onto bigger, better things that occupy our time and our head space, but this, my son, is at times how we give birth to regret and by no means indicates that these are things I'll ever truly forget.

Love, Dad

CHAPTER 19

Curious and Afraid

Adam

"GET THE HELL off my property before I call the police," says Dad.

With both hands Henry pushes Dad, and Dad stumbles back but manages to catch his footing before tripping over the root of a maple tree—the one he'd been staring at earlier.

"What the f…." Dad holds his tongue when he notices Mia standing at the door.

"Dad, what's going on?" she asks, eyes scanning the scene.

"Ameleiah, get back inside."

"But Dad…."

"Now."

With her head hung, Mia retreats into the house and peeks out from behind the curtain, curious and trembling as she tries to hold the curtain open.

"This is your last warning man, leave now," says Dad.

Looking rather embarrassed with a red face at having been caught by Mia pushing our father, Henry walks away. When he gets to the end of the driveway, he turns around for one last jab at Dad.

"You can't keep me from seeing her, you do know that right?" He tilts his head to the side, "You don't own her, man."

Dad takes a step closer towards Henry as he continues his rant.

"I don't need you to get to her. Keep her locked up if you will, and that's fine if you don't want me to see her, I have her number, I'll just call her. There's other ways for me to get to her, I don't need YOUR permission," he says, as he waves his phone in the air and grins.

Dad clenches his fists, but remains put. Hidden behind the curtain still, Mia sighs and releases the breath she was holding, then she hobbles into the kitchen and searches the fridge for something to eat while Dad remains outside brewing over his thoughts, and for the first time he's glad that Mom has left the island.

An hour later, the two are sitting at the kitchen table together. "This is great sweets, thanks," says Dad, while he eats the pasta that Ameleiah prepared. Mia remains silent, staring down on her still—full plate. "Do you want to play a board game together tonight?" He waits for an answer, but again is met with silence. "Okay then, I'll do the dishes since you cooked dinner." Dad stands, picks up his plate and utensils and carries them to the sink.

"Dad, we need to talk."

Dad sighs but sits back down next to my frowning sister.

"What's up sweets?"

"What was that about?"

"What?"

"Dad, don't pretend, okay? You know what I mean…out in the yard with Henry?"

Dad moans. "Ameleiah, it's complicated. Can you just leave it alone? You won't understand."

"I'm not a small child anymore, you haven't treated me as one in a long time, why start now?"

Dad picks up what is left of his drink, takes a sip, then sets it down, straightens his back and leans into the chair. He rubs his hands over his face, lets out a blow with his breath. "It was over your mother."

"Finally, your talking now, but I could've guessed that much,"

"How?"

"I see the way he looks at her."

Dad nods. "I see it too, and I don't like it."

"As in you're jealous, Dad?"

"Ameleiah, you must understand something. Before your mother arrived here, I wasn't exactly happy like I once was before your brother died, but I had moved on, learned how to live without her, without both of them. And she shows up here suddenly and my world once again turns upside down. At first, I wasn't sure how I would react to seeing her again after all these years, but I quickly got used to having her around. It was awkward at first, don't get me wrong, and she got on my nerves plenty of times, still gets on my nerves, but if I must be honest with myself, I like having her here." He lowers his head as if to hide his expression from my sister. "I miss her already and she's been gone only a few hours. Geez. What am I going to do? I feel as if I must begin the entire grieving and separation process all over again now. Does any of this make sense or am I confusing you?" Dad looks up to Mia now, tears running down her face. "Sweets, why are you crying? I certainly didn't mean to upset you."

"Dad, you are the one who doesn't understand. You have no idea what this means."

"What does it mean?"

"Oh gosh, you are such a guy."

"No offense sweetie, but I sure hope so; I'm your Dad after all."

They both chuckle and I sit between them smiling; Dad always knows when to crack a joke, even during a serious conversation—it's one of his strengths.

"Why didn't you ask Mom to stay longer?"

"It's complicated, it's not that easy to just say those words."

"Why do adults always say things are complicated? They're only complicated if you make them complicated. It's like my algebra homework for example; if I try to solve a problem without thinking it through, it's overwhelming and I'll stop trying, but if I break it down—you know, baby steps—then it's not so difficult after all. Why can't life be more like algebra?"

Dad pats her on the head, "Good analogy sweets, but let's resume this conversation in about ten to fifteen years, and I'll ask you that same question, and we'll see if you're still wishing life were like algebra."

Mia considers this comment but doesn't respond. Dad decides they need to lighten things up, so he goes to the living room cabinet where the boardgames are kept and pulls out Monopoly, Mia's favourite boardgame. Half hour into the game, and Ameleiah has already acquired The Boardwalk, the property demanding the most rent. "I give up," says Dad, raising his arms.

"No way, you can't give up this quick; we are only just getting to the good part."

"Another half hour and I'll be broke," says Dad, as he waves his Monopoly money at her. "I'm quitting while I'm ahead. I need some air; do you want to take a little stroll with me."

"I noticed how you used the word 'stroll' and not walk," she says, smiling. "That's Mom's word."

"Come on let's go, before it gets dark."

"All right, but I want to finish the game when we get back, so don't put away the pieces."

It's a silent night as most nights on the island are, there isn't anyone out at this time of day. Many homes have their outside lights turned on as their owners sit out on the front porch, drinking tea, sipping wine, or listening to music through a portable speaker. This is what people do here in the evenings—there's nothing else *to* do. The wind carries sound far, so Dad and Mia keep their voices low. "Dad, why are you seeing Michelle? I mean, she's not even your type."

"How do you know what my type is?"

"I know more than you think, besides, Mom is more your type."

"Really, how so?"

"Well, for starters: crop top with low rise jeans, low scooped neckline, large hoop earrings. And how does she even walk in those heels—seriously? Sometimes, I want to give her my crutches because she's surely going to need them soon." My sister's eyebrows raise as she describes Michelle's everyday attire. "Don't even get me started on the fake eyelashes. It's not that there's anything wrong with the way she dresses, I myself love crop tops, it's just different from Mom. Mom doesn't dress like that, she's more conservative and elegant in her fashion choices."

"We've been there, your mother and I. We had our time, and in the end, it didn't work out."

"Yes, but only because you're both ridiculously stubborn and gave up easily," says Mia as Dad gawks at her. "What? It's true, and you know it, you just don't want to believe it or see it for the reality that it is."

My sister is distracted by her phone, constantly checking it like it has a life of its own. Dad notices and asks her about this, but she doesn't tell him that she has been sending Mom texts that are not being answered. At first she dismisses this, as she knows Mom is driving, then she assumes she has no phone service on the boat, but Mom would be home surely, judging by the time.

"What's so important on your phone that you keep looking at it?"

"Nothing Dad, nothing at all. Let's go back and finish that game before it gets late and I get too tired to kick your butt."

Bright and early, Dad heads out to Michelle's house. He rings the doorbell twice before she answers, still in her silky, see-through nightgown and robe. Opening the door and realizing it's him, she ruffles her tidy hair trying to mess it up, but I'm not sure why.

"Oh, hey you, what a surprise. You didn't mention you were coming over, not that I'm complaining," she says as she lifts the bottom of her robe up, exposing more of her long, sunburned, bare leg—she must be hot and needs air.

Looking away from her, Dad says, "We need to talk."

She straightens her robe, and gestures for Dad to come in. "Wait here one second, I'll be right back," she says pointing to the couch, and heads into the bathroom leaving Dad in the hallway alone scratching his chin.

A minute later she re-enters the room, but this time her lips look different, they are coloured a deep red and her hair is much bigger than it was. She sits on the couch and pats at the seat beside her, inviting Dad to sit close. "Okay, I'm ready. You caught me off guard first thing in the morning; women do like warnings about surprise visits sometimes."

Hmm, that's an odd comment for her to make. If she was warned, it wouldn't be a surprise.

"This isn't really that kind of a social visit."

She raises her eyebrows, "Is that so?"

She already knows what has brought him here so early in the morning, she already knows what he is here to say, and she doesn't like it, so she tries to distract him and not give him a chance to speak the words she hopes will remain unspoken.

"Are you hungry? I'm starving," she asks as she heads into the kitchen. She goes on and talks about her day as she pulls a carton of eggs out of the fridge. "It's early, so I'm assuming you haven't eaten yet?"

"Michelle, will you stop and listen for a minute."

"I'm listening," she says as she breaks open eggs into a bowl, adds milk and whisks vigorously as if the eggs have done something to upset her.

"Stop, please."

She puts down the whisk and looks at Dad with a frown. "What?" she demands.

"It's over, I can't see you anymore. I'm sorry, but I shouldn't have let this go on as long as it has."

Michelle doesn't speak at first and casually goes back to whisking the eggs, ignoring Dad.

"Did you hear me?"

Still whisking and not looking at Dad, she says, "This is bullshit, this is her fault." She's whisking so fast that egg spills from the sides of the bowl.

"What is whose fault?"

Michelle stops whisking, and with a spatula still in hand approaches Dad. "She has turned you against me, hasn't she?"

"Who, Ameleiah?"

"No not Ameleiah. I'm talking about Clairah."

"You're not making any sense right now. Clairah isn't even here. She left yesterday morning."

Her expression brightens. "Really? Clairah is gone, as in no-longer-on-the-island?"

"Yes. She's gone."

"But then…I don't understand. If she's gone, what's the problem?"

"This has nothing to do with her, the problem is that I don't feel for you what I should. Look, you're a nice person and all, it's just that I…. We don't have a connection."

Michelle paces, waving the spatula in the air, and storms back to the couch where Dad is. "We don't have a connection?" Her words blare into his face while she waits for him to answer, hands on hips.

"Come on Michelle, don't pretend that you don't know this."

Michelle raises her arms up in the air. "It certainly feels like we connect each and every time you're in my bed." She places the spatula on the kitchen counter, and unwraps the robe, letting it hang loosely and revealing uncovered legs. I close my eyes briefly; I don't want to see this part.

"That's the only connection we have, and that's not enough. It's not sustainable."

"Since when is that not enough?"

"It's never been enough."

"It's enough for me." She begins to pull the robe off her shoulders now, starting with the right side, the side Dad has a view of, as if showing off her shoulders is all it will take to get Dad to change his mind.

"No, it's not enough, you only think it is."

"It's enough for now. The rest will come later. We've only been seeing each other for less than two months." Shoulders are now exposed.

"It won't come later."

"Well, not if you give up on us it won't," she says with a strained voice as she drops the robe to the floor, letting it fall around her feet—I guess she doesn't care to show Dad her feet, they remain covered.

"There is no us, there was never an us. Look I'm sorry, but I have to go." Dad walks out the door leaving Michelle and me alone, her arms still outstretched.

When Dad is outside, and out of ear shot, Michelle screams, "I hate you Clairah. I hate you with a passion." She punches the wall in her hallway, breaking her index finger. She's got a contorted look on her face and it causes her fiery red lips to bleed into the sides of her mouth creating a mask-like effect—instead of appearing ladylike and put together like my mother, this look reveals Michelle's true rage. Her pointy chipped fingernails make their way up to her face to try to salvage the situation, but as she brings them away from her line of vision and up to her face they, too, are covered in fiery red rage from her punching the wall. Adults can be complicated; I've had enough, so shortly afterwards I leave her to wander the Earth alone, cloaked in darkness.

Dear Adam,

Anger is not something that I'm proud of, it's not something I want to carry around with me, I try to let it go, try to eliminate it from my life, but at times, even my own wishes are ignored and rage surfaces inside me in ways that I didn't see coming. It happens to us all, and at these times, the anger evolves out of nowhere, springs to life in a sudden roar as if unleashed like a cannonball—destroying everything in its path, replacing the things destroyed with nothing.

Love, Dad

CHAPTER 20

Paris

Clairah

AFTER BEING AWAY for a little over two weeks on an island with not much to do but lots to see, it's strange to be coming home to my quaint town of Paris. My little town has a population of just over twelve thousand, so it, too, is small; but as I drive through the country from Tobermory, I can instantly feel the differences between the two. The air is purer on the island, untainted; unlike here. There's a special presence about the island that draws you in, allows you take deeper, fuller breaths, and forces you to stop and look, sometimes at nothing—it's in those moments you see it all. I prefer to drive through the back roads instead of the highway, as I'm not a comfortable driver in traffic. The back roads at least allow me to pretend for a little while longer that I'm still back on the island, although the differences are vast, and pretending is difficult.

As I drive closer to home, closer to my street, my heartbeat increases as I prepare to walk into the house alone. When I pull up to my house, all the things on my To Do list come flooding back into my mind, reminding me of what I've neglected over the last couple weeks. But it's not as if I had a choice, my daughter needed me. And besides, this time at the island has done wonders for my brokendown, non-existent relationship with John. At least it's summertime, and I don't have to go to work so the time off will allow me to tackle some of the much-needed tasks that wait undone on my long To Do list. I'm used to spending my summers alone so this isn't new to me, but this time, walking into the already empty house without my daughter here has a bigger impact. Goosebumps cover my skin despite the warm weather, so the first thing I do is check the thermostat to make sure the air conditioner is not set too high. It's set to twenty-two degrees, so it's warmer than most keep their homes set at. I grab a thick Adidas sweater from my bedroom and put it on hoping I'm not coming down with a cold. I plug my phone in as the battery is almost dead, unpack, and draw a bath, turning the single lever a little too much to the left so as I lower my body into the hot and soapy water, my muscles and mind relax as the heat penetrates my skin. This feels heavenly and maybe I'll just stay in here all night. I let out a big yawn and realize it's later than I had thought it was, but despite the late hour I let the warmth of the bath soak me until it reaches deep within my bones.

Well over one hour later I'm still lying in the tub, and my skin looks as wrinkled as a wet cloth left out to dry while rolled up. I pull myself out and wrap a towel around me. Water still drips off my skin when I hear my phone going off; it's the sound of texts coming in, multiple texts and within seconds apart.

Ameleiah: Mom, where are you

Ameleiah: Mom, why are you not answering your phone

Ameleiah: Mother!

Ameleiah: Hello?

Ameleiah: Okay, I have called a few times again and you're not answering, I'm getting worried, call me back or text me please! If you don't, I'll tell Dad your MIA. I swear I'll tell him!

So, there's her threat and it comes with an angry-face emoji after her last text, that's how I know she means business, so I dial her number.

"Mom! Thank goodness, are you okay? I have been calling forever."

"I'm sorry honey, my phone was in the other room, and I've been in the bath so I couldn't hear it."

"Who has a bath for an hour and a half? That's how long I've been trying to call you."

"I was reading a really good book and lost track of time." I lie, as I don't want her to know the truth; that I was simply lying in the water with my eye's closed, thinking about Adam.

"What book"?

Oh shit, think quick, "*The Woman In The Window*, by A.J. Finn

"That's a good one, a page-turner, I've read it."

Oh shit, I haven't read it, I only thought of that book as it's been sitting on my nightstand for months, waiting for me to get to it. If she asks me any questions about the story, she'll know I'm lying. "So, do you miss me already?" I say at a bad attempt to change the subject.

She ignores my question and asks her own, but thankfully it's not about the book. "Mom, are you okay?"

"Of course, why wouldn't I be? What are you up to honey?"

"Dad and I were playing Monopoly, we just finished and I'm getting ready for bed now."

"Sounds like you two had a lovely evening together." I continue to pat myself dry. "Oh honey, I have another call coming in, can I call you right back? I don't recognize the number so it might be important, maybe it's Jim, wanting to talk since my car is in the driveway."

"Sure Mom, love you, bye."

"Hello," I say to the unknown caller, only, it's no unknown person on the other end—the voice pulling me into my past is Henry's voice. Shit. I had forgotten that he somehow found my number before we even went out for coffee.

"Henry, what a surprise. What's up?" I say trying to sound confident and composed.

"Hey, good surprise I hope! Are you up for some company tonight, I know it's really late, but I can't get you off my mind, so thought I'd ask? I went by the house earlier, and even tried to call you a few times, but you never answered."

"Just a random surprise, is all. Henry, I'm not on the island anymore."

There's silence as I wait for him to respond, the quietness seeping through the speakers is thicker by the minute.

"Henry, are you still there?"

"Since when?" His voice sounds hurried. "I hadn't heard that you left."

"I left earlier today."

"Really? Why? And without even saying goodbye, without telling me?"

"I'm sorry, it was sudden, I actually just got home a couple hours ago. I was considering staying in Tobermory overnight as I didn't want to drive home in the dark late at night, but thought against it, so I'm beat and heading to bed now. You do realize that you're calling me after midnight?" Why am I apologizing to him?

"Why didn't you tell me you were leaving so soon? I went by the house to see you and was caught off guard when John wouldn't let me see you, but he didn't tell me you left. That wasn't very nice Clairah. You could have at least told me about your plans."

His reaction to my leaving catches *me* off guard.

"I'm sorry I didn't let you know. You knew I'd have to be leaving soon." Wanting to put an end to this conversation, I lie, "Listen, I have to go Henry, Ameleiah is on the other line calling."

Henry ignores my lie and presses on, "Why didn't you tell me you were leaving so soon? I went by the house, I kept calling, my calls were never returned. That was cruel Clairah. Not nice at all," he repeats.

"I didn't know I owed you an explanation. Listen, I have to go Henry, I have Ameleiah on the other line." I lie again to get out of the call and hang up. Henry is persistent and calls again an hour later, but this time I recognize the number, so I ignore it—fear prickles my skin. I begin to think about the past, the time that Henry and I first met and the few times that we dated, before John—the sudden shift in his approach, his controlling nature then…and possibly still now.

I was at the Queen's Inn with my parents on summer vacation when it all started. It seems that all major events in my life revolve around the Queen's Inn. It was midweek, and Henry was there working on the landscaping—he owned a landscaping company, still does. Henry is a few years older than me; I was eighteen at this time, it was four years before I met John, Henry was twenty-one. I was on the second floor library of the inn, located directly at the top of the stairs, browsing through all the classic titles on the bookshelves. I loved that part of the inn, it brought me comfort, sitting there, looking at the books. The bookshelves were floor-to-ceiling and built into the wall, so they looked more original to the house than just random bookcases placed up against a wall. Halfway down the shelves drawers extended from one end of the shelves to the other, then underneath the drawers, more shelves housed even more books. The bookshelves were made of dark oak and had panelling and crown moulding along its side. Kelly was so generous and offered for her guests to read the books if we promised to return them to where we found them. She had all kinds of titles including some favourite classics: *Pride and Prejudice* by Jane Austen, *Wuthering Heights* and *Jane Eyre* by Charlotte and Emily Brontë. The room had two brown leather couches and a glass coffee table over top of a large, burgundy Victorian-style rug. A landscape painting hung on the side of the wall that faced the front yard and water. The painting reminded me of the island itself, and as I'd study the fine lines and intricate work of the artist, I wondered if it had been painted by a previous guest or someone local. Since the library was on the second floor, there was a clear view into the back from the window behind the couch. To say I was in love with being there, and in that room particularly, is an understatement.

I had picked out *Jane Eyre*, a book I had already read twice over, sat on one of the two couches in the library and got to page three when I heard the loud bang outside. Looking out the window, I saw Henry working in the gardens, he looked up and smiled, I smiled back and returned to my reading. Later that afternoon, he came looking for me, he asked me out to dinner, but I declined. The next day, he came around again, even though his job there was done, he asked me out again, and once again I declined. He seemed like a nice enough guy, but there was no chemistry between us, no initial spark. It wasn't until the following summer that I agreed to go out with him, the day he cornered me at the restaurant; I did this mainly because I felt bad about turning him down repeatedly. I figured that one dinner wouldn't hurt, so we went out for dinner, with my parents' permission of course, and we had lunch the following afternoon. My parents were a bit skeptical, being Portuguese and old-fashioned at times, they didn't much like the fact that I was going out with a boy. I found that I liked the company though, and he helped to pass the time—that was it. By the end of the week, we had been out several more times, been swimming together, gone for a few short walks, and I was growing comfortable around him. We exchanged phone numbers just before my family and I left the island, and he called me each night. To me this was just a friendship, we had never kissed, held hands, or had any special moments that made my heart flutter. But his daily phone calls quickly became too much for me once I was back home—he was slowly suffocating me from afar. If he called and I wasn't home, he demanded to know where I had been, who I was with. He questioned me endlessly on my whereabouts as if he owned me. After a month of this nonsense I told him that the time we had spent together on the island was nice, but that the friendship would never work, he lived on the island year-round, so we were hours apart from one another. He wouldn't accept this and continued to call every night for two more months. By that time it was late fall. One afternoon, after another interrogation from him, I got the courage to confide in my parents. My father immediately got involved—he called Henry himself and told Henry that he needed to stop harassing me. After this, the nightly calls, while they didn't stop completely, reduced gradually. I only heard from him once a week, then once every other week, and eventually, as more time passed, not at all. By the next summer I hadn't heard from him in months, and I had forgotten all about Henry and I had thought he had forgotten about me, but I was wrong. The following summer, back on the island, I ran into him again at the inn. He had a weekly contract to maintain the landscaping and I should have known it was inevitable that I would run into him again, but I hadn't really given it much thought. By the time I saw him again, to me he was just another guy from my past and meant nothing, in fact, he had never meant anything to me at all—even then. I had thought that in the beginning we could be friends, but he soon proved that he wasn't capable of being just friends.

When Henry first laid eyes on me the summer after he and I hung out, he dropped his shovel and ran to hug me, squeezing me a little tight. He tried to kiss me, and I backed away blocking him. He had assumed we would pick up where we left off one year before and once he knew I was back had made plans for us to have dinner that night. I don't know if he was expecting me that day precisely, but I had been coming to the island at the same time each year, so his anticipation of my return wasn't completely unfathomable. I knew better this time around than to make the same mistake, so I shut him down right away. He persisted, and two summers later when he saw me and John together, I couldn't help noticing he balled his fists at his sides.

These memories are so old; they happened so long ago, but I wonder as I reminisce, why I had agreed to have coffee and dinner with him again now. I should have remembered about his possessive nature; I should have stood my ground, but I had pushed these memories away, tucked them deep into the part of the brain that files information that's not needed. I should have recalled all this; I should have made myself stay away.

As I pull myself out of my ruminating thoughts, I check my ringing phone; the same number, Henry's number, he's called four more times. I set the phone on silent, thank goodness he doesn't know where I live.

That night, exhausted from the journey and drama, I tuck myself into my own bed and let sleep take me to a dreamless world.

CHAPTER 21

Back to Old Habits

Clairah

THE NEXT WEEK goes by without much incident, except that Henry continues to call every night like he did all those years ago; he's back to old habits. I answer once in the entire week I've been back, hoping that finally talking to me will satisfy him, but it only opens up the invitation even more. I try to keep the call cordial and friendly, but Henry has a way of reading into things with a clouded and skewed perception. He speaks of coming to Paris to visit me, and I shut him down right away, telling him it's not a good idea and also that I'm leaving on a work trip and not sure when I'll be back. I'm not sure when I got so used to lying; although, he didn't buy the lie, this I know by the way he keeps saying, "I see…" So, I decide to be blunt and tell him I don't want to see him. I'm hoping this message gets delivered nice and clear, and when he hangs the phone up on me after I say this, I think that perhaps finally the message has set in; because he doesn't say, 'talk to you later', he just hangs up.

I haven't heard from John since I left, but I do talk to Ameleiah daily, ether by phone call or text. She's doing well, still using her crutches but managing better than before. She's getting a little annoyed at having to have the pins sticking out of her leg still, and I remind her that it could be worse. When she asks me how that's possible, I tell her that it could be winter, and she'd have to try to manage wearing long pants with the pins sticking out; she grunts at that thought and doesn't complain about the pins again. Since I haven't heard from John at all, I'm surprised when I see his number appear on my cell, it's lying on the coffee table and I jump off the couch a little too eager to answer it before it goes to voicemail.

"Clair," his voice blares through the speakers, "I hope I'm not catching you at a bad time, but we need to talk."

"What's up, is it Ameleiah?" I scratch my head with worry.

"No, she's fine, but what exactly is going on with you and Henry? Are you two together?"

"Gosh no, what kind of question is that?"

"It's a fair one to ask."

"He's called me a few times," I admit, but refrain from telling him that it's a few times a day, "but I've only actually spoken to him once since I left." Actually twice, but now that I've said once, I'm sticking to it. I stop to allow John to say something, then continue. "I'm ignoring his calls."

"So, you're not seeing him, romantically that is?"

"I already told you, we had coffee and dinner, that hardly constitutes as being together."

"Well, according to what Henry is telling everyone here, you are. In fact, he's telling everyone about a lot more than just dinner and coffee. Listen, Clair, if you are dating, or whatever, I'll figure out a way to be fine with it. You are a grown woman; I get it that you have moved on. Just don't lie to me or keep me in the dark. You know I don't like that."

I sit back on the sofa again, phone close to my ear. "I haven't kept you in the dark about anything."

"Whatever, just...."

"Just what?" I ask with irritation in my voice now. "What have you heard anyway?"

"The next time I hear Henry bragging to one of the guys at the marina that you're great in bed, I don't want to have to punch him in the face again if, in fact, you are happy and in a relationship with the jerk. It's your business, but I just worry because of the history with you two from before, I know how possessive he once was." There's a pause as John waits for my reply, but I give him none. "Clair, are you there still? Hello..."

I hang up the phone before he has a chance to say anything else. I immediately press the call button on Henry's number, it's easy to find because it's in my missed calls list many times. I want to know what the hell is going on and why he's spreading these lies about me.

He answers on the first ring, "Hey gorgeous, you've finally come around and called me back. Miss me?"

"Why are you telling people we slept together?" I say with a loud voice and it echoes through the phone.

"Hey, calm down gorgeous. I didn't say we slept together. I was talking to Timmy over at the marina and he asked how I was. I was telling him I missed you because I do. I went on to tell him that I want to spend more time with you, have you wake up in my bed next to me. This is all true. There are no lies in what I said."

"You knew, didn't you?" I shout into the phone.

"Knew what exactly?"

"Don't pretend to not know what I'm talking about. You knew that John was there, overhearing the conversation, didn't you?" There's silence on the other end, so I provoke him to answer. "You *knew*, didn't you?"

He lets out a big sigh and says, "I had no idea your possessive lunatic of an ex-husband was nearby until his fist met my jaw. Good thing Timmy was there to break up the fight or I would have destroyed him. He needs to mind his own fucking business. You can tell him I said that."

"Henry, I need you to listen carefully."

"I'm listening, gorgeous."

"We have nothing, we are nothing. I don't want you to call me again. Stop talking about me, and stop trying to make John miserable, he has been through enough."

"It's always about John isn't it? At the end of it all, it's always about him."

"No, this has nothing to do with him, this is about me."

"You still don't know who the better man is, but you will soon. I'll make sure you do."

"Stop. I don't want to hear anymore. Don't call me again. I'm blocking your number." I hang up the phone and text John back.

Clairah: I'm sorry I hung up on you. I called Henry, we talked, and I told him to stop this nonsense. He should no longer do or say things to upset you. There's nothing between us and he understands this now.

As I press the send button on the text, a fleeting odd feeling passes through me. I *hope* Henry understands. My phone dings, indicating an incoming text.

John: I don't like the man, he irritates me

Clairah: Get over it. He's just being Henry; he obviously has not changed.

John: I tried to tell you that, but once again you didn't listen to me

I type a smart reply, and my fingers hover over the send button. On a whim, I backspace it out to remove the message and instead send him an emoji with a tongue sticking out.

That night, I dream of our wedding day.

Neither of us comes from a large family, and so we got married at the Queen's Inn since the size of the venue was perfect. The reception was held outside, under the dreamy sky on the front lawn. There were chairs covered in white cloth setup for the guests, and a little wooden pergola stood at the end of the lawn welcoming guests as they walked through. A second white pergola took up space at the alter where we stood and exchanged our vows. After the ceremony I noticed him, Henry, standing down by the water's edge, watching intently, hands in his pockets.

John notices me stiffen my body and follows my gaze down to where Henry stands.

"That's it, I've had enough," he says, as he makes his way down to Henry, arms swinging wide at his sides. I follow behind, grabbing one of John's arms in mid-swing back.

"Honey, don't bother, let it be. He's harmless."

"I'm not letting him ruin our special day."

"Nothing can ruin this day," I say, softening my voice and rubbing his arm.

John looks at me and back at Henry and says, "He actually can if he tries hard enough, but I won't let him."

As we approach, Henry clears his throat as if he is getting ready for a screaming match. "I guess congratulations are in order."

"Stay the hell away from my wife. I'll have you arrested if you so much as come within fifty feet of her."

"Arrested? What for? For being out in public, on a public path, minding my own business? Seems unlikely I'd get arrested for that." He says as he turns and walks away smiling, leaving John breathing heavily.

"Come on honey, let's get back to our guests."

"I hate that guy."

"I know honey, but please let it go, for me."

John takes my hand in his and squeezes it. As we walk back up to the inn, John tells me how he wishes Henry would move away and off the island. "I just don't have a good feeling about him."

The reception was held in the inn's spacious dining room. There weren't many people present: my parents, my aunt and her husband, John's brother whom we don't see often drove in with his wife and kids from Toronto to be there, some friends from back home, a few friends from the island, and of course Kelly and her husband. We had rented the entire inn to have rooms for all the guests. Of course, John and I stayed in the Victoria room, the grandest of the rooms and my favourite. We used up all the rooms between the guests and their kids. We had dinner catered and setup buffet-style on the large kitchen island. The living room which is generally not part of the inn but used by Kelly herself, had been graciously donated to us and cleared for a dance floor so that we could enjoy some music and dancing after the food. The Queen's Inn had been transformed for our magical day. Purple irises in full bloom lined the staircase that led to the second floor, the floor where our room was. The irises lining the stairs continued up through the hallway and also on the bookshelves, leading right into our room that was located at the end of the hallway to the right. At the end of the night, as we ascended the stairs as husband and wife for the first time, John reached down, scooped me up in his arms and carried me down the hall. Using one arm to open the door and his foot to keep the door open, he carried me across the room and placed me on the elaborate king-size bed. He told me to stay put while he poured champagne, but I was in too much awe to stay still; I immediately got up to look around. The spacious ensuite bath to the left of the bed had a white clawfoot tub, and inside the tub were more irises floating in a warm bubble bath. In the room itself, irises hung from the chandelier creating a tent-like feeling. Romantic.

"Wow, this is amazing," I said.

"Perfect for my sleeping beauty."

Candles lit the room, creating a soft ambiance. This was a lovely night filled with stars in the sky, and when all our guests had retreated to their rooms, John and I grabbed a bottle of red wine, two wine glasses and a tray of cheese and crackers left over from the dinner party and sat outside on the balcony off the second floor. The balcony was right outside our room, in fact, our room's window faced the balcony, affording us views of the calm sparkling water from the lights shimmering off the boats moored and waiting to be taken out on a nighttime sail. White lights hung all around the white railings of the balcony, creating a soft, romantic space. Two large vases were filled with more purple irises. The inn's red roof had also been transformed and rimmed in the same white lights, casting a shadow-like effect for those looking up from the outside.

These are the memories I had remembered these last few years, not the ones of Henry following me, constantly calling, and harassing me. That was the reason I had agreed to go to coffee and dinner with him, but I wish I had remembered more than just the bliss and joy.

The next morning, I wake up early and plan my day by making a To Do list: shower, go get groceries, eat at some point, exercise, and pull weeds from the garden, in this order. A visit to the pharmacy is also necessary; I need to refill my prescription. I must try to get my life under control and back to normal. There are only a few weeks left before I go back to work, back to my classroom, my students and second family. School doesn't begin for another six weeks, but I have to be there a few weeks earlier to get ready, setup, prepare lesson plans. So, I have four weeks to get myself together, to try to form some type of routine. Yes, routine is good, I decide, it keeps me accountable and on track. Truthfully, I'm trying to keep busy so that I don't think about the empty house, about Adam, Ameleiah and, if I must admit, even John. I need a few weeks of thinking of only myself. This is my time to reflect on nothing while thinking of everything.

The day turns out to be a good one, I managed to accomplish all the items from my To Do list. I even eat three meals. This small victory leaves me with a sense of encouragement; I can do this.

Three weeks later, one week before I start work, I'm deep in thought making colour selections one afternoon as I sit outside in my backyard that faces the Grand River, painting for the first time in years, when Henry shows up in my backyard. I'm so startled to see him standing before me that I knock the canvas off its stand and it flips over, fresh paint littering the grass and what would have been a great painting of a canoe on the river is an unrecognizable mess.

"Hey sexy, I didn't mean to startle you."

I'm frozen, glued to my chair.

"No hello? No warm greeting for me?"

"What the hell are you doing here? How do you even know where I live?"

"Nice to see you too, gorgeous. I've missed you." Henry waits for me to say something more, but I bite my tongue, afraid to speak. "I'm worried about you. You never return my calls, so I had to come see for myself if you are okay." He places both hands in the pockets of his jeans.

For a few moments, I don't speak or move; Henry has never physically hurt me before, but his constant harassment after that summer that he and I dated caused my father to get the authorities involved. They couldn't do anything because Henry did nothing more than call and show up constantly, and since he had never threatened or physically hurt me it was all fine, they had said. I remind myself of this now. He didn't hurt me then, and he most certainly won't hurt me now. He's just possessive and doesn't take no for an answer, nevertheless, I need to take precautions and so, I find my voice. "You shouldn't have come, I have plans tonight, so I can't see you, in fact, I was just wrapping up here and was going to have a shower and get ready to leave, I'll be gone for the night. I'm sorry, but you need to go."

"Plans?" he says raising his eyebrows.

"Yes, I have plans," I repeat with a steady voice, "and I meant what I said on the phone, I can't see you anymore. You need to stay away from here, away from me. This is not healthy for you Henry."

"Don't get all overdramatic about me being here. I'm not here just for you. Yes, I worry because you won't answer my calls, but I'm also here on business, well not specifically in Paris, but Toronto. There is some new equipment for garden maintenance I'm here to see, and I'm also attending a gardening show. I figured I'd make the drive down to see you while I was close by, and I'm here for the whole week."

"Toronto isn't exactly close by."

"It is when you consider the distance between here and Manitoulin Island. It's all about perspective, gorgeous."

"Still, you shouldn't have driven here."

"Well that's for me to decide, now, isn't it?"

"Leave Henry. Now." I decide to be firm and straight to the point.

"He was stupid to let you go, to leave you. I wouldn't have left you."

"Leave now." I repeat louder this time and with a shaky voice.

Instead of leaving, he takes two steps towards me; I hold my breath.

"Don't come any closer to me," I say, but without conviction.

My neighbour, Jim, hears me, crosses the lawn and comes to stand beside me.

"Clairah dear, everything okay?"

Relieved to see him here, I say, "Hey Jim, I think so, but if you don't mind sticking around for a few minutes to make sure there is no trouble, I would appreciate that." My eyes are pleading for him to help me and he nods his head in response, understanding my fear.

"Sure, thing Clairah dear. I'm not going anywhere," says Jim waving his garden ho. "You let me know if you need me to do anything."

I nod in return and face Henry, standing even closer now. "Henry, please don't force me to call the police. My father had to do that once, all those years ago, I don't want to have to repeat that process again. We aren't kids anymore."

I back away from him even more and manage to put my hand in

my pocket and grab a hold of my phone. Henry seems to consider my words, looks from me to Jim, and nods his head and leaves. I watch him get into his truck and before driving away he says, “This isn’t over.”

I let out the breath I didn’t realize I was still holding.

“What was that all about?” Jim asks after Henry’s truck is no longer in sight.

“I wish I knew, Jim, I wish I knew.” I drop the phone I’d been clenching back into my pocket. That same evening Jim and his wife, Mary, invite me to for barbeque chicken and I accept, not wanting to be alone. During dinner I fill them in on my history with Henry. After dinner, as I’m making my way back home, John texts that it’s time for Ameleiah to be heading back soon. We usually try to have her return home at least a week before the start of the new school year so she can get settled and prepare. This year however she’s still in a cast and it will take longer for her to adjust, get her supplies and be seen by a doctor here, so he thinks she should return a couple weeks earlier. He also says in his text that he will be accompanying her home sometime through the week. When I read that, I immediately press the phone icon next to John’s name. He answers right away, “Hey Clair.”

“I’ll come get her,” I say as quickly as he says my name upon answering.

“Really? Why?”

“I think that would be best.” I’ve arrived at my house and before going in, I peek into the backyard, just to make sure there are no unexpected visitors, phone still glued to my ear.

“You really want to come back here again? I mean, that’s fine and all, I just figured it’s easier for me to bring her to you.”

“It makes more sense for me to go there and get her John, you have a job, I’m not working right now. I still have almost a week before I start work. It’s easier for me to come get her. In fact, I’ll be leaving in the morning.”

“As in, tomorrow morning?”

“Yes.”

"Well, that's sudden. I didn't mean that Ameleiah had to leave right away, I was thinking next week, what's the hurry?"

"I want to do it while I'm off. I'll only stay a night, give you two a chance to say goodbye. I'll stay out of your way."

"That's not what I'm worried about."

"Then what?"

"You left so suddenly, you couldn't wait to leave and now you can't wait to get back here again. Something is not right.... I know you Clair, you're running away from something there. What is it?"

"Nothing," I say with a quivering voice.

"I think you're lying to me."

Darn, why does he know me so well? "That's bullshit John."

"Is it?"

"Yes, and you and I both know it."

I walk through the front door and secure the lock behind me, double checking to make sure it's locked. I walk to my desk and open my laptop and type in the address for the Chi-Cheemaun ticket centre. "I'm not running away from my own home—there's no reason why I would—I just want to be helpful when it comes to my daughter."

"Our daughter," he corrects.

"Our daughter," I say with an apologetic tone.

"Fine, you come then, but I don't think you will get on the morning ferry, it will most likely be full now."

"I've ordered my ticket as we speak. I'll be there."

"I really don't understand you sometimes, but okay, see you around eleven in the morning I guess?"

"Yup, see you then."

"Do you need me to pick you up at the dock?"

"No, that won't be necessary, I'll get myself there."

"You remember the way?"

"I got myself back to South Baymouth on my own, did I not?"

"Yeah, I suppose you did."

"All right, see you tomorrow before lunch sometime. Goodnight

John." I hang up the phone before he has a chance to respond or say goodnight back. I want off the phone as fast as possible—I worry he'll hear the fear that seeps through me through the phone's speakers.

That night, I pack my bag and set my alarm for two a.m. This gives me five hours before the boat leaves; that should be plenty of time, even considering that I must be there an hour before as there shouldn't be much traffic through the night, so I shouldn't hit any delays. I don't sleep though, not at all, I'm up all night sitting in the living room waiting for the alarm to go off, watching the door with a bat in hand and extra chairs underneath the doorknobs, just in case. At one point through the night my phone chimes; it's a text from John. My eyelids are heavy, and I can barely keep my eyes open, so I struggle and squint to read the incoming text, the time on my display reads twelve fifteen in the morning—one hour and forty-five minutes before I must get up. I press my thumb and index fingers onto the screen, enlarging the text to help my sleepy eyes.

John: Everything will be all right. Keep your door locked and make sure you don't miss the ferry in the morning. I'll be at South Baymouth waiting

I blink a few times and re-read the text to ensure I didn't misread something, but I didn't. I'm not sure what this message is about or what it means. Does he know that Henry was here? That's impossible, he can't know, how would he know?

I type a quick reply, eyes half shut so the text remains enlarged.

Clairah: Okay, I'm going to try to get some sleep now. Have to be up soon. Goodnight

John: Good, get some sleep, you can always crash when you get on the ferry and in the car. Goodnight Clair

John: And don't worry about anything

He knows…something is wrong. My eyes shut instantly, and I'm dreaming before I even have a chance to turn off the ringer and realize what I've agreed to.

CHAPTER 22

There's Something Wrong

Adam
(Earlier the same day)

"TOMORROW?" ASKS MY sister, as she puts her hair up in a ponytail to get more comfortable. "She's really coming here. Tomorrow? I'm really confused Dad."

"As am I sweets, as am I."

My father and sister are both in shock that Mom is coming back to the island, but I'm not. I know the truth, as I stood beside her shaking body last night when Henry appeared unexpectedly. Mom wants to leave Paris, as she is afraid that Henry will return. She feels safe on the island, always has and always will, only, she doesn't know and won't admit to herself that it's her safe haven.

"Did she say anything else?" asks my sister.

"Nope."

"There's something wrong Dad, I know it. Wait. I got it," says Ameleiah.

"Got what?"

"Mom doesn't want you at the house."

"Why do you think that?"

"Think about it, Dad. You left five years ago, and that was the house you two shared—that was our family home. Mom spent the last five years sulking and being depressed, she hasn't done anything to the house since you left. She doesn't want you to see it that way. She doesn't want you to see that it's exactly how it was when you left. She's trying to protect herself, protect her feelings from you."

Dad pulls the top of his jeans up. "I thought she was happy, keeping busy, painting, and doing all the other things she loved to do. That's what she's told me, anyway."

"Oh Dad, you can be so naïve at times. Mom hasn't painted since you left."

"Wow. I had no idea. You never told me she was unhappy."

"You never asked. In fact, neither did I so I shouldn't talk."

"Then how do you know she's unhappy?"

"I just do. She doesn't have to speak the words for them to be true."

Dad scratches his chin, nods his head and says, "I suppose you're right. I never did ask."

"No, you didn't so there was no way for you to know."

My sister's theory is a good one, but she is off base, and I can't correct her. It's true that Dad never asked about Mom after he left—he couldn't ask, he was hurt. She blamed him for my death, and as much as she doesn't want to admit it, her blame pushed him far away.

My father looks out the window, staring into the night, wondering about what my sister revealed.

His thoughts are interrupted when Mia speaks. "Hey Dad, can we have dinner at the marina tonight? I have a craving for their juicy burgers."

Mia waits for a reply, but Dad continues to stare out the window at nothing, thinking about everything. "Dad, did you hear me?

"Sorry sweets, what did you say?"

"Dinner tonight at the marina?" Mia repeats.

"Sure, sweetheart."

As my father and sister sit across from each other at the marina restaurant later that evening eating a burger, the waitress and another couple, one my family doesn't recognize, are at the nearby table discussing business. The couple is talking about the landscaping and asks the waitress who takes care of the marina grounds. "It all looks so well kept and so lovely," says the woman wearing an oversized sunhat and sunglasses.

"Henry's landscaping business, actually. He's a local and has lived here his whole life."

"We love hiring locals to do work. Do you think we could have his card? We have a rather large property on the west end of the island, near Meldrum Bay. It's about, oh, less than an hour's drive from here and we are looking for someone to maintain the property once a week."

"Sure thing, I can get you his card, but he's away on business this week, off the island down south in Mississauga or Oakville, one of those cities. I don't think he will be back for at least a week."

Dad's head jerks back so fast when he hears the waitress' words that I'm afraid he will snap his neck.

"Well, no worries, just leave his card if you have one here and we can call him next week, dear."

"I didn't know Henry was so close to Mom. Good thing he doesn't know where Mom and I live. I wouldn't put it past him to go and try to see her while she's alone," says Mia innocently, as she takes a sip of her Coke.

"Why would you say that?"

"Oh, come on Dad, I'm not stupid—I've told you before that I see how he looks at her. And don't pretend that you don't either."

They finish their dinner in silence. After they eat, Dad stops in at the marina shop to pick up some paperwork he needs for work, there's a phone number he needs to find for one of his clients he needs to call this evening. He tells my sister to wait at the restaurant, so she doesn't have to walk far, and Dad walks next door. Inside the shop, Dad meets Bill, another mechanic, cigarette dangling from his lips.

"Hey Bill, you still here? It's getting late, you should go home," says Dad.

"Yup, just locking up. I had a repair I had to finish on a motor that the owner is picking up first thing in the morning. I'm heading home now, cracking open a beer and sitting my arse down on the couch for the night."

"Sounds great. I think I'll do the same. I'm just grabbing a phone number."

"Oh, hey John, by the way," he says, putting out the cigarette knowing he's not supposed to be smoking in the marina shop, "I hope it's okay that I gave Henry Clairah's home address."

Dad's face reddens, eyes bulge, he stares blankly at Bill. "You did what?"

"Relax man, it seemed innocent enough. He says he was going to be close by on business and wanted to stop in on her to say hello, he said he wanted to surprise her so that's why he didn't get her address from her directly."

"So instead, the bastard came here, and you gave him the address, just like that?" Dad's fists are balled at his sides.

"Yup, sure did. Why is that a problem? They're seeing each other and all."

"No, they aren't. Is that what Henry told you?"

"Yup, sure was. Listen, either way, he knew we had it on file from when you lived there. Is this going to be a problem or not?"

Without answering, Dad storms out of the room, slamming the door behind him. He knows the truth—he tries to control his breathing while his blood boils at rapid speed. He doesn't, however, tell my sister that it's the reason Mom is coming in the morning—that she is scared; he doesn't want to worry her.

At night while Dad lays in bed trying to sleep, he picks up his phone and texts Mom.

John: Everything will be all right. Keep your door locked and make sure you don't miss the ferry in the morning. I'll be at South Baymouth waiting for you

Mom's reply comes quick.

Clairah: Okay, I'm going to try to get some sleep now. Have to be up soon. Goodnight

John: Good, get some sleep, you can always crash when you get on the ferry and in the car. Goodnight Clair

John: And don't worry about anything

Dad re-reads the last few texts and knows for sure that she's frightened. At the same time, he receives another text. It's from Michelle, but without reading it he flips the phone upside down on his nightstand.

Dear Adam,

Did you know, Adam, that you were the one who taught me compassion? It's true my son. While you were a baby you suffered from colic syndrome and so you cried—a lot. Sometimes you'd cry so much that I worried I was doing something wrong while taking care of you. Your mother, she was the smart one, the calm one—the one who knew what to do to soothe your whimpering cries; I on the other hand, just worried. I'd sometimes stare down at you for a long time and wonder what was going on in that little head of yours, what were you feeling inside, was the pain unbearable? Soon, I'd find myself changing your clothes thinking that perhaps the fabric of your current outfit was rubbing against your skin, scratching you. I'd let your bottle sit for an extra minute to ensure the milk wasn't hot so it wouldn't burn your tongue. I'd even run out in the middle of the day to buy you new tubes of cream for your bum rash, afraid the old one had lost its effectiveness, even though the expiry date wasn't for another two years. Your sister was different, Adam, she didn't cry much, she mostly ate, slept and during the waking hours she was content laying on a blanket staring at the ceiling. I didn't have to push deep within myself to help her, that came naturally to me. But you my son, you pushed me to the limit, forced me out of my comfort zone, and made me the person I am today—it's just a shame that you are not here to see me now—to see me take action on things that have long been left idle.

Love, Dad

CHAPTER 23

Everything Will Be All Right

Clairah

WHEN THE ALARM rings at two in the morning, I'm already awake—I haven't slept much at all. I try to remember all the benefits of waking up early, and chuckle because though I often try to be part of the 5:00 a.m. club, it always fails. But today, even I'm up before the early morning risers. I remember the text from John late in the night and question if I imagined reading it. Scanning my phone for reassurance, I find it, staring me in the face in black text.

> **John:** Everything will be all right. Keep your door locked and make sure you make the ferry in the morning. I'll be at South Baymouth waiting for you

Everything will be all right, he said in his text. Why would he say this, unless he knew something was wrong? Perhaps I gave it away with how I acted during our last call—the urgency to leave Paris and return to the island—that must be it, has got to be it. I stumble to the bathroom, splash water over my sleepy face, brush my teeth, change my clothes, and decide to put on some tinted CC cream to give my appearance a bit of a lift. Looking at myself in the mirror, I decide to add some blush to my cheekbones and mascara to my lashes as well, then shake my head, unsure of why I'm fussing over my appearance so much, especially at this hour. I grab my bag and purse before glancing one last time at myself and walk out into the dark night and into my car. The drive to Tobermory will be long and lonely, so I set up my music ahead of time to keep me company. I stop at a Tim Hortons on the way in Cambridge on Hespeler Road, and order an extra large double double dark roast coffee to keep me awake and make my way towards Guelph, up Highway 6 to Tobermory. It's just me and my music, which is on shuffle so I never know if I'll hear an eighties hair band like Skid Row come on, or John Mayer; each time a song ends the next one is a surprise. After all this time, it feels comforting to be listing to music again. I drive faster than I normally do, afraid of falling asleep at the wheel, and make it to Tobermory in record time. It only took me three hours and twenty minutes as there was no traffic, so I have time to spare since the ferry doesn't leave until seven. I stop at a restaurant serving breakfast, order another coffee, eggs and bacon, and toast. As I wait for my breakfast to arrive, my phone dings, another text—it's from John again.

John: Morning! Are you there yet? I hope you are, or you will miss the boat

Clairah: GM! I'm here, at the restaurant just having breakfast as I wait

John: Good. Don't bring your car over; leave it in Tobermory, it will just be a hassle leaving it parked at South Baymouth. I'm picking you up remember, so you won't need it while you're here

I hesitate for a minute before replying. John will expect me to disagree and to argue and bring it anyway—that's what the old me would do, so, instead I send the following reply.

Clairah: Okay. See you soon

I'm about to put my phone down and another text comes in.

John: Try to get some sleep on the boat

Clairah: I'll try

On the ferry, I find a window seat away from tourists, lay my head back while clenching my purse and bag tight, and with eyes shut. I must have fallen asleep and not have heard the announcement notifying passengers to make their way back to their cars, as I only remember being shaken awake by one of the ferry crew members telling me that I must get off the boat now. Picking up my bag and purse, I look around and realize I'm one of the only passengers left. How had I fallen asleep so deeply? I apologize to the staff and make my way out, but I don't even get five feet away before I see John standing by his truck, frowning, arms crossed over his chest. When he notices me, he uncrosses his arms, his face relaxes, and he makes his way towards me; with a gentleness I remember from before, he takes my bag from my arm, and says, "You okay?"

I'm so embarrassed and about to cry, and I try to hold back tears that threaten to well up, but the lack of sleep through the night is catching up to me and I break down in a full-out sob as he places the bag down on the ground and takes me into his comforting arms. He eventually picks up the bag and leads me to the truck with his arm resting on my shoulder, then puts the bag in the backseat and opens my door for me, gesturing for me to step in.

He buckles my seatbelt and reclines my seat back and says, "Try to get some more sleep. I'll wake you up when we arrive." He shuts the door and walks around to the driver's side, and before he even gets into the vehicle, my eyes are shut and I'm oblivious to my surroundings.

CHAPTER 24

I Can Read Her Thoughts

Adam

MOM IS MORE shaken up about Henry's visit than she even admits to herself; I know this, not only because I can read her thoughts, but also because of the way she lets her guard down in front of Dad—this is unlike Mom. She is used to being the strong one in front of Dad, the hefty rock that can't be carried away, but holds the world down to a solid form—this is the image she hopes to portray to Dad, wanting him to think she's okay and doesn't need him. Watching her collapse into Dad's arms breaks my unbreakable heart. She sleeps the entire ride back to Dad's, peacefully dreaming about me. It's during these dreams that I try to sometimes enter into her subconscious and give her some sign that I'm here for her, here with her. She understands me when I do this, although she doesn't think about this in her waking state, but only in her dreamlike bliss.

Back at the house, Mia waits patiently on the front step. She had wanted to come with Dad to pick up Mom, but Dad asked her to stay behind. Dad wanted to give Mom the opportunity to talk about the situation that had her frazzled, even though it didn't work out that way in the end, sleep consuming her for the entire drive. Mia understands, she has a mature mind for her age, always has. When she sees the truck pull into the driveway, her eyes light up, it has only been a few weeks since she last saw our mother, but the excitement running through her bones is as if it has been a lifetime. Dad notices her excitement and places his finger on his own lips to quiet her as she is already trying to prance her way to the car, hopping on one foot because her crutches fell over, eager to see Mom.

"She slept the whole ride here. I don't think she slept last night," says Dad, as he picks up Mom from the passenger seat and carries her inside the house, leaving Ameleiah outside standing alone in the tall grass.

Two hours later, Mom makes her way into the bright kitchen. The sun is at its full peak this time of day and rays sneak in through the opening in the curtains, illuminating the counters and floor and revealing a light layer of dust. The table is set for three, and the smell of bacon, Mom's second favourite breakfast food, lingers in the air. It's after lunchtime, and Mom is famished having had breakfast at five forty-five back in Tobermory. She doesn't complain that she's already had bacon and eggs once today.

Dad is at the sink loading the dishwasher with the dishes he used to prepare the late lunch. He turns to face Mom when he hears her approach, "Hey there sleeping beauty, do you feel more refreshed? Are you hungry?"

Dad hasn't called Mom 'sleeping beauty' since before I died. We all have breakfast together as one sort-of happy family; even I take a seat at the table for this one. Later at night, they have a frozen pizza, since lunch was so late, and no one is hungry until about seven. After dinner, Mom and Dad both clean up the kitchen and Dad suggests they go sit out by the water and get some air; Mom doesn't reply at first, but eventually agrees.

The night is clear, and many bright stars fill the sky as the two of them walk down to the water side by side. "Look, there's Cassiopeia," says Dad, pointing to the sky. "Do you see it?"

Mom squints to get a better look. "No, I don't think so."

"There, look to where my finger is pointing. See the lines almost forming a 'W'?"

"I'm not sure, oh, wait…there?" Mom points to the sky in the direction that Dad points.

"That's it!"

"I see it now. Oh, and look there," says Mom, pointing to another area of the sky. "Isn't that Orion?"

"Hey I'm impressed," says Dad.

"Once upon a time, I learned from the best."

"Yeah, it was once upon a *long* time ago, wasn't it?" says Dad, emphasizing the word long.

They walk a little further ahead and sit on a bench near the water; Mom shifts in her seat, unable to get comfortable. "Thank you for picking me up today. I don't think I would have made it, driving myself after not having any sleep through the night."

"Clair, you don't have to thank me, it's just something I do. It's my job to be there for you."

"No, that's not true. Perhaps, as you put it, 'once upon a long time ago' it was, but not anymore. I'm not your responsibility now; I haven't been your responsibility for years. So yes, I must thank you."

Dad clears his throat before replying. "I know about Henry."

"John, I don't want to hash that out again."

"No, not about that, I know that he was there, in Paris I mean."

"I had a feeling you knew because of your late-night text, but how?"

The wind has picked up slightly and Mom's long hair blows uncontrollably so she tries to hold it down with her hands.

"Bill, one of our mechanics, he mentioned that Henry asked for your address, he knew the marina had it on file from when I lived there."

"Oh, and he just went ahead and gave it to him? Just like that?"

"Yeah, that's the trouble with small-town and being a lifelong local—everyone assumes it's okay to share other's personal information."

Mom doesn't comment but looks down at her hands, willing them to stop shaking.

"That was shortly after our phone call when you announced you were coming in the morning. At the time, I didn't know this, but I suspected something was off. After talking to Bill, I put two and two together. I can't tell you the rage I felt at that moment. I wanted to be there for you, I wanted to break every bone in his body, but at best I knew it would be almost seven hours before I got to you. The ferry was done for the night, so I would have had to driven around the lake—from Little Current up to Espanola and around the lake through Parry Sound —it would have taken too long. I also had Ameleiah to think about."

"I'm glad you didn't leave Ameleiah alone."

"Did he hurt you?"

"No, he didn't have the chance."

"I think we should get a restraining order."

"I thought about it last night, trust me, I really did. But he left when I asked him to. He didn't touch me, so I don't know that we have enough cause for one."

"So, he was there then, he actually went to the house? You saw him?" Dad leans in closer as he asks this.

Mom didn't want to tell Dad the truth, but she did. "Yes, he was at the house."

Dad balls his fists, fingernails digging into his skin leaving fingernail marks. "That bastard, I'll kill him."

"John, relax, he didn't hurt me."

"Not this time." Dad looks out into the dark night. "That does it, we have history and now this, you're getting a restraining order." He waits for Mom to argue, but she doesn't. "It took him years to get over you, don't you remember that? Him calling constantly, even after we were together, the lurking around on our wedding day trying to ruin it. Damn him, the guy was obsessed with you. It seems that all it took was seeing you once more, years later, for him to pick up where he left off. Part of me wishes that you never came back here because of him, but the other part of me is glad, as I got to see you again."

He stops speaking long enough to catch his breath. "This is why I was so upset when you first agreed to go out with him. I couldn't understand for the life of me what the hell you were doing with the jerk. You, of all people, know what he's like, you were a part of the history. What the hell were you thinking?"

Mom looks at the sand gathered around her feet. "I don't know myself what I was thinking. It had been so many years ago and I gave him the benefit of the doubt, I suppose. I was going with the 'people change' mentality, but I know it was dumb of me."

"Hey, since you used the word dumb and not me, I can agree without pissing you off, right?"

Mom chuckles and slaps Dad's arm lightly.

"It's nice to see you smiling."

"It feels good to smile."

"I think you should stay here for a few weeks, until we sort this out. I'm not comfortable with you going back knowing he's still close by."

"I don't have a few weeks, John, I have to start getting my classroom in order. Ameleiah needs to go back-to-school shopping, we have to get back to our lives. You were the one who had suggested she leave a bit earlier this year."

"Yeah, I know, but things have changed now. Will you think about it at least?"

"We can't run away from our problems—from our lives."

"I'm not asking you to. I'm only asking you to consider staying at least for the week, when Henry returns, you can leave. How's that? Can we compromise?"

"That's cutting it close to the start of the school year."

"Yeah it is, but safety first, right?"

"Yes, I suppose you're right. Okay, that sounds reasonable, I'll stay until the end of the week, but then, whether he's back or not, I have to go."

"Good, glad we agree on something. I'll ask around and make sure I get the actual date Henry's conference is over. I'm also taking you to the police station to file a report, just to have this incident documented. I know he didn't hurt or threaten you, but his behaviour is obsessive, and that can lead to other things."

"Okay."

"That's it? You're not going to argue this one either. Wow, I'm on a roll. What else can I negotiate today?"

"Don't push your luck," says Mom with a giggle in her voice. "Listen, John, I want to tell you something. I tried to tell you that day at the coffee shop and again a few days later, but you shut me down then too."

"I wasn't ready to talk then," says Dad, moving his line of vision away onto the boats.

"Are you ready now?"

"Depends on where the conversation goes. I suppose we can't avoid it forever." He turns to face Mom. "What's on your mind?"

"John, I don't blame you. I know I said I did, but I never in my heart truly believed that you were responsible for the accident and for Adam's death. I needed to find someone to blame to make myself feel better, to be able to go on, to live. I needed to know that there was a reason he died, and I needed to hate someone for it. It was wrong, I know that now. But at the time, and for many years, I was trapped in that turmoil and grief and couldn't think straight. Losing Adam was like losing a piece of my soul, like it was ripped out aggressively from deep within me. I didn't know how else to cope with the pain." Their eyes are locked on each other's and Mom clears her throat before continuing, "I blamed you because you were there, and you made it easy for me to blame you. I have never told anyone this, not even my therapist, and I really want you to know that now. I know it doesn't change anything, too much has happened, and what we had is in the past, but I just want you to know I'm sorry for pushing you away," she pauses for a moment, "I pushed you so far away that you couldn't find your way back to me."

The wind has died down, it's calm once again, a peaceful night. The water, which is only three feet away from the old wooden bench where they sit, is as still as a rock. Dad stands, walks to the water's edge, picks up a flat but round stone and tosses it into the bay. It skips three times across the water before making a final splash and disappears from the water's surface. To the right is a path that leads around to the marina entrance, and a couple are walking by hand in hand. They look young, in their early twenties—visitors, surely. Dad looks at them and back at Mom. "They remind me of us, the way we used to be when we first met, do you remember? We used to sneak down here at night. You always wanted to be by the water."

"I used to love the water, I still do and yes, I remember us all too well."

Dad makes his way back to the bench where Mom sits feet up and arms crossed over her knees. "Are you cold? Do you want to go back?" he asks her.

"No, I'm good right here. There's no other place I'd rather be." says Mom, shivering.

Dad takes a seat next to Mom. "You were right to blame me. It was my fault. I killed our son. I was the one sailing the boat. I was the one in charge. It was my fault and you were right to blame me. I left you and moved back out here because I hated myself for not being able to save him; you only gave me the push to leave, gave me the confirmation that I was to blame. You made it easy for me to leave because you hated me as much as I hated myself."

"That's not true, I never hated you."

A tiny piece of paper blows their way and lands by Dad's feet. He bends to pick it up and fidgets with it through his fingers. "In your own way you did hate me. I felt it. And you had every right to hate me. I should have been able to save him; it was my job to keep him safe and I failed at the most important job of my entire life."

"Oh, John," Mom places her arm on Dad's.

"You know something?"

"What?"

"I haven't been on a boat since, other than to work on one."

"Really? I didn't realize that."

Dad shakes his head from side to side, "I can't do it anymore; I don't think I ever will again."

Mom considers his words briefly, then asks, "Do you still think about that day often?"

"Not a day passes that I don't relive it."

Mom reaches down and takes Dad's hand in hers, so he drops the paper he'd picked up and was fidgeting with. "Adam died because of an accident due to a storm no one saw coming."

Dad looks away from Mom. Mom reaches out to take his face and turns him towards her.

"It was an accident; do you understand me? I was wrong all those years to blame you. You are not to blame for his death."

We all want to hear the buried truth until the shocking words hit our sensitive ears, then we wish we never heard the words at all as sometimes the truth is hard to swallow—like now, years lost because of the buried truth.

Tears run down Dad's face so fast that he can't keep up with wiping them away and they blur his vision. "I think about him every day."

It's true, he really does think of me everyday. Sometimes I wish he would think of me less often, as it will help him to heal, help him to get back to the way he used to be before. Will what once was, ever be again? Even I don't know and only time will tell.

"So, do I. That's normal. We are his parents, we will always think of him, but we need to shift our perspectives. We need to remember the happy times, the fun times. We have many great memories on the boat, and we need to try to focus on those. It's what Adam wants us to do—Adam died, but his memories live forever. Somehow I know this to be true; although I do admit it's easier to say the words than to live by them."

"I tried going to counselling for years after I left. I was never able to open up to the therapist the way I just did with you." Dad is still sobbing uncontrollably, and his breathing is fast, and short.

"I think I'm to blame for that," says Mom. "I still blamed you, and as long as I did, you would never open up and forgive yourself." She raises an eyebrow at him. "Am I right?"

"Yeah, I think you are."

"I feel as if Ameleiah's accident was meant to happen, like it was fate."

"What do you mean?"

"Well think about it. We probably would never have seen each other again had it not been for her accident, right? Just think about it, John. Maybe we would have seen each other at her graduation, and wedding, but that would be it. Her accident has, in a way, freed us both from the pain we have been each carrying around for years. Don't you think so?"

"Yeah, I think you're right Clair. It almost feels like it was supposed to happen."

"I really think it was," says Mom, as she reaches out and takes Dad in her arms; he continues to weep uncontrollably while she holds him. He is the one who needs comforting now. They continue to sit on that bench under the stars at the little beach area, for the next two hours. There isn't much talk about me after this; instead, they talk about other things: work, hobbies, life. They catch each other up on how life has been for them the past five years—their real lives and not the fake lives they've pretended to live; they search the sky for more constellations and they sometimes just sit in silence, each wondering and trying to guess what the other is thinking, but afraid to ask. It's a calm night now, not even the tops of the trees move. At half past midnight they make their way back home, back to Dad's home.

Mom goes to my old room, changes into her pajamas, and goes

back out to say goodnight to Ameleiah, who is still up on her phone at this hour. She meets Dad in the hallway.

"You're still up?" she says to him as his bloodshot eyes stare back.

"Just saying goodnight to our daughter who refuses to get off her phone."

"Yeah me too. I'm pretty tired, I'm heading off to bed."

"Clair," says Dad, as Mom walks away.

She stops, turns, and faces him, "Yes," she whispers with hope.

"I'm glad you're here. I'm glad we talked. I know things can never go back to how they were before, too much has happened and too much time has passed, we are not those same young adults anymore, but I'm glad to have you back in my life, even if only for a while. I need your friendship—I want that."

At the word friendship, Mom flinches but not enough for Dad to notice. This is not what Mom wanted to hear. After tonight, she had hopes of more than just friendship. But if friendship is all he can give, she will gladly accept what he offers.

She avoids his eyes. "I'm happy to be here too," she says as she walks back into her room, closes the door behind her and quietly weeps into her hands, her back to the door, firmly shut.

Dear Adam,

You were about nine months old, your mother had a headache and we needed food in the house, so I took you and your sister to the grocery store. This was adventurous of me, considering I didn't often do groceries—that was your mother's department. But today she needed me so without hesitation I bundled you two up and off we went to No Frills. I had it all planned out, I was going to make her some grilled salmon, fresh vegetables, and basmati rice. You were being fussy when we first left the house, so I was in a hurry and failed to check if I had my wallet. We got to the store and I realized I didn't have a loonie for the cart

return, so instead I gave your sister a basket and I took one myself, you hung off my other arm in your car seat. We hurried through the aisles filling our baskets with everything I thought I'd need to surprise your mother with a nice dinner, your sister complaining that her basket was heavy, even though it was still empty—mine overflowed. When we got to the check-out, I set your car seat that you were in down on the conveyor belt and reached into my empty back pocket—wallet missing. I might have let a certain swear word spill from my lips when I realized it wasn't where I expected it to be. When the cashier saw the look of horror in my blazing eyes she said, "Oh dear, someone is having a bad day." You chose that moment to let out a cry so loud that it drew the attention of many shoppers. Your sister came to my rescue; she reached into her tiny pink purse she carried with her everywhere she went, pulled out a dime and handed it to the cashier, she turned around to the many shooting eyes disturbed by your wails and said, "Baby brother sad." Needless to say, Adam, that the nosy shoppers all turned red in the face and went about their own business. The cashier told me to take the groceries and come back later whenever I could to pay for them. This my son is what humanity should be like, each of us extending a hand to one another in times of need, it really does make the world go around.

Love, Dad

CHAPTER 25

Poking Around

Adam

"HEY JIM," SAYS Mom into the phone, dripping wet as she had to rush to the bedroom to answer it since she's spent the last thirty minutes in the hot shower, the warm water penetrating her skin.

"Clairah, my dear, sorry to bother you, but that man that was here the other day threatening you, was here poking around again last night. I didn't like the way he looked at you then. If he comes around again, I'm calling the police next time."

Mom had called her neighbours to tell them that she was back on the island so they wouldn't worry, they look out for my mother and sister, for that I'm grateful.

"Jim, it's okay. John is taking me to the police station today and we're filing a formal report. I'm staying here for the next week, so you don't have to worry about me. By the time I return, he'll be gone and there'll be a safe distance between us."

"All right, well, I walked over and told him to leave your property since you were away, so I don't think he'll be around anymore. He gave me a bit of a hard time, threatened me if I didn't mind my own business."

"You told him I wasn't in Paris?"

"Yeah, figured it would keep him away if he knew you weren't around."

Mom's skin prickles, she rubs her arm in an attempt to soothe it. "You didn't tell him where I was, though, did you Jim?"

"Of course not Clairah. I only said that you were away, was all."

"Good," says mom, as she lets out a sigh.

"Well, listen here Clairah, the wife is calling, she most likely has a list of things she needs me to do for her, so I must run. Ring us when you're back in town, so we know."

"I will, and thank you Jim."

Although Jim didn't reveal Mom's location, she still wishes that he hadn't told Henry that she was out of town. She worries that he will figure it out, come back to the island, guessing that's where she returned; she's hoping not to run into him while she's here. If she knows Henry at all, he will come straight back and that will defeat the purpose of her being on the island. And if she must admit this to herself, she doesn't want to leave, not yet, despite what she says to Dad. Mom decides to get dressed in a pretty pink sleeveless sundress, something I haven't seen her wear before. She blow dries her hair straight, applies some pink blush to her cheek bones and black mascara to her eyelashes, something I barely see her do, and heads towards the living room, I follow closely behind. Once in the kitchen, she looks around for Dad and Mia but finds neither, so she pours herself a cup of coffee and takes it outside. As she steps off the porch onto the lawn, the morning wetness from the night envelopes her bare feet—she stands for a few moments, allowing her skin to absorb the coolness from the earth as she wiggles her toes into the tall grass. Slowly sipping her coffee, Mom sits on the step, listening to the sounds of the island; the birds singing as they visit the water's edge for a drink, the boats as their sails are lifted and prepare to leave the marina for a day of sailing, the trees blustering with the light wind over the cliff on the other side of the bay. Mom blows gently into her coffee mug—it's a little too hot to drink—then looks up at the sound of an engine; she recognizes the brown truck: it's Henry's truck. Upon recognition of the truck, her hands shake, spilling the hot liquid onto her exposed legs. "Shit," she says, as she wipes her legs dry with her dress.

Henry climbs out of the truck, slams the door, and rapidly approaches her. "You took off on me the other night," he says, looking straight into her eyes with raised eyebrows.

"Henry, what are you talking about?"

"I went back for you, to see you again, and your nosy neighbour came around to tell me you were gone, he said you left town for a few days. I figured you came running back here," he says as he approaches Mom even closer; he's only standing a few inches from her. He places his left foot on the first step, almost touching her leg. Mom pulls it away and brings it up to her chest while swallowing the saliva that accumulates. "So, why'd you leave?" He rests his arm on the railing, inches from her face.

"I don't think it's any of your business Henry. What are you doing here anyway?"

"I happen to live here, or have you forgotten that?"

"I mean here, on John's property. You've crossed the line, literally."

"Well, I came to see you, gorgeous. Isn't that obvious?"

Mom places the coffee mug on the step next to her and stands. "You need to leave. I want you to leave," she says with a shaky voice.

"I don't think you do." He reaches out to touch her chin, Mom pulls back, and knocks his hand away.

"How the hell do you think you know what I want?"

"Come on, gorgeous, I'll buy you breakfast. You look way too pretty, sitting here alone in that slinky dress."

Mom turns to leave and walk back into the house, but Henry reaches out his arm and grabs Mom and pulls her back into him.

"Get your hands off me." Mom is trying to break free from his strong grasp, but he holds on too tight for her to get loose.

I don't worry though; I don't have to worry; because I know that Dad hears her from inside the house and is on his way out. Dad had been in his room getting dressed when Mom came down to the kitchen, but he hears her yelling now, and within a few seconds Dad's at the front door and forcing it open, allowing it to slam back into the brick wall of the porch. He takes one look at the scene before him: Henry holding Mom's arm with one hand, his other arm around her waist, Mom trying to break free, pleading that he let her go—the vein on Dad's temple bulges, he doesn't wait another second before walking right up to Henry, his nose inches from Henry's face, and knocks Henry's arm free from Mom's, throws a punch, making his fist connect with the side of Henry's jaw. Henry swings his right arm towards Dad but misses, and Dad punches him a second time. From within the house, Mom is on the phone dialing the police. By now, other neighbours have come by to witness the fight, and one of the older gentlemen from a few houses down holds Dad's arms back, preventing him from getting to Henry again. Henry uses this opportunity to make Dad even more mad saying things like, "What's the matter? Did you lose your spark, Johnny boy?"

Within minutes, the police arrive—Mom is standing at the end of the driveway in tears, her freshly applied mascara is smudged on her face, giving her a raccoon-like look. Mia has woken up with the commotion and is also outside in her butterfly pajamas, comforting Mom. Henry and Dad are on the front lawn, each giving the police officer their statements, both speaking out of turn and eventually the police officer threatens to take them both down to the station if they don't settle and co-operate. They know this police officer, his name is

Jeffrey, all 3 men having grown up on the island, and so they are both on a first name basis with the officer. Nevertheless, the officer demands silence from each of them, and only allows them to speak when they are directly asked a question. He has not yet spoken to Mom and leaves her report for last. When he approaches, Mom clears her throat, readying her voice for the statement.

"Clairah," says the officer as he puts his pen away in his notebook. "It's nice to see you after all this time. I'm sorry about Adam, I know it's been years, but I haven't seen you since."

"Thank you, Jeffrey."

"Can we sit?" he gestures towards the two red Adirondack chairs crammed in on the front porch.

"Sure."

They both have a seat—Mom is fidgety and plays with the hem of her dress.

The police officer, Jeffrey, places his hand on Mom's arm. "Relax Clairah, I'm here to help."

"Okay," says Mom while wiping her nose with the back of her hand.

"Can you tell me what happened?"

"You mean with Adam?"

Jeffrey raises his eyebrows, "No, I don't mean Adam, I mean with Henry."

"Yes, of course," says Mom shaking her head, "of course, you mean Henry."

Dad and Henry are reminded several times to keep their distance as the officer listens to Mom's statement. Both men stand back, Dad with his arms crossed over his chest, listening intently and protectively to every word Mom speaks, and Henry staring rudely. Once finished, Jeffrey says he has all he needs and asks Henry to stay away from Mom for the time being.

"If you feel at all threatened, you should bring Clairah to the station and file a restraining order especially if he comes around again, okay? I think there is enough here to warrant one, at least with the history and all. Although I still think he is harmless," says the officer, pointing at Henry, "and just a little obsessed, but one can never be sure."

"Thanks Jeffrey, but what good will a restraining order do if he lives next door?"

"It'll keep him off your property at least, and prevent him from going to Clairah's house once she leaves."

"That's true," admits Dad.

Jeffrey nods towards Dad, waves at Mom, gives Henry one last warning telling him to leave, and gets back into his cruiser and drives away as Henry pulls out of Dad's driveway and into his own.

Dad walks up to Mom, takes her into his arms and she lets the tears fall freely as her body melts into his.

"Dad," says Mia, standing by the door, "do you want me to put on more coffee?" Both my parents had forgotten that Mia is here.

"Yeah, that would be great sweetheart, go and do that, we'll be in soon."

"Okay," says Mia, leaving Mom and Dad alone outside, Mom enveloped by Dad's arms.

Dad holds Mom's arm, the one that Henry grabbed, and inspects it for bruises. "Did he hurt you?"

"No, not really, not physically anyway."

Dad's jaw is tight as he continues to inspect my mother's arm. I follow Mia into the kitchen, wanting to give my parents privacy, they deserve that even from me. As I leave them Dad says, "He won't touch you ever again. I promise." He plants a kiss on her forehead.

Mom nods hesitantly and then rubs the spot where his lips touched her skin.

In the evening, during dinner, Mom suggests that she and Mia should leave tomorrow.

"Why are you in a hurry?" asks Dad, dropping his fork.

"I came back here to get away from Henry, but he's here, so what's the point in me staying? I'll just cause more trouble if I stay any longer."

"Clair, you're not the one causing trouble."

"He'll get to me faster if I'm here."

"I'll protect you."

"I know you will, but still, there's no point in delaying the inevitable, is there?"

Dad clears his throat before he gets up and walks away from the table, placing his dirty plate in the dishwasher. Upon closing the dishwasher, he looks out the window, avoiding Mom. "No, you're right, there isn't. You should go."

Mom's eyes flash towards Dad's, she's surprised that he gave in so easily—she expected him to protest, insist they stay longer. She had hoped that would have been the reaction, anyway. "Well then, it's settled. Ameleiah, can you have your stuff packed soon? I can book passage for us the day after tomorrow, first crossing."

"I can't Mom, I need more than one day. I want to say goodbye to everyone before I leave."

"Okay, I'll book the last ferry so that gives you all day tomorrow and the afternoon the following day."

"What's the hurry Mom?"

"You heard your father; there's no point in delaying things any longer." Mom gets up, lips glued together and leaves her dirty dishes on the table; she walks out of the room and into her own. Mia examines the table and cleans up Mom's dirty dishes without complaining.

She stays in there alone for the rest of the evening, and that night she dreams of me.

It was the night of the accident, the night I died. Mia and my parents were on board the rescue boat, and Mom had just slapped Dad across the face, blaming him for killing me. I was still in the water, floating further and further down shore. There was a second rescue boat, searching for me. Mom wrapped herself in a blanket, rocking with the waves as the boat transported my family back to shore. She kept reliving that moment, panic surging through her like an electrical wave, as she realized that I was gone—shock rather than blood filled her veins. Mia, too, was wrapped up in a blanket, huddled next to stone cold Dad, who stared, white-faced, across the water, searching endlessly for ghosts.

Throughout the night, the wind picks up and there's a screeching sound coming from outside—this wakes Mom. She sits up in bed contemplating the time, reaches for her phone, touches the screen to bring the display to life—it's two thirty in the morning. Deciding she is thirsty, she leaves the comfort of the warm bed and heads into the kitchen for a glass of water.

"Hey," she says, as she sees Dad sitting on the couch, whiskey glass twirling in his hand.

"What are you doing up?" he asks.

"I could ask you the same."

Dad tips his glass towards Mom, "Thirsty?"

"As a matter of fact, I am, that's why I'm up, but that's not exactly the kind of drink I had in mind."

Dad considers her comment for a second then asks, "What could be better?"

"I think I just want water," says Mom, as she grabs a bottle from the fridge and takes a big gulp.

"So why did you get up?" asks Dad, taking a sip of his own drink.

"I had a nightmare. I was dreaming about the night Adam died and I was startled awake by the wind. It sounds like it's horrible outside," says Mom, peeking out the window.

Outside, debris and sand blow around everywhere, the tops of the trees dance rhythmically with the wind. Mom covers the window back up with the curtain and turns to face Dad. "Is there a storm coming that you know of?"

"Yeah, actually there is. They say it's supposed to hit tomorrow. Heavy rain and winds up to one hundred kilometres per hour, so don't wander off far on your own, just in case. I don't want to have to come save you again." Dad takes a big swig of his drink, setting the glass down gently, eyes on Mom.

"Who said I need saving?" Mom tilts her head to the side, and Dad peeks at her bare shoulder that becomes exposed the more she stretches her neck.

"Sometimes we all need things we didn't know we even wanted."

"Is that so? What is it that you want John?" Mom takes a step closer to Dad. He takes one more sip of the whiskey, sets it back down again—looking at Mom intently, with purpose. There is no one else around, just the two of them, the only people in this world at this moment. Dad reaches for Mom's face and runs his fingers down her contoured lines, her nose, her cheeks, her lips—Mom swallows the saliva that accumulates. Dad brings his hand around the back of Mom's neck and pulls her shivering body forward towards his; he plants his lips on hers and the kiss lasts for a few seconds, growing in intensity the longer it goes on for. Mom is about to bring her arms up to wrap Dad in them when, suddenly, Dad pulls away, breaking the moment, ending the kiss. Thank goodness, I was worried this was getting out of hand and had prepared myself to shut my eyes.

"I'm sorry Clair, that was…uncalled-for."

"No, don't be sorry John," Mom reaches out to take his hand, but he backs away. Mom's eyes flinch at his reaction.

"It was a mistake, in so many ways, I just can't, I'm sorry," his hands are in his hair now, aggressively running back and forth from root to tip. "I think I had too much to drink, just forget that ever happened."

Mom stands frozen with her fingers over her lips staring at the floor, not wanting to meet Dad's eyes.

"I'm off to bed, I'm going to try to get some sleep before work, my head is pounding." Dad walks towards the bedrooms and stops, "I really am sorry about tonight, I shouldn't have kissed you, it was a huge mistake." He waits for Mom to speak, but she's still trying to hold on to the kiss, the hot sensation he left on her lips.

"Good night Clair," says Dad when Mom doesn't respond, and turns his back and walks away.

Mom wants to call out to him, but she's afraid that if she speaks, she'll lose the sensation, the memory that lingers on her lips, and besides, Dad is already down the hall and in his room with the door closed—shutting her out of his life once again. Mom remains frozen for a long time afterwards, standing with her back towards the wall, her fingers still running across her lips.

The morning news is the first thing that Dad hears when he walks out of his bedroom. The television is blaring, and he cringes at the sound and rubs his head. Turning the corner of the hallway into the living room, he sees Ameleiah on the couch holding a bowl of what looks like Chocolate Cheerios.

"Morning Dad. Whoa, you look like shit today," says my sister, honestly.

"Gee thanks, sweetie, you look lovely though."

"Did you sleep at all; because you look like you were up all night."

"A bit I think, but not as much as I should have, apparently. That nasty wind kept me up a lot, it was loud from my room." Dad stayed up all night thinking of Mom and that's why he didn't sleep, although he blames the wind.

"I woke up a few times because of it too. Have you heard the latest breaking news? There's a huge storm coming."

"I think the entire island has heard the news with that volume," says Dad, pointing to the television.

"Oops, sorry, is it really loud?" Mia reaches for the remote and turns down the volume from a setting of forty-three to twenty-two. Dad pours himself a coffee and sits next to her on the couch as they both watch the storm tracker on the news channel, the volume no longer piercing Dad's ears, but last night's whiskey still rings in his head.

"I'm going to miss you, sweets." Dad rubs Mia's head, but she swats his hand away as she has already run the straightener through it this morning and doesn't want it messed up.

"I'll see you at Thanksgiving, it's not that long away Dad, but I'll miss you too."

"Will you promise me to keep an eye out for your Mom? Push her to paint often and do the things she used to love."

"I'll try Dad. But sometimes Mom can be stubborn and if she's convinced about doing something, or not doing it, I can't make her change her mind."

"Fair enough. I'm not expecting you to perform miracles here, kiddo, I just want to know that someone will be encouraging her and pushing her to live."

"She needs more pushing to live, she hasn't lived in five years. Is it possible, Dad, to live without actually living?"

"That's a pretty deep question, you're getting all philosophical on me now, are you? But yeah, I imagine it is possible to live without actually living, it's often called depression."

Mia considers this. "I'll keep an eye on her, Dad, I will, don't worry. You know, if you are that worried, maybe you could come visit sometime?"

"You want me to go to Paris?"

"Why not?"

"When you and your mother leave here tomorrow, I don't think I'll ever see her again, at least not until your high school graduation and your wedding…in about thirty years."

"So, you're just like her. Stubborn in every way."

"Your mother is way more stubborn than I am."

Mom walks into the living room, and as she passes the spot where they kissed the night before, her eyes linger for a few seconds, questioning if she dreamed the kiss. She hears their conversation and raises her eyebrows at the two of them sitting on the couch, side by side discussing her stubbornness.

"Really? This is the morning greeting I receive? And for the record,

I'm not that stubborn, I just know what I want, when I want it, and how I'm going to get it…usually."

Both Dad and Mia look at each other and roll their eyes while smiling—Mom makes her way into the kitchen to get coffee.

"Have you started packing yet?" asks Dad, leaning back on the couch, both arms over his head.

"Yeah, last night. I have a load of laundry to do, and that's the last bag. So, I'm pretty much done," says Mia.

"I'm going to try to get off work at noon today so that I can be around to take you anywhere you need to go; I know there are some friends you want to say goodbye to in person."

"That's great Dad, thanks. I was thinking maybe the three of us could go to Rocky Raccoon for dinner tonight, since it's our last night here."

"Sure, that's fine by me, but ask your Mom if she's up for it, and if so, I'm in." He gets up to stretch, "I better go shower and get to work if I have any chance of getting out at noon." Dad reaches down to kiss Mia on the top of her head and heads towards the washroom.

Dear Adam,

Is there really such a thing as coincidence, or is everything meant to happen the way it's been planned by a higher being? Are we really in control of our own thoughts, our actions, or our emotions? Or are we simply vehicles put on this earth to deliver a message, and guided by powers beyond our comprehension? Do we have control over our own lives, our own bodies, or are we puppets put here to act a certain way, to play out a pre-planned, well developed, but sometimes difficult script called life? Hmm…this I wonder…

Love, Dad

CHAPTER 26

Conflicting Feelings

Clairah

I DON'T HAVE MUCH stuff with me, so packing takes all of half an hour. I lay the clothes that I'll wear tomorrow out on the bench in the room I'm staying in, Adam's old room, and take one last look around to make sure there aren't any stragglers lying around. Satisfied I got all the items I brought with me, I zip up my bag, making sure I leave enough room for the clothes I'm wearing today and my pajamas that I'll wear tonight. I have conflicting feelings about leaving, I know that it's best for us to leave, for me to get back to my own routine, my own life again; this is not my life here anymore, this has not been my life for many years and the more time I spend here, the more I'm reminded of what I lost all those years ago, of what could have been. My hardened heart is once again softening, and I'll do all I can to keep it as hard as possible—it's easier to manage this way. The conversation that John and I had the other night at the beach rings in my ears like a bell calling me to action. I was surprised by how deep in discussion we got. Generally, when we try to speak to one another we're having the same conversation, but each of us is speaking a different language and it's not one that the other of us understands—that night, however, had been different, enlightening, healing.

Rain crashes down outside the window on all things, both living and still, as if its only mission is to kill upon impact. It's a good thing the storm is hitting us today and not tomorrow, allowing us to still leave.

"Mom, come here… quick." I hear Ameleiah yelling from the living room.

"What is it honey?" I ask on my way to her.

"They cancelled the ferry for the next forty-eight hours. Listen," she says, pointing to the television and grabbing the remote to return the volume back to its original level of forty-three.

From the TV, the weather announcer, a tall, pretty blond woman who looks to be in her late twenties, stands before a map of northern Ontario, pointing to the areas that are to be hit the hardest by the storm that's coming; not today now, as first expected, but tomorrow. She informs the viewers that the wind from last night and rain we have today is just a precursor, and that the eye of the storm will make contact tomorrow, mid-afternoon. As a precaution, all ferries to and from the island are cancelled until further notice, at minimum for the next two days, if not longer.

Darn, I should have driven myself rather than leave my car in Tobermory. The woman continues on about how this is anticipated to be the worst storm in the history of storms for the island. Rain of up to sixty centimetres is expected to fall in a few short hours alone, rain changing to pellets at times. Winds strong enough to cause severe damage, however, are the most feared. Most homes on the island are older homes and are already in need of repairs and updating, a storm of this magnitude could cause severe damage to the neighbourhoods. I walk back to the window and stare out into the long street, to the front of us is the lake and I can see that the waves are in as much of a panic as I am, rolling uncontrollably especially for a protected body of water, crashing against the boats.

John's truck is in the driveway, he walked to work as he often does. I consider calling to ask if I can use the truck to drive Ameleiah around to say goodbye to her friends now, before the weather gets worse. I'm still determined to leave on the first ferry that's available after the storm, and I don't want her seeing her friends to delay us anymore than we will already be by then, but as I contemplate calling, a figure emerges from down by the water, and I realize it's him, making his way to the house. Water drips quickly from his clothes and hair, and so I grab an umbrella that's in the front hall closet and, without taking a jacket, fight my way through the heavy rain and wind to get to him.

As I approach, he yells, "What are you doing out here?" He has to raise his voice as the wind and rain are so loud they drown out the words spoken.

"I saw you walking from the window and you didn't have an umbrella."

"Clair, I'm already wet, what difference will the umbrella make now?" he says, gesturing towards his body, then lowers his voice and leans in closer to me, "but thanks, that was…sweet of you."

He takes the umbrella from me, it's hard to hold on to due to the wind pushing against it. The wind is forcing it away from me and reversing it, so instead of forming a protective shield allowing the water to cascade down over it, it creates a bowl-like shape that water accumulates in instead.

"Great idea with the umbrella, so glad we have this," he says, shaking it closed with a smile and for a split second our eyes lock—once again my mind goes to the kiss.

We walk back together, exposed to the elements as the cold rain beats down on our skin giving me shivers. The temperature has plummeted significantly, and I regret not grabbing a jacket before I left. The short walk to the house takes longer than it should due to the elements we are fighting, and as we walk in the front door I grab my hair into a ponytail and squeeze it to let the excess water drip onto the porch rather than onto the floor. Ameleiah comes hobbling through the front door with two towels, and upon seeing how wet we are, stumbles back to get two more.

Once inside, John turns to the television to listen. "Apparently this is only the beginning, and it's only getting worse, so we all need to take precautions and stay indoors," says the pretty news lady. I tell John about the cancellations and I'm not sure if it's my imagination or not, but he seems to smile.

"Dad, Mom wants to leave as soon as the storm is over and the ferries are running again, so I want to say goodbye to my friends. At least to Nena and Julie, so can you drive me there now?"

"You really want to go out in this weather?"

"Please, Daddy."

"I can take her if you let me use the truck," I offer.

John turns to me, "It's fine, I'll take her." He turns to Ameleiah, "Get your jacket, I'm going to get changed out of these wet clothes, and I'll take you."

"I'll come too, if that's okay." I say, as I take off my wet flip flops. "I'll be two minutes."

Now that I'm in dry clothes and no longer freezing, I grab one of John's jackets this time, having learned my lesson earlier. Ameleiah climbs into the back cabin of the truck, so I get in the front seat. The rain pelts down onto the window faster than the wipers can clear them away. There are no other cars out today, and we, too, should be at home where it's safe.

By the time we get back to the house, it's midafternoon, and everyone is starving as we have not yet had lunch. John decides to go back out to the grocery store to pick up some food. "It's a good idea to stock up anyway, who knows what tomorrow will be like, especially if it ends up being as bad as they predict. You two can wait here."

"I'll come with you," I say. "I want to pick up some snacks also."

"Suit yourself," says John, already half out the door. Ameleiah decides to stay home.

As we walk into the small grocery store, I run straight into Michelle—she stands with her back to me contemplating an avocado, but I can tell from her stance and the back of her big hair that it's her. As if she can feel me looking at her, she turns and drops the avocado back in the pile while she keeps her gaze locked on me, jaw dropped, shocked to see me. John must not have told her that I'm back.

In an instant, John is at my side, and he can surely feel the tension as it's thick, circulating in the stuffy air. "Let's go," he says, and grabs my arm before Michelle has an opportunity to say anything. She's left standing alone with a long face, next to the avocados. I'm not sure why John doesn't even acknowledge her, have they broken up? John leads the way to the freezer section, we didn't get a shopping cart but rather only grabbed a basket and soon, its contents spill over, reminding us that we underestimated how much food we need. I want to ask him about Michelle but bite my tongue—it's none of my business anyway. In the granola bar aisle, we overhear two workers talking and one of them is saying that the store owner is closing up tomorrow in preparation for the storm. This makes John want to buy even more food and soon, not only is our basket overflowing, but we also each have arms full as well. Placing all the items down on the conveyer belt we see Michelle once again, only this time I avoid eye contact and pretend that I don't see her, but I can still feel her gaze on me, burning a hole into my skin, deep within—her gaze scorches like fire. John, I notice, ignores her too: trouble in paradise it seems, a tiny smile forms that I try to hide.

Back at the house, Ameleiah and I each help carry in the bags so that John doesn't have to go back outside, although Ameleiah can only manage one small bag. The rain is not as heavy as it was earlier, and this gives me hope that perhaps the ferry will be running tomorrow after all. Still, the rain is heavy enough that just carrying the bags into the house leaves us each dripping wet again. For the third time today I change my clothes, and so this means that I'm no longer neatly packed like I was this morning. With clothes hanging from the side of the tub drying, I take a moment to sit on the cold floor and wonder if I caused this delay in my wanting to stay longer. I got what I wanted, what is it that people often say? Be careful what you wish for. Did I create this situation by putting these thoughts out into the universe? As I collect all the wet clothes, deciding that I'll put them into the dryer instead, I hear John and Ameleiah in the kitchen; they are making grilled cheese, one of Ameleiah's favourites, next to the chocolate cheerios. I don't care for it as much, but it's fast, easy and I'm starving so I eat the one that they prepare for me served with a side of sour cream chips. As I'm about to take another bite of the grilled cheese, there's a loud crashing sound coming from outside, I drop my sandwich and run to the front window to have a look, John and Ameleiah at my heels—a tree fell over on top of a parked car on the side of the road.

"What the…" John yells as he runs out the door. "Stay here, I'm going out to check if the car is empty."

Ameleiah limps her way to stand beside me, still eating her grilled cheese, arm swung over the crutch, her other hand slipping in through my own. "Mom, this weather is scaring me."

I pat her on the head, like I used to when she was little; she doesn't shy away this time like she normally does when someone tries to touch her hair. "It's okay honey, it's only a storm. It'll pass soon enough."

She squeezes my hand. "It doesn't seem like just a regular storm to me." We watch John searching the car as the alarm continues to blare.

Within minutes John returns, drenched again; there is no keeping yourself dry, not in this weather. He confirms the car was empty and suggests we stay clear of the windows.

"There are many mature trees out front, that wind is growing stronger and stronger each minute."

I grab him by the arm as he walks by and squeezes water out from his shirt. "John, are we okay?" I ask quietly so that Ameleiah can't hear. I don't want her frightened anymore than she already is.

He whispers back, close to my ear, "It's bad out there, I'm not going to lie or sugar coat it. This is one of the worst storms I have seen here yet, in fact, this is the worst storm I have ever seen anywhere."

Ameleiah has turned up the TV volume again and listens intently for updates.

It's a good thing we went to the grocery store today, but no longer having an appetite I throw out the remainder of my grilled cheese and go sit next to Ameleiah. John clears the dishes and joins us. The three of us are tuned into the news, watching and listening to the devastation happening all through the island. There are many car crashes reported, trees knocked over, hydro lines down, and within a second of hearing about many areas with no power, the TV shuts off. So does the running dishwasher, and lights; it all goes black and silent, save for the sound of the thunder roaring.

"Mom," I hear someone whisper in the dark.

"Ameleiah, is that you calling for me?"

"No Mom, I didn't say anything."

CHAPTER 27

She Can Sense Me, Feel Me

Adam

IT WAS ME who called out to her, me who tried to get her attention. It seems that it's when Mom is most in pain that she can sense me, feel me, hear me. She is panicky at this moment; her enlarged eyes give it away. She also won't stop playing with the hem of her dress, rubbing the fabric in between her fingers, letting it slide comfortably back and forth. She does this when she's nervous. It's still early evening, but the weather has caused darkness to blanket over the island, and so the house is dark, too. Dad is cautiously opening drawers and cupboards looking for candles to light, while Mom and Mia remain seated on the couch, arm in arm.

"Found some," says Dad, referring to the candles. He brings over three votives and lights them each with a matchstick. It takes him a few tries before he gets all three lit. Placing one on each end table and one on the main coffee table provides enough light so that my family can see each other's pain again.

I join them, sitting on the couch next to Mom. At one point she reaches out her hand and swipes the area where I sit, her hand going through my body as it searches for something but finds nothing. I miss them, all of them. I miss being able to give my big sister a hard time on purpose just to see her face redden when she gets angry, I miss my mother's warm and affectionate hugs, I miss my father's words of wisdom and guidance; sometimes I pretend that I'm still here physically and I talk to them like I would if I were alive, I even anticipate what their responses would be to my silly questions and quirky ways. I miss my family being a family, having them all together. This summer, I have witnessed many things that I haven't since before the accident; they have laughed, cried, cooked dinner together and, in some ways, lived like a family. I had high hopes that they would be able to overcome the tragedy of my death, enough to be able to embrace one another once again and admit their feelings. My parents have always argued over who is more stubborn, but the truth is that they are equally just as stubborn as the other, neither admitting what they feel for each other, still.

The wind outside intensifies and screams through the streets, taking with it everything in its path: signs, cars, railings; nothing is too strong for the wind today. My family can't see what I see, they don't know the things I know, so they have no idea that a few streets down a house is smashed to pieces, trees are torn from their roots and crushed like pieces of candy. The wind is no friend of ours today, the wind has a mind of its own and destruction is its only companion.

My sister is hyperventilating and breathing into a pillow, tears rolling down her cheekbones, so I walk up to her and with my finger wipe her tear. She reaches up to place her hand over the spot I just touched, only she feels nothing there, not even the tear she shed. Dad is struggling to take control of the situation, because he, too, doesn't know what to do. I try to give him an idea, to board up the windows, I put this thought into his mind and focus hard, until it penetrates into his thoughts.

"Wait here, I just got an idea," he says and walks to the back closet, carrying one of the candles with him to provide light. Seconds later he returns with a few pieces of wood and a drill and begins to secure the wood over the living room windows. It works to keep them safe, for now. As the evening progresses, so does the storm's intensity. With no radio or TV to hear the news, my family is living blind not knowing how severe this storm really is. Mom checks her phone periodically but doesn't receive any service. We're huddled together in the middle of the room, all four of us, and each one of them is wishing we had a basement to hide in, to keep us safe and protected.

There's a screeching sound. Down the hall, in the bedrooms, the windows shatter one by one and sharp glass flies everywhere, landing on the beds, dresser and floor. "What was that?" Mia cries, looking up into my mother's desperate eyes, only she can't see them as they are still in the dark due to the votives having long burnt away. Hopelessness hangs in the air.

"I'm not sure, sounds like glass shattering," says Mom holding Mia tight.

"I'm going to check, stay here," says Dad.

"No, please don't go. Stay," pleads Mom, holding his arm.

Before Dad can respond, there's another loud roaring sound, this time it's from the kitchen, and the wind that's destroying anything in its path outside is rapidly blowing through the inside of our house. The next window to smash is the one from the bathroom, the only windows left are the ones that Dad boarded up earlier. Before my family can even fathom what is to happen next, there's a gust of wind so strong that it caves in part of the house, causing floorboards to disengage, and walls to come tumbling down. Part of the roof is gone, leaving my family fully exposed to the elements outside, to the danger lurking about making its way in, to us. Dad grabs onto Mia with all his might, and crushes her under his body, protecting her from the flying debris.

He is momentarily knocked out but when he comes to, he calls for Mom. "Clair!" Dad yells in a panic as he continues to lie over top of Mia. "Clairah, where are you?" he repeats, but is met with nothing but Mia's anguished screams underneath him. Dad and Mia got separated from Mom when the kitchen roof caved in, and she, unfortunately, was blown across the room.

Dad tries to move to relieve some of his weight off of Mia, but he can't as he is trapped himself, forcing her to remain buried. The wind is deafening as it navigates through every room, whistling as it passes my family, like it's singing to them on high volume. Outside there is more destruction: boats come lose from the dock and sail away on their own with no one to guide them, sand kicks up and covers pathways, doors to buildings blow away. Listening to the wind holler, Dad closes his eyes and, in his mind, composes his daily journal entry to me.

Dear Adam,

I'm helpless. Lost. What I wouldn't give to have your mother and sister safe at this moment. I'd trade it all, my life and everything with it... then you and I at least could finally be together again Son. We could finally do all the wonderful things we talked about doing before you were ripped from my life. Wouldn't that be a glorious day to be together once again?

Love, Dad

CHAPTER 28

Trapped

Adam

IT'S WELL AFTER midnight and the storm is finally diminishing, decreasing its destruction while it makes its way out across the lake. The wind that only a few hours ago caused my father's house to look like a wreckage yard is a mere sixty kilometre per hour wind. The rain that pelted down on all things living and dead is now only a light shower.

The house might as well be empty to anyone who walks in, not a sound is heard from any member of my family; however, I can still feel their heartbeats beating in place of mine, I know they're alive, buried under the debris, fighting for their lives. Part of the house is gone, the roof is no more, and there is nothing recognizable in sight—it no longer looks like the loving family cottage we used to spend our summers in. I'm desperately searching through piles of rubble and debris, hoping to find my family. The debris is so thick, piled high, layer after layer, it's making finding anyone or anything impossible—I search again for their heartbeats, and even their thoughts, trying to find them that way.

It's Dad's voice I first hear in the faint distance, calling out my mother's name, his voice is a scratchy, desperate tone. He calls for her again, and for a third time but receives no response. I follow the sound of his voice and approach apprehensively, even though I'm invisible to them. It's dark anyway, so even if they could see me, they wouldn't be able to, not in this pitch-black destructive night. Dad is lying over top of Mia, protecting her frail, small body from sharp, piercing objects all around. Mia is quiet, not moving, so I reach into her mind trying to determine if she is all right; I learn that she is. Dad struggles using all his force to push two-by-fours off his back releasing some of the pressure off my sister, and takes a look around at the surroundings, his enlarged eyes revealing his shock. "Oh my God," he says, and our thoughts connect, and I can hear him screaming and begging for help inside his mind. He reaches down and gently touches Mia's shoulder; she's lying on her stomach.

"Sweetie are you okay?" he says, waiting for a response. When Mia doesn't answer, he shakes her again, this time a little firmer. "Ameleiah, wake up."

Mia moans for a bit, so this relaxes Dad some, it takes her a few minutes to speak and during this time, Dad keeps asking her questions, trying to keep her awake. "Dad, what happened? Where are we?" she says, finally coming to after Dad's last attempt to wake her.

"Thank God, are you all right? Are you hurt?"

"My shoulder hurts, and my back, and I have a headache but other than that, I think I'm okay." She brings her hands to her head rubbing her temples. "What happened here?"

"The house got hit by what I think might have been a tornado. Are you sure you're not seriously hurt?"

"I don't think so, other than… ouch, my head… that hurts more than I thought."

"Did you bump it," he asks.

"I think so. I might have slammed my head into the ground when you were on top of me." She looks around the destroyed room, the exposed sky, still with a hand on her head. "Where's Mom?"

"I don't know sweetie, she isn't answering me," he says. "I've been calling out to her a lot."

"Where was she right before…we got hit?"

"She was beside you, wasn't she?"

"I thought so, but…. Ouch, my head."

"Lay your head down, stay here, I'm going to look for your mother." Dad yells for Mom several more times but is met with more silence. "Clair, where are you? Are you hurt? Clairah, answer me." There's no response from Mom, and Dad's breathing quickens. He can't see anything, so it's impossible for him to search for her, and within a few minutes, he tells Ameleiah that he's dizzy and tells her not to move again and to stay put. He lies back down on one of the two-by-fours he pulled off his back earlier and closes his eyes.

I keep searching, weaving my way in and out of the piles of wood, dust litters the surface—her mind and thoughts still closed off to me. Finally, after what feels like forever, I find her, Mom, she is trapped under what is left of the large wood kitchen table. Her body lies sandwiched—pinned between the plank of wood and the far end of the wall that remains standing. I can feel her breathing, her heart beats slow but steady in the dead air. The top of her forehead is cut open, blood dripping from the wound down her face. I reach down and wipe it, look at my hands but they are still clean and not a trace of blood on them. I look over the rest of her body. Her legs, too, are cut, blood spilling onto the pile of mess she lies on. She is on her back with one arm outstretched over her head while the other remains tucked under her back, also cut open. Her eyes are closed. I enter her mind, this time she lets me in—she's dreaming of good times, of us being a family.

On the other side of the room Dad stirs, so I make my way to him. He, too, has his eyes closed, but at least appears to be in better shape as I don't see any visible cuts or blood. His body no longer covers my sister's so I can see what shape she is in—she has one cut on her face, but other than that, appears intact. I hope she, too, is okay.

Deciding that I can't do much more than I am, I head outside to check on the neighbourhood, it's daytime, I don't know what time it is, but it must be early morning as the sun is peeking through the clouds. The rain has stopped, and the wind is quiet once again; the tops of the trees no longer dancing in the breeze. There are several trees knocked over—they soon will meet their death. There are signs on the road, garbage and debris everywhere, but other than the destruction to our house the night before, there is only one other house destroyed to the extent that ours is. I take stock of my surroundings and realize that my family is lucky, they are all still alive, and one look at the house, or what's left of it, suggests that no one could have survived inside. From a distance, sirens blare from the first responder trucks as they make their way carefully up our streets, zooming past us to the next neighbourhood that needs help. Another emergency vehicle speeds down the street, this time a firetruck, but they, too, don't stop. I rapidly wave my arms in the air, hoping to catch their attention but I know it's a helpless cause, they can't see me, I'm invisible to all. We just need to be patient, wait our turn, we are only one family in need.

I keep walking a little further, surveying the streets again; the next street over is in much the same shape as ours. I begin to make my way back to our street, feeling anxious about being far away from my family and by the time I get close, neighbours from across the street are outside, frantically screaming, calling my parents' names from what used to be the front door. I tell the couple that Mom, Dad and Mia are alive, but Mom is hurt and needs medical attention and they should call for help, but they don't listen to me, no one listens to me anymore. I look over at Henry's house and it, too, got hit but doesn't appear to be as bad as ours. There's an oversized maple tree leaning on part of the roof, but other than that, the house is undamaged. I haven't seen Henry around at all though, but he's not my concern, only my family is so my thoughts don't linger on him. More people gather on the streets to check out the damage and I overhear one middle age man calling for help. "It won't be long Mom, hang in there, help is on its way," I say to the wind as it carries my voice and dissipates before it makes its way to her.

Dad, still lying next to Mia, continues to compose his letter to me in his head, eyes still closed.

Dear Adam,

When you were little did you ever have a dream that felt so real that upon wakening, you questioned if it was really a dream at all or if the events that played out so meticulously in what you thought were just in your head, really happened? I think this is happening to me now—I'm not sure—I can't be sure of anything anymore. I know Son that you understand; because when you were four years old, you woke up screaming one morning saying that you had a nightmare that you wet your pants in front of the entire class. You didn't remember that while you thought it was just a dream, the day before I had to drive to your school to bring you a change of clothes. So, you must get it, my son, you must understand the confusion and fogginess inside my own head unable to differentiate between a dream and reality.

Love, Dad

CHAPTER 29

The Deep Stabbing Pain

Clairah

THE FIRST THING I become aware of when I open my eyes is the deep stabbing pain coming from my head; I try to move, but I can't—I'm trapped underneath something, but I'm not sure what that something is. What has happened here and to me? Where am I? I can't seem to place my existence, and I don't remember what happened just before…just before what? I rack my brain for the last memory from before I ended up here in this place, in this moment, but my mind is empty, like a broken heart. Where's Ameleiah and where's Adam? I wonder—as if he hasn't been gone for years. I try to move my legs again but end up getting myself pinned deeper into the trap that has me stuck. My arms are tingling, almost numb, and my legs feel like they are no longer part of my body; I look down to see if they are still there, but they, too, are covered by wood, chairs, and by what looks like pieces of drywall. I try to concentrate to listen for sounds that might provide me with a clue as to where I am and what has happened to me, but there's no sound that will help me, other than commotion outside; although I can't make out any voices, nor do I understand what's being said. I look up and above me, where there should be a kitchen ceiling is the bright blue sky of an early morning day. I try really hard to remember, to think of something, anything that might help me to understand my reality, so I close my eyes and concentrate.

I am thirty-six-and-a-half weeks pregnant and heading out to the grocery store—worrying thoughts enter my mind as a mild pain forms in the centre of my navel. "Ouch," I say to John, as I hold my stomach. "You don't think that this could be IT, do you John?"

"Clair, you have almost four weeks to go, don't be so paranoid all the time. I'm sure it's just gas pains."

"Gas pains? That's your answer to everything. Besides, how many babies have you carried before?" I tease in between the stabbing pains.

"Yeah, yeah, I know I'm no model example here. Listen, on a serious note, it's too soon, don't worry, but if you're going to be panicked about this, I can go with you."

"No, it's fine, I'm fine. I'm sure you're right. I'll be back in about an hour."

"Okay, besides you're the one who's been through labour once before, I'm sure you'll know when it's happening again."

I consider this last comment and convince myself that he is right—surely, I'll know when the time comes. So, I head out to the grocery store, feeling less than perfect. And sure enough, once I arrive I know I am not fine by any means and, in fact, I am worse than before I'd left the house—the pain has intensified severely. I consider turning back, but I am here now. Why did I listen to him? Why didn't I just go with my gut feeling? Because John is always telling me that I'm uptight, overprotective, and that I need to let loose, that's why, so this is me trying to put one foot in front of the other to walk into the grocery store holding my stomach—all so that I can prove something?

By the time I get to the entrance, I can barely walk. I sit on the curb for a few minutes, contemplating what to do—walk back to the car, drive home, or go into the store, get what I need…and fast. I decide that I'll go for it, it's what John would do, so I follow suit. I figure I can be in and out before the next wave of pain hits. But the moment I pull the cart out of the cart return area, I feel a stab so deep I know this has to be more than just Braxton Hicks contractions. I bend over the cart, preparing myself for the next blow. Needless to say, the contractions are getting closer and becoming consistent. I manage to get my purse open and fumble inside, looking for my phone, counting in my head until the next blow. When I locate the phone under the mess in my oversized bag, I manage to slip open the phone case and unlock the screen with my passcode, but I can't dial my home number because the dial pad is a blur, one big jumbled mess of numbers. I try to rack my brain to remember where the numbers are situated on the screen and get the number wrong—someone I don't know answers, and before even apologizing for dialing the wrong number, the phone slides from my hand and smashes as it makes contact with the cement floor at the store's entrance. The next thing I know I'm on my way down too, but I manage to hold onto the cart as I tumble down—this helps break the fall. Still awake, sirens blare in my head; I hope they are coming for me. Strangers loom over me telling me to relax, saying help is on the way, encouraging me to breathe. During the next contraction, big manly hands reach for me and within minutes I'm picked up off the floor and on a stretcher and being carried to the ambulance; the paramedic asks me who they can call. "My husband, John," is all I can manage to speak before the pain takes over and I no longer remember the number I need to give them.

Two hours pass and I go through a completely different experience this time. Adam Bennet is born in the Brantford General Hospital weighing seven pounds, four ounces. As I hold my beautiful baby boy in my arms, my frantic husband rushes into the room, hair all dishevelled. He takes one look at me and his glance shifts to the baby, his face softens the moment he notices him. "Clair, oh my, I'm so sorry."

"Shush," I say, placing my hands to my lips.

"I should have listened to you. I'm so, so sorry. I convinced you that it was nothing when you clearly were in labour."

"John, don't." I say, waving my arms to silence him. "You had no idea, and the chances of me going into labour with almost four weeks to go and no prior history of an early delivery were slim. You couldn't have known. I didn't even know and I'm the experienced one here."

"I know, but still...I should have been more cautious," he says, kissing me on the forehead.

"Would you like to meet your son?"

His smile widens as he takes Adam from my arms and holds him tight, pressed up against his chest like a protective father should.

My thoughts are interrupted by John's frantic voice screaming my name.

"Clair, where are you? Can you hear me?"

I can hear his anguished screams, but I can't answer as I don't have the energy to speak. I barely manage a soft whisper. "John, I'm here." I wait for a response, some indication that he can hear me, but his desperate pleas continue to bounce off the debris.

"Clair, Clairah, for God's sake, where are you?"

"Is Mom not okay?"

"I don't know sweetie; she's not answering. Stay here, don't move it's dangerous."

"John, I'm here," I whisper a second time.

"Where are you going Dad?"

"I have to try to find her. She must be stuck under something. Stay here. I mean it, you could get hurt moving around here. There are many sharp objects."

John must be shuffling through the rubble; I can hear him tossing things aside, but instead of getting closer to me, his voice, as he continues to talk to Ameleiah, grows further and further away. Breathing is difficult—I realize I'm barricaded between two hard objects, and the leg of a chair pushes up against my chest, suffocating me slowly.

CHAPTER 30

Lost Track of Time

Adam

"HAVE YOU FOUND her yet?" asks my sister as she lays in the exact same spot, waiting for our father to return and hopefully with our mother, unhurt, safe.

"Not yet sweetie, but don't worry, I'll find her."

"Dad, I'm scared."

"I know, but you need to trust me and stay put, help should be here soon."

"How long have we been stuck here?"

"I'm not sure sweetie, I lost track of time, I've been in and out myself, but it looks like it's morning now."

"What if the entire island is destroyed, like our home is? What if there's no one left to help us? What if we're all alone."

"Sweetie, stop. It's not, I peeked outside, there's minimal damage to the other houses nearby, looks like we got the brunt of it."

As Dad continues to turn over every piece of drywall, wood, and furniture, his spirit sinks but he tries to remain positive for Mia's sake. He continues to call out for Mom, with no response. He's limping, his leg is injured from being crushed under the television cabinet, but he doesn't stop, not at all. I try to put thoughts into his head, to get him to shift direction, he's moving away from where Mom is trapped, instead of closer to her. My attempts at trying to reach him must have worked, because suddenly Dad starts turning over the wreckage in the opposite direction, heading towards Mom. He finds pieces of the television shattered, an unrecognizable object, and he finds the wall unit from the hallway smashed in the kitchen, instead of where it belongs. He looks around trying to remember where they were all sitting just before the storm hit and he turns his head to the right and spots the coffee table, flipped upside down, its legs pointing straight up to the sky—there is no more ceiling in this part of the house to act as a barrier. He makes his way to the coffee table, feeling hopeful as he knows this is most likely where he'll find Mom. He repeats her name once more, and this time when she answers, replying with just his name whispered ever so faintly, he hears her.

"Clair, I'm coming for you, don't move" He looks back behind him to speak to Mia.

"I found her, sweetie, she's here." He continues carefully making his way through the mess to get to Mom, to save her.

Dad tries to push the table off of Mom, but he's weak, he stops for a minute to think of another alternative, another solution, but nothing comes to mind, so with one more attempt, he takes a deep breath and gives it all he's got and pushes the table off of her, revealing her in a broken-like state.

"Clair, thank God, I found you," says Dad as he bends down to examine Mom closely. He frowns when he notices her cuts. "Can you talk? How bad are you hurt?"

"I feel like I got hit by a truck."

John smiles at her attempt at a bad joke at this time.

"Well, it wasn't a truck, but it was a tornado, I think."

"I'm so glad to see you John."

"You have no idea how happy I am to see you," says Dad, placing his hand on her face.

The two sit within inches apart, not saying a word for about half of a minute—eyes locked on each other; sirens break the silence and their moment is interrupted by three firemen with determined looks on their faces who are barging their way inside, looking for survivors. Dad breaks the trance he and Mom are in first by looking away from her and clearing his throat, signaling to the firefighters to come help. "Thank goodness, help is here," he says as he pulls Mom into him, holding her tight and kissing her forehead. The three firemen approach quickly and survey the area, but Dad stops them, "Please, one of you, help my daughter."

"Where's your daughter sir?" asks one of the firemen looking around the destroyed space.

"Right over there." Dad points to where he told Ameleiah to stay put.

The one fireman leaves to go to Mia, the other two stay to help my parents.

The older of the two rescuers bends down and speaks first. "The ambulance should be here momentarily; can you move at all?" he asks Mom looking over her wounds.

"A bit, but it hurts…a lot."

"All right, don't move until the paramedics get here, just in case something is broken."

The firefighter that went to tend to Mia returns. "Your daughter is fine, other than a few scratches and she's shaken up. She is, however, worried; she told me about the prior concussion after the accident, so we do need to monitor her for another one, but she's fine otherwise."

Dad lets out the breath he was holding. "Thank God, where is she?"

"She's outside sitting on the step, waiting for the ambulance."

Within minutes, more sirens blare and two ambulances are parking in front of our house. One of the paramedics tends to Mia first, making sure she is okay and takes her to the first ambulance; he then joins the others inside who are busy helping Mom. They place her on the stretcher and carry her out to the ambulance. As she passes me, her eyes shift up and down, measuring the length of me, then she says, "Just like when Adam was born." She shuts her eyes and reaches into the empty space where I stand as the paramedics carry her away—I follow closely behind, never leaving her side, she needs me and she knows I'm here for her, she is the one most open to allowing me in.

They place her inside the second ambulance with Dad; Mia is in the first ambulance and already on the way to the hospital. Mia's initial examination doesn't reveal anything problematic, but the paramedics want to take her in to be sure her leg isn't rebroken. I hop inside the same ambulance as my parents, keeping myself occupied, giving them privacy and space in this confined, small area. It's late afternoon by the time we arrive, and Mom is immediately taken in for an x-ray. Dad is fine, he was examined upon arriving in emergency; he just has a sore leg from being hit by furniture. Mia, too, is examined; she suffers minor scrapes and scratches but nothing else—Mom is the most injured; she suffers from a concussion due to being slammed into the wall, and requires several stitches on her forehead, leg, and arm. But nothing is broken, so the main concern is the concussion, and for this, she's admitted for at least forty-eight hours so that they can monitor her condition closely.

Michelle is on duty today; I've seen her running through the halls; the storm was less intense at this end of the island and Michelle had been working during it. Dad and Mia hang around for the next several hours and decide to leave as they need to figure out where to go now that we have no home. The emergency room is full, some patients hold their heads, others nurse a sore arm, some limp around—it will be a long day for the medical staff today. Dad reaches into his back pocket for his phone; it's still there and works, despite the many cracks that run from end to end, so he makes a call to the Queen's Inn to talk to Kelly.

He wants to know if the inn is damaged and if he and Ameleiah can get a room for a few nights. Kelly assures him that they are fine, and tells him she has one room available since some guests left due to the storm warning the day before. Kelly loans Dad her husband's truck, as he has a work vehicle and doesn't use it much, which she and her husband drop off at the hospital. The keys to his own truck are lost in the rubble. Kelly has a short visit with Mom, then gives Dad a credit card to use to buy food and new clothes; since his wallet wasn't on him at the time of the storm, it got lost. After saying goodbye to Mom, Dad and Mia drive in silence to the inn, with me in the backseat, both shocked by the events of the night before. When they pull up to the inn, there are several trees knocked down and there is cardboard blocking two of the windows at the front of the house, the two windows to the right of the front door, but other than that the inn appears to be untouched by the ravenous storm. It was also confirmed by Environment Canada that whatever hit our house, and one other house in our town, had not been a tornado like Dad thought, at least this is what the preliminary findings are—Environment Canada has confirmed that winds of up to one-hundred-and-three kilometres per hour came sweeping through our island; this is considered a violent storm that can cause widespread damage, so we are lucky that there wasn't more destruction.

As Dad unbuckles his seatbelt, my sister reaches out her arm and grabs him, preventing him from leaving the truck. He turns to look at her red, blotchy and tear-streaked face. "Oh sweetie," he says as he pulls her into an embrace.

"I'm scared Dad, so scared," says my sister, barely able to get the words out from in between the sobbing.

"I know sweetie, I know."

"Mom and I have a home, we have a place to go back to in Paris, but you…you're homeless now. What are you going to do? Where will you live Dad? Have you thought of this?"

"We've only just left your mother at the hospital; I haven't had a chance to think of myself yet."

"But Dad…"

"Listen to me, I need you to let me be the parent here, okay?" Dad climbs out of the car, Mia following closely behind. "I'll figure something out, but I don't want you to worry about me. It's my job to worry about you, not the other way around. Got it kiddo?"

Since I can read Dad's thoughts, I know he's acting tough but inside he's thinking to himself, *What the hell am I going to do, where the hell am I going to live?*

That night, after they each get settled into their double beds in the Catherine room of the inn, they lay in silence, thinking. Neither of them gets any sleep tonight.

Part way through the night, Dad awakens to search for a pen and piece of paper.

Dear Adam,

How much can one person be pushed, challenged so greatly that it reaches deep inside your core? There must be a breaking point, like a drop in a song. I'm still waiting for my moment for things to turn around…

Love Dad

CHAPTER 31

Hospital

Clairah

"I'VE SEEN MORE of this hospital this summer alone than I have all the years we used to come here for vacations," I say to Ameleiah, who sits on the edge of my bed carelessly flipping through the pages of a magazine.

She looks up briefly, still flipping pages. "How long will you be here for?"

"I'm hoping only one more day, honey. They want to make sure that I'm okay from the concussion I got from smacking my head."

"Does that mean we're still leaving tomorrow?"

"Well, if I do get discharged tomorrow like I'm thinking I will, we'll most likely leave the next day. At least, that's what I'm hoping for."

Since we already had a ferry passage booked that got cancelled, I was able to rebook it without providing identification. The only problem is that I don't have my car keys, and so once I get off the ferry I'll have to find some way to get new keys cut before I can drive home. John says he'll help me with that from here, make some calls for me. He also told me not to worry about the money, Kelly had loaned him a credit card to use until we could sort out our lost credit and bank cards.

"Where's your father?" I ask, looking around the room, realizing that I haven't seen John in the last little while. The last thing I remember was him saying he was going to get a drink of water, but he never returned.

She puts down the magazine. "I'm not sure, but I can go find him if you need him."

"That's okay honey, I was just wondering. Has he mentioned anything more about the inn? Did it suffer much damage from the storm? I know that's where you two stayed last night and where you're staying again tonight, but I'm just curious how it held up."

"Dad actually talked to Aunt Kelly this morning about him staying there for a while, until he can reconstruct his house, and yes, it's fine; other than a couple broken windows and knocked down trees, it didn't get touched."

"That's a relief. I'm also glad that your Dad has a place to stay, I was worried sick."

"Trust me Mom, so was I."

"Wasn't the inn full though, how did Kelly manage to have a vacant room?" I think back to my failed attempts at trying to book a room myself earlier in the summer.

"Kelly said that a few of the guests checked out just before the storm hit, they didn't want to be stuck here on the island during the storm."

There's a light knock on the door as it opens wide. "Hey, there's my girls," says John, all smiley and chipper—or at least he's trying to appear chipper. "How's your head feeling Clair?"

His words echo in my ears—he just said, 'my girls' and I wonder if he even realizes his choice of words. He used to always refer to Ameleiah and me as 'his girls' when we were a family; I haven't heard him say that in five years.

"It still hurts quite a bit, but not as much as yesterday," I say, holding my head out of habit now.

"That's good to hear. By tomorrow it should be even less painful." His expression softens and he sits on the edge of the bed, reaches out and takes my small hand in his large one. "Clair, I have to tell you something." He clears his throat once, "Henry is gone, he didn't make it."

I search his face, and his eyes reveal it all.

"He's dead?" I ask.

"Yeah, he is. He hit his head on something sharp at one point during the storm, he lost a lot of blood quickly, and he was dead by the time he was discovered."

I don't say anything, I just keep my eyes focussed on my hand inside of John's, not knowing what to feel and yet feeling overwhelmed all at once.

"He won't bother you anymore now, Clair. It's over."

"I know, but still…" It's my turn to clear my throat. "He still didn't deserve death."

John doesn't respond but instead turns to our daughter. "We better go kiddo, it's getting late and we have to get some food into you soon. It's been a while since you've eaten."

"I'm not hungry, and I'd rather stay here a bit longer with Mom."

"Your mother needs to rest, too, let's go. Actually," says John with pleading eyes, "can you give your mother and I a minute alone?"

She grabs the magazine and clutches it tight. "Sure, I'll wait outside. I love you Mom, I'll be back in the morning,"

"I love you more, honey."

My daughter bends slightly to kiss my forehead, like a mother kisses her child before bed, and John and I are left alone, once again. I look over the top of his shoulder, pretending I'm focusing on a nurse, trying to get her attention, trying to forget the kiss. John turns around to see what I'm staring at and finds nothing but the sink at the front of the room by the door.

He raises his eyebrows. "What are you looking at?"

"Nothing, I thought I saw my nurse pass by, that's all," I lie.

"I can go get one if you need something," he offers as he gestures towards the door.

"No, that's okay, I can talk to her later. It's not important. So, what did you want to talk to me about?"

"What do you mean?" he asks, scratching his chin.

"You told Ameleiah to give us some time alone." My voice is low, afraid that Ameleiah might be outside the door listening.

John pauses for a moment. "Nothing in particular, I only want a few moments alone with you, that's all. How are you feeling about Henry? Now that you've had a few minutes to process it."

I lower my gaze to my feet; they peek out from under the blanket and dangle at the edge of my bed. "Well, I'm safe from him I suppose, although I'm not sure what I'm supposed to feel right now. I feel sorry for him, he had issues, he needed help."

"Yeah, he did, but I'm glad you'll be safe now."

I risk a glance at his face, and his eyes stare back at me, pleading with me; my pulse is racing, my heart beats fast, and I worry that the monitor that I'm hooked up to will alert the nurses of my racing heart. I curl up my lips in a fake smile and casually look away and back down at my feet, waiting for John to say something, but the only noise is the sound of the machines beeping in the next room, and announcements about different colour codes coming through the PA system.

The silence is broken when the door bursts open and in walks Michelle with a stone-cold expression on her face. John whips his head around to see who I'm staring at. "What are you doing here?" he asks in a sharp voice.

"I saw Ameleiah out in the hall, I worried you were hurt, so I wanted to make sure you were okay," she says, shifting her glance from John, to me, and back to John again.

"I'm fine, so unless you're here for a medical reason, you need to leave."

She frowns, turns around, and before she walks out the door looks over her shoulder to shoot sharp daggers at me with her eyes. Once we're alone again, John breaks the silence. "I'm sorry about that. Do you want to be left alone?"

Do I want to be left alone? I really don't know. I want more than anything to reach out and touch his arm, his face, to feel the warmth emanating from his skin. I want to pull him into my arms and tell him that I appreciate him, that I'm thankful for him, that I…that I love him…still. In my mind I picture the kiss, in my mind I can feel his lips on mine, but I remember losing him, him pulling away—telling me it shouldn't have happened.

"That might be best," I finally say, as he waits for an answer.

"All right, I'll go." He gets up to leave.

"John wait, I think I'm just tired. I'm sorry. I do want you to stay, but I think maybe it might be best if you leave just so that I can get some rest," I say not meeting his eyes—I don't want him to see the truth in them. He sits back down on the edge of the bed; he doesn't respond, he only looks at me, searching for the truth, the truth that I'm trying to hide from him. He clears his throat readying his voice, opens his mouth to speak, but closes it again leaving everything unsaid. He gets up off the side of the bed, pulls the covers up to my neck, kisses my forehead, and turns to leave. As he gets close to the door, my already racing heart beats even faster. What am I doing? Why am I pushing him away, again?

In a sudden panic I call out his name once more, "John."

He turns and says, "What is it?"

I hesitate, then say, "Tell Ameleiah I love her."

He looks at me for a moment, searching, turns back around, gently closing the door behind him. I want to tell him that I love him still, that I need him, but I remember the last five years and instead of calling his name again to ask him to come back, I bury my face into my pillow, wetting it with the many tears that fall for what once was that can never be again.

Partway through the night I'm awakened by a nurse tugging at my arm; she's trying to check my vitals. Looking out the window I see the dark sky and the stars gazing down on Earth, illuminating the world with their brightness. My phone hadn't been on me when we got hit, so it was lost in the debris along with my credit cards and identification. John had bought me a new one, a pay-as-you-go with the credit card Kelly was so kind to lend him. John felt that the phone was important so that I could keep in touch, so I take this opportunity to check the time—it's still early morning, or late night, depending on the perspective. I'm about to put the phone down on my nightstand when I notice a message on the screen, swiping the screen to unlock it, I read the text message from John.

John: Clair, I'm sorry if I made you uncomfortable earlier today. I only thought that maybe, just maybe we could have talked, but I know that was selfish of me after what you've been through—being trapped and the concussion and all

Then I read the second message.

John: Anyway, you're probably asleep now, and I hope you have sweet dreams. Ameleiah and I will see you in the morning

And one last message.

John: Goodnight Clair, sweet dreams

The last message was sent at just after two thirty in the morning and it's two forty-five, so only a few minutes ago. What's he doing up at this time of night? I stare at the screen, debating whether I should text back. On a whim, I decide it's easier to hide behind the screen of a phone rather than speak in person, so I type using one hand as the nurse finishes taking my blood pressure on the other arm.

Clairah: What are you doing up at this time? I was asleep, but don't worry, the sound of your text coming in didn't wake me—it's routine time here at grand central. LOL. ☺ And you didn't make me feel uncomfortable; I was in fact uncomfortable, but not because of you, because of me. I have so much that I want to say, need to say, and I can't bring myself to commit to any of it

My fingers hover over the send button before I press it.

The dots appear, showing he's typing. I hold my breath waiting for his reply—the dots disappear for a few minutes, then they appear again, and his reply comes in.

John: Can't sleep, keep thinking about you

His last text makes me open my sleepy eyes wide, I read it again to ensure that I didn't misread it. 'Can't sleep, keep thinking about you', he texted. Does this text really contain these words? These six words could change, will change everything.

Then the next text comes in seconds later.

John: I mean, I worry that you are okay. You are okay right, from the head injury?

Of course, he's concerned about my health that's all. I read too much into it, read too much into the kiss.

Clairah: Yes, I'm fine, or I'll be fine after I get some sleep

John: I better try to get some sleep too

Clairah: Goodnight John

John: Goodnight Clair, sweet dreams

Clairah: Sweet dreams!

I included an emoji of a sleepy face to lighten the conversation; after placing the phone back on my nightstand, I wait for the nurse to leave before I close my eyes and wait for sleep to take me.

CHAPTER 32

With a Frown and Heavy Heart

Clairah

I WAKE UP AT seven with the sun beaming in through the oversized windows, and the first thing I do is pick up my phone and hold my breath as I check for messages from John—there are none. With a frown and a heavy heart, I place the phone back down and close my eyes for a few more minutes. I only manage another fifteen minutes of shut eye before breakfast arrives—scrambled eggs, brown toast, strawberry jam, orange juice and coffee. Leaving everything else untouched, I open the coffee lid, add a package of sugar, and close my eyes once again as I take that first morning sip—the best sip of the day. The lack of sleep will definitely show on my face today, so after breakfast I head to the restroom to wash my face. I'm relieved of all monitoring devices and intravenous fluids, so it's much easier to walk around. My nurse comes to tell me that the doctor is expected around ten and if he's satisfied with the charting results, I'll be released and will get to go home.

Home. I ponder that word for a moment—home sounds so final, so distant. At least the home that I'm thinking about—my home back in Paris. Suddenly I remember the storm, the heavy winds, the destruction, the cottage, and I realize I'm lucky to still have a home of my own. The thought of losing the cottage brings a rush of tears to my eyes, even though the cottage isn't mine, it's still a part of me, a part of my heart, a part of my family's memories. I remember the day we bought the cottage, it was so long ago, but feels like only yesterday.

John and I had only been married for six months, but we knew we wanted a cottage on the island; we always knew we wanted to spend our summer months here and celebrate our holidays by the lake. Manitoulin has always been home to the both of us. We wanted our children, our future children as we were still newly married at this time, to grow up near the water, to learn to swim here, ride bikes here, hike. We wanted them surrounded by friendly, semi-retired neighbours who spent the majority of their days sitting out on their front porch with a cup of hot tea or coffee. John had found out about the listing for the property from a real estate agent we had hired to do some searches for us.

John is home from work early and comes running through the house still with his dirty shoes on, screaming, "Clair, Clair, where are you? I found it. It's the one!"

I'm out in the garden weeding and raise my eyebrows at him when he rushes through the back patio doors with a smile reaching from ear to ear. "What's the one?"

"Oh Clair, you better sit down for this."

He holds a piece of paper in his right hand, his left swings at his side, unable to contain the excitement at showing me whatever it is that he has. I wipe my hands on my jeans, they are dirty from digging in the dirt. His words scare me, but his expression reveals happiness, excitement. "John, you're not making any sense. What's that you got there?" I point to the paper he holds tight.

"Here," he says, handing me the pamphlet with a shaky hand. I toss the shovel aside onto the front of the garden and stand next to him. I take the pamphlet from him and stare at what looks like a rundown, beaten up old cottage. "What's this?"

"This, my love, is our second home. Our cottage."

I search his face for signs that he's joking, but I find none. "A cottage?" I squint my eyes from the glare of the sun, examining his face again. I study the pamphlet, flipping through the pages. "You want to buy this piece of shit? I mean, look at it?" I glance at him again, sure that he'll see the same thing I see, but the only thing that stares back at me is his somber expression. "I mean, look at it. You did look at the picture, didn't you?"

"Clair, just hear me out for a second, you're going to love it. I promise."

"You think I'm going to love this?" I say, handing the pamphlet back to him. "This looks like both a time and money pit to me."

"Clair, you have no imagination. This isn't what it will look like after we move in. We'll make it our own, you'll see."

"Oh, okay, I get it now," I say, smiling.

"You do?"

"Yes, you've won the lottery. That must be it and how we'll pay to completely rebuild this old house." I say teasingly, knowing full well that he didn't win the lottery.

"Clair be serious. What's the problem with this one?"

"I guess I just expected something a little newer, a little nicer."

"We either pay significantly less for a rundown, fixer-upper that we can work on over time, or we'll be paying more than we can afford up front for one that's exactly what you want. We'll work on this house slowly, we will make a list and knock off one item at a time, it's more affordable that way. Within a couple years, you'll see, we'll have the cottage of our dreams and without having paid an arm and a leg for it," he says, raising his eyebrows, waiting for me to comply. "I can do most of the work myself. Come with me, I'll show you."

He takes my hand and leads me into the kitchen, opens the junk drawer and pulls out a pad of paper and pen and he begins to draw the plans he envisions in his head. It's not that the idea of the cottage is new, we have spent many weeks discussing it, and looking at properties, but I have a different vision in mind when I picture my home away from home and this rundown thing is not it.

I'm hesitant at first and unsure due to the look of the place. I'd always wanted a summer beach house with a white kitchen, a large white wrap-around porch with oversized steps big enough to sit on, and more gardens. But I also realize that he's right, a cottage like that would cost more than what we can currently afford. So I muse over the summer house on Water Street down the road from my beloved Queen's Inn.

I consider the plans laid out before me and take a deep breath, hoping I won't regret my next words. "Okay, we'll go look at it," I say, throwing myself into John's arms—he catches me easily. We make an appointment the following weekend to go look at it and also book the ferry, and the Queen's Inn for the weekend while we are going to be on the island. It's not peak season, so rooms are available.

After walking around the entire cottage, we both stand in the centre of the kitchen hand in hand. "Can we redo the kitchen? Not now, I know that, but eventually?"

John looks deep into my eyes and takes my face into his hands, "Anything for you, my love," he says. "If you want a kitchen with white cabinets, you will get it. If you want a big porch, I'll build it for you." He reaches for me and takes me in his arms then.

"Don't go making me promises you can't keep," I tease.

"Dance with me?" he asks, and we waltz to the silence in the air in the kitchen of the cottage.

"We're already dancing silly, but there isn't anything else I'd rather be doing and no one else I'd rather be doing it with than you."

In our room at the Queen's Inn we stay up until almost midnight making our list—and a long list it is. Then, sitting the next morning at one of the many dining room tables of the inn, I pick up the list and read through it as I sip on my first cup of coffee.

John and Clair's Cottage Renovation List:

Inside Renovations:

1. *Gut the kitchen. (completely) Replace the old dark oak cabinets with light coloured cabinets (preferably white) complete with dark granite counter tops, and an oversized island with stools to eat breakfast—enough space for four stools, stainless steel appliances, and hardwood maple floors*
2. *Paint the entire interior—ocean blue (reminds Clairah of her favourite spa)*
3. *Redo the bathroom, adding in an oversize soaker tub for the nights that Clairah wants to sit and read in the bubble bath. A full-length mirror would be nice too*
4. *Pull up the old carpet throughout, replace it with maple hardwood. The real stuff, not the click engineered stuff they are selling at Home Depot and Lowes*
5. *Add a shoe rack to the front hall and fancy/decorative hangers for the children's (the kids we will eventually have) jackets*

Outside Renovations:

6. *Add a white picket fence around the perimeter of the house*
7. *Add a fancy mailbox and next to it, a Little Free Library (Clairah loves these)*
8. *Replace the old broken-down railing with bright white ones*
9. *Replace the tiny dining room window with a large bay window*
10. *Add a sign reading "The Bennet Family" to the front lawn—somewhere where it's visible for all to see*
11. *Plant more trees for privacy*

As I read through the list, I smile knowing this list is long and expensive—one that will most likely take us ten plus years to complete. This is, after all, still just a cottage, not our permanent home and I don't know how much we'll be able to complete realistically.

John walks down the inn's staircase rubbing his eyes, watching me look over the list. "Good morning sweetheart." He kisses me on the forehead. "So, what do you think? Did you sleep on it?"

I had told him the night before that I needed the night to think about it, to be sure this is the right decision. I take one more look at the long, crazy, ridiculous list we created and answer him right away and with more conviction that I ever thought I'd have.

"Let's do it."

His eyes brighten. "Really, are you sure?"

"John, there is no one else I would rather go through this craziness in life with than you."

When John and Ameleiah walk into my hospital room, my memory fades and I'm brought back to reality, back to present and remembering that I'm in the hospital and the cottage is still destroyed. We never did get to many of the items on the list, in fact, in all the years we were there together we only ever painted, replaced the carpets in the bedrooms, and laid hardwood in the front entrance, but that was enough because we soon had Ameleiah, and a couple years later, Adam. By that time our home, hearts, and souls were full. Year after year we made empty promises that we'd get back to the list, but we never did; life was busy, other priorities took place. After we separated, I wondered if John would finally redo the cottage, since he took it over to live in full time—that's what he got in the settlement—I got the house in Paris, and he got the cottage; it was a good arrangement for the both of us, it created a much-needed distance between us. But John never did do anything more with the cottage either, I realized it only this summer, having never asked my daughter about it before.

John stands a few feet away from the bed as if he's afraid to come closer. "You haven't touched your breakfast." He's looking at the leftover food sitting on my tray, cold.

"I had coffee."

"That's not breakfast, here eat this," he says, passing me a piece of toast while still keeping his distance.

I grab the slice of bread from him and take a bite to avoid an argument. "Happy now?" I say, sticking out my tongue, trying to lighten the mood. He reaches towards me and wipes a crumb from my mouth, just like he used to years ago when we were an us, when we were a family, happy. His features relax and he brings his hand back down quickly and away from my face; there is a dull moment when neither of us speaks. Ameleiah stands a few feet away, watching us intently, not saying a word.

John clears his throat before allowing his voice to escape. "I've made all the arrangements with Kelly at the inn, we have a room there, so you'll stay the night with us. That is, if you're okay with that? I'm assuming you would be unless you have a better offer?"

"Yes, that's fine John, it's not like I have many other offers," I say, looking around at the almost empty room, waving my arms.

"Even if you did, no other offer would stand up to mine, after all, I'm offering you the Queen's Inn," he says with a smile from ear to ear. "When will you be discharged?"

"As soon as the doctor clears me. He hasn't been here yet, but I'm told he makes his rounds by ten each morning."

"Well it's a good thing we brought crossword puzzles." He reaches for the bag that Ameleiah holds, takes it from her and places three crossword puzzles and three pens on the breakfast tray and finally sits on the bed. Ameleiah pulls up a chair, still quiet in her own world and not speaking to either of us, while John and I sit on the bed solving crosswords and wait for my discharge order.

CHAPTER 33

Grief and Sorrow

Adam

MY SISTER'S HEART is breaking and so is mine; she's trying to remain strong and not cry in front of our parents, and so in an attempt to protect herself she remains quiet, afraid that speaking will reveal her true feelings of grief and sorrow. She has wished for the last few years that our family could have one more chance at happiness, and after seeing our parents here in this hospital showing concern and emotion for one another is confusing to her. She doesn't know whether to be happy or sad and if this can ever be more than what it is now. After tugging at her ponytail, that sits high on her head, she carefully turns away from my parents and heads towards the window where the sun's rays shine through, allowing the warmth to soothe her skin, she remains facing the sun and wipes a tear that has slipped from her eye. After she does this, she glances up to check if our parents have noticed her tears, but they are consumed with their puzzles to notice—Ameleiah might as well be invisible at the moment. Anyone walking into this room would think that the three of them were a family, a real family — one that lives together in the same house and shares each other's lives. Anyone would assume that Mia's grim face was due to boredom rather than sorrow. They would think, *What a picture-perfect family*. The only problem is that a picture never tells the real story; it's only a snapshot of what we want the world to look at. What lies hidden behind the picture that we show the world is the truth we don't want anyone to know about or see.

Mom doesn't want this moment to end; she's deep in thought pretending to focus on the puzzle, but every so often she steals a glance up at Dad and pretends she is just stretching. She's also thinking that when she gets back home, she might take up painting regularly. Dad also ponders over buying another sailboat—it's cute watching them, like little kids. It's so obvious to me what's happening and what they are doing, but to each other they are oblivious to the signs right in front of them.

Dear Adam,

Some moments in life pass us by without a second thought, replaced instantly by the next thing, the next memory—never to be thought of again, while others linger, clinging to our minds like a child in need—like you my son. For me this is one of those moments that I don't want to let go of; instead I want to cherish it for life, hold onto it forever, or at least for as long as I live because I know all too well that nothing lasts indefinitely.

There's no time like now to be in the present moment, letting go of the past and not thinking ahead into what's yet to come. I wonder my son if you have memories of your own up in heaven? Surely you must at least remember me.

Love, Dad

CHAPTER 34

Break the Silence

Clairah

I DON'T WANT TO break the silence between us, it's soothing, relaxing even, but I know that the doctor will be here any minute as it's already a quarter to ten. Once we leave here, things will be different, I'll be busy: confirming passages, making sure Ameleiah is ready, saying goodbye. This is the last opportunity for us to be together like this, like a family. I glance down at the crossword puzzle on my bed.

"John, can we stop off at the Loco Beanz when we leave, I want to say goodbye."

"To whom?"

"No one, just the place."

"You want to say goodbye to the business, to the building? I don't understand."

"More like…to the memories."

"Is that supposed to be a sentimental thing that women do?" he asks, shrugging.

Of course he'd ask this, he has no idea. "Something like that," I say, closing the crossword puzzle because the doctor has walked in.

John and Ameleiah leave while I have my examination which consists of several questions: my name, address, do I have any pains, and do I remember what happened. Satisfied that I answered the questions with a sound mind, the doctor signs off on my release. Ameleiah and John re-enter while I'm in the washroom getting changed into my new clothes that John picked up for me so that I don't have to wear the clothes I was wearing the night of the storm; the night I was trapped. I shake off that train of thought. Their voices are loud, so I can hear them talking, laughing over something that Ameleiah has said.

As I step out of the hospital's automatic doors, I can't help but lift my head to the sky—the sun is out full-force today, many traces of the storm from two nights ago linger, reminding me that the horrible night really happened; I move my head a bit too quick and the pain throbs from the back to the front, once more, reminding me that it was real, all too real to not believe.

John notices my discomfort and takes my hand. "Clair, you all right?"

This breaks my trance. "Yes, just a little dizzy, I need coffee."

"You know, Mom," says Ameleiah, vigorously shaking her head, hands on her hips; she's decided to join in the conversation after being silent for so long, "coffee doesn't cure everything. It's not the answer to all world problems."

"You're right honey, it's not, but it certainly makes dealing with problems a little less painful."

The Loco Beanz isn't full today, there are only three other families here besides us; the nice weather is not enough to bring back all the tourists that left, as part of the island is still in a state of reconstruction. The people who are here, though, seem unaffected by the storm. Next to us, a family applies sunblock; across from us, a couple shares a special moment while staring out to the water; and the last family has small children and they run away from their mom while she tries to feed them sandwiches. If only life were this easy, this pure. This was my life once, I remember when the children were little, before.... No. I won't allow my mind to go there any longer, I can't do it anymore. If I'm not happy with where I'm at in my life, then I must be the one to do something to change it, or nothing changes. For the past five years, I've been stuck like glue to a life I no longer want, a life that's not truly mine. Today is a brand-new start for me, a new day, a new opportunity, a new beginning. Why haven't I painted much the last five years? I had tried that one time after leaving the island, the afternoon Henry showed up, but other than that, painting was a lost memory to me. I ask myself this question when I already know the answer. This needs to change; I need to change. I will change, in fact, I already have.

"What can I get you, Miss?" asks the barista behind the counter, waiting impatiently to punch in my order even though we are the only family in line.

"Mom," says Ameleiah nudging me with her elbow. "Wake up, are you daydreaming?"

"Oh, so sorry," I say to the frowning barista, "I'll have a large-sized soya vanilla latte, no foam, no water please." After our orders have been punched in and the total calculated, I say, "Actually, I changed my mind, make that a green tea instead of the latte, please." The barista rolls her eyes ever so slightly, but I still pick up on her annoyance with me.

"Green tea? Mom, since when do you drink green tea?"

"Today is a good day for a change," I say, closing my eyes and letting the deep breath escape from my lungs; for the first time in the last five years a feeling of satisfaction with a decision I have made washes through me.

"Green tea, yeah?" says John, looking me up and down. I'm unsure if he meant this as a question or an observation. "When I first met you that was the drink of your choice."

"Yes, I remember," I turn towards him, "sometimes we just need to go back to basics, back to the roots."

Wanting Ameleiah to have some time with her dad, I insist on her sitting up front, so I'm in the backseat, my head pressed up against the window. The drive from the hospital to the Queen's Inn is quiet, save for the soft music from the easy listening station John has the radio set to. Ignoring the music, I focus on what's outside the window; I really just want to be alone with my thoughts and memory. John isn't driving really fast, so this allows me to soak in the island views, the greenery, the blue lakes, the full rounded trees.

There is so much beauty here it's breathtaking at times, even after so many years of seeing the same landscape—the island never gets old, its beauty and grandness only grows into something more precious with age, like a fine wine, bottled and waiting to be enjoyed. On a whim I pull out my phone and check the battery life, twelve percent; that will do. As we wait at a red light, I snap about ten photos of a lake so mesmerizing it almost seems enchanted with the shimmering water shining and blinding me. A passage from one of my favourite books comes to mind, "The Lake of Shining Water," as written in *Anne of Green Gables.* The photos won't do this beauty any justice, but I want to capture this moment, this memory because I want to paint this lake when I get home. As we continue to drive, I snap a few more photos of interesting landmarks and even take a few short video clips along the way. These are more than just photos and videos of my drive, this is a real and solid reminder that today I made the decision to paint regularly again, today I decide that for the first time since Adam died, I'll actually finish a painting. When I'm back in Paris, if I question whether I wanted this change in my life, all I have to do is look at my phone and the evidence will be here, reminding me of the change I want to make—the change I will make, must make, before not changing kills me.

I'm glad the Queen's Inn escaped the treacherous grasp of the deadly storm, its historical landmark and beauty still preserved for visitors to enjoy for years to come. It was kind of Kelly to give us a room, despite the storm I'm sure she had a waiting list this time of year. The inn is the place to stay if you are heading to Gore Bay, there's no other place like it, at least for me. There's no other place that contains that same enchanted state of mind that you are instantly pulled into when you step foot on its glorious, well landscaped grounds that will no longer be maintained by Henry: no other place contains its magical vibe. As John pulls the truck up into the driveway and parks along the side of the inn—the side that faces the kitchen window—I'm put at ease and instantly relax my stiff muscles. John drops us off and goes out to the store to pick up a few essentials for me; toothbrush, face wash, skin cream, and another phone charger. While he's gone, I confirm our passage for the next day, we are taking the first boat out in the morning, seven. We need to wake up by about five to make the drive, in time to be there early. Later in the day, we go to the marina for something to eat, it's reopened after having been closed yesterday for some minor repairs.

It's still early evening when we finish dinner, and when we get back to the inn, I tell John and Ameleiah that we are leaving early the next morning. This doesn't come as a surprise to either of them, they both know that this day, this moment, is coming. While I was in the hospital, John and Ameleiah had gone back to the house to try to save whatever belongings of Ameleiah's they could, but with most of it still being covered by debris, it was a useless effort. That night I sit out on the balcony and take more pictures and videos, more proof of the change I want to make just in case I find I need it back home. Before putting my fully charged phone away for the night, I remember to set the alarm for the morning, bright and early, 5:00 a.m. When the sun has fully set on the Earth, I head up to the room with the double beds that we are sharing. Ameleiah and I each take one and John sleeps on the small couch on the far side of the room. That night I sleep the most peaceful sleep I have slept in five years and, instead of dreaming about Adam, I dream of the lake that I have seen for years, but for the first time fell in love with earlier this afternoon.

When the alarm sounds playing my favourite jazz music, I'm already awake, feeling refreshed from a good night's sleep and ready to leave.

While I love it here, this is not my home, this is John's home now, and I have already stayed longer than I should. With no hesitation, I leap out of bed, already in the clothes I'll be travelling with, since I have no other clothes to wear, I head to the washroom to brush my teeth and wash my face with the supplies John picked up for me last night. John and Ameleiah are up by the time I leave the washroom. We all head downstairs together and find that Kelly has left us some home baked banana muffins on the kitchen peninsula. I'm about to make a cup of coffee, then last minute decide on tea again, remembering my promise to myself. I take a muffin with me, wrapping it up in a paper towel. We don't have any bags to carry, as almost everything got destroyed, so it's just the three of us in Kelly's husband's truck, with the quietness of the early morning drive once again. I'm not sure if it's because they are tired or just want the calm drive, but neither Ameleiah nor John says a word as I slowly munch on my muffin. When we pull up to South Baymouth, the ferry is already here, and people are lined up ready to board. They haven't yet opened the ferry's mouth to allow passengers in, another twenty minutes the announcement had said, so we decide to go to the souvenir store and restaurant to kill some time. I expect John to leave now, but he doesn't; instead, he announces that he'll come with us.

"You don't have to," I say with a soft voice.

"I want to."

Ameleiah has walked on ahead saying she wants to get a few souvenirs for some of her friends back home; John and I are left alone outside the store. There's a moment, a brief second in time when he looks me directly in the eye, and for that instant, I wonder if he will ask me to stay, if he will kiss me again, but this time not say it was a mistake. I hold my breath, waiting for the words to leave his lips but they remain hidden, locked inside; instead, he shakes his head slightly from side to side as if he's tossing away a thought that he doesn't want to have. He reaches to open the door and we walk into the store side by side, the moment between us lost, forgotten—like the last five years.

CHAPTER 35

Contemplating Life

Adam

PASSENGERS WAITING TO board are called upon to enter the ferry and find their places onboard. Dad is sweating despite the cool breeze from the early morning wind thrashing across the lake. He reaches up and wipes a bead of sweat as it trickles down his face. He's contemplating life, past and present, and worrying about the future. He needs to make some serious decisions concerning his lifestyle, including where he will live. Kelly has offered to have Dad stay at the inn as long as he needs to get back on his feet, so he's not homeless, but the inn is no permanent home—he must decide if he wants to rebuild the cottage with the insurance money he will surely receive, or start over someplace fresh—perhaps even off the island. Memories of me and my sister happily running through the cottage seep into his cloudy mind, making the decision all that much more difficult. He knows he needs to let Mom go—despite what his heart tells him; his head warns him to stay quiet and not speak the delicate words that sit trapped inside his heart. He has realized over the course of this summer that Mom is in love with the idea of no longer being in love. He sees a transformation in her since the night of the storm, and especially today, a change that brings both hope and sadness at the same time. He can't pinpoint what the change is and why, but he can only speculate that it has something to do with the events of the storm, and him. Sometimes, when one goes through a traumatic event it changes a person, and he's convinced this trauma is changing Mom's outlook on life. She seems different, not happy but content and eager; yes, it's eagerness that has been the biggest difference today. She seems eager to go back, eager for something, eager for anything…just not him.

Still inside the store, Mom takes her time picking out a bracelet, she's made up her mind on two bracelets that she wants, but she says she can't decide between the two. Her thoughts are more protected today, unlike most days when I can read them clearly; I'm not sure why she hides her true feelings when usually she's an open book.

"Mom, hurry up, we'll miss the ferry," says my impatient sister with a loud voice, causing strangers to stop and stare.

"What do you think, the pearl-like pink one, or the seashell one?" she asks, holding both bracelets up, one in each hand.

"The pinky pearl one, let's go."

She hesitates for a moment still holding both bracelets up, and places the seashell one back in its original box. She puts the pearl bracelet on her right wrist and moves her arm in several directions as if she expects the bracelet to take on a new form.

"Girls, it's the last call for passengers," says Dad, waving his arms and pointing out the window in a panicky voice.

"I think Mom's having a nervous breakdown over bracelets." Mia looks at Dad with a questioning look, eyebrows raised. Dad scratches his chin.

Mom lowers the bracelets and turns to the both of them as they stare at her. "I'm not having a nervous breakdown, in fact, I feel great.

I'm in a good space. Let's go," says Mom, pulling out Kelly's credit card to pay for the bracelet. "I've decided."

"Do you need a bag, Miss?" asks the cashier as she wraps the bracelet in tissue paper.

"No, in fact, you don't have to wrap it at all. I plan on wearing it now."

"Well, here you are, Miss, enjoy your new piece of jewellery."

"Oh, I plan to, I really truly do."

I'm blown away by this exchange as I didn't realize that jewellery meant so much to my mother, it never has before, at least not that I noticed. As my mother unwraps the bracelet from the tissue paper, Dad opens the door for his girls.

Mom slips the bracelet on her wrist, stops for a moment, looks up, takes a deep breath, and says, "I'm ready now."

Dad and Mia turn to look at one another, both silently wondering why Mom is acting so strange. A family with a baby buggy passes us and Dad stares at them for a minute too long, watching the three of them walk by in peace. He turns to Mia and says, "Kiddo, look after her for me, will you?"

"Of course, Dad,"

"I'll see you at Thanksgiving. Hopefully by that time I'll have another place." Dad lowers his head so that Mia doesn't see the tears forming.

"Dad, who will take care of you?" Mia bends her head to the side as they speak.

"I'll take care of myself kiddo."

"But…where are you going to live in the meantime? What are you going to do? I'm worried about you."

"You know I'll be at the inn until I can find someplace else to live, who knows maybe I'll rebuild."

"Really?"

"Maybe!" says Dad as he takes Mia into his arms. Mom watches the two of them joined together, and for the first time jealousy runs deep within her; she's imagining herself in Dad's arms—this she doesn't hide from me. Dad and Mia remain in an embrace long enough for one more announcement about passengers boarding. "All right kiddo, get going, I love you."

"I love you too Dad," says my sister as she turns her back and walks through the opening of the ferry's mouth, giving my parents time alone to say goodbye. Dad turns to Mom, but she doesn't take a step closer towards him.

"What a summer it's been!" says Mom, her eyes still glued to her new bracelet.

"Yeah, it's been quite the adventure that's for sure." Dad looks down at the bracelet also, still wondering what its significance is; he reaches into his pocket and pulls out a piece of paper.

"Here, before I forget," he says, handing it to Mom.

"What's this?" She looks at it and pulls a flyaway hair back behind her ear.

"It's a photo of when the kids were little that I found on the ground, outside the house when Ameleiah and I went back before picking you up from the hospital. It's a bit torn, but I thought you'd like to have it."

Mom lifts her head, her hand still on her hair, looks Dad directly in his eyes after looking at the photo. "They were so little. I don't think I've ever seen this photo before, so thank you," she says gripping the photo tight. "Some of it I wouldn't trade for anything, and other times I wouldn't wish upon anyone," says Mom, referring to the events of the summer.

"Yeah well, all good things must end, right? Isn't that what you once said to me, after Adam died?"

"Yes, I did say that once." Mom takes a half a step forward, she wants to embrace Dad, to have him hold her like he held Mia, but she also knows this would only lead to more insecurity, more unanswerable questions between them, more hurt, so instead she pretends to be shifting from one foot to the other. She glances at her bracelet again and draws strength from the roundness of each pearl-like piece. "Take care of yourself John."

There's a moment when I wonder if he'll speak the words trapped in his heart; will he say the things she wants him to say, but knows he shouldn't? Will she beg him to let her stay? There is no noise around them, no sound, no other voices even though there are many people around talking—it's just the two of them presently, alone in the world.

Then suddenly there's a shift again, and the world resumes its loud banter as Dad says, "Take care of yourself, too, Clair." He turns away and walks back towards the truck leaving Mom standing alone, hoping, waiting for him to turn around and take her into his arms. To tell her that he still loves her, that he forgives her for blaming him about my death all these years—to say that they will rebuild the cottage together, live happily ever after as family; to say that the kiss meant something and wasn't a mistake.

Dad, however, doesn't turn around, instead he walks with his back straight and shoulders pulled back, exuding a new confidence that wasn't there this morning. For a split second he almost turns around, he stops in midstride, then forces his right foot to move forward, leading him away from her, away from the life he knows he wants but shouldn't have, can't have. He wonders if she is still looking at him and waiting, but he fights the urge to turn around to check; instead, he pushes himself forward towards his future. It's only when he arrives at the truck that he gathers the courage to look up at the spot where Mom was only moments ago when he left her—tears welled in her eyes then. The spot where she stood teary-eyed is vacant; an emptiness fills his heart, and his glance shifts to the boat where he spots her walking onto it, back to her old life: a life without him. Satisfied that he made the right choice to not turn around before now, he starts the engine of the truck and puts it into reverse to back up and drives away from the life that he used to know: a life without her.

Dear Adam,

Goodbyes are not something that I have ever been good at, yet I seem to have much practice with them. Having your sister here with me this summer was therapeutic, she brings a new energy to the room, gives me hope and strength. Your mother, too, in her own way has helped me to understand life a bit better—she has brought a sense of clarity. While she says she has forgiven me for what happened, and for what I was never responsible for, I can see in her eyes that there is a hesitation, a piece of her still looks at me and sees you. Because of that I need to let her go, I need to set her free. For many years your mother was a bird who had lost her wings, only they have re-grown, and they are stronger than any wings she ever had before, and I must let her learn to use those wings once again—only then can she be free to be mine once more—only then will she see me as me and not you.

Love, Dad

CHAPTER 36

My Feet Remain Planted Here on the Ground

Clairah

(Earlier, just moments ago)

MY ENTIRE WORLD has come to a standstill as I watch John walking away from me, away from us. I'm surrounded by a large ferry, a few tourists, other families, but I'm alone. The boat behind me is taunting me to get on board and pulling me towards it to move on as I had planned I would, but my feet remain planted here on the ground, watching and waiting for John to turn around and come back to me. He stops for a split second, I hold my breath thinking this is it, this is the moment he will turn around and see me looking at him. This is the moment he will run towards me, take me in his arms and tell me he forgives me for blaming him for the death of our son all those years ago. My breath is still caught between my lungs and throat, ready to escape at any moment, the moment he runs back to me and embraces me, I will let myself free, but he continues on his way, stepping forward and never looking back.

"Please John, please, please, please look back at me. If you look back at me now, I'll know, and I'll run to you." I say in a whisper under my breath—begging. But he continues to walk forward, away from our life together and back to his own.

The tears that I fought while he stood before me fall freely from my face—only he can't see them, but despite the moment, the sadness and the tears, I look down at my bracelet, my new anchor, my strength, and I smile. I'm well aware that it was so close, he was so close to coming back to me, but even though he didn't turn around, I haven't lost him, in fact, I have found him again, just in a different way. While we might not be husband and wife again and live as family, I have found him after all these years. He's Ameleiah's father and I'll forever have a piece of him that no other woman will ever have, not even a future girlfriend or someday possibly even a new wife. We share Ameleiah, our first born, and that can't be replaced, even if he does have more children with someone else. I might not have him the way my heart hopes I would, in my bed, lying next to me at night, but I know that deep down, I'm still in his heart and he's in mine, forever. The two of us have a bond that will never be broken, a bond that will last forever. With one last look down at my wrist, I draw strength from the pearls and turn around and head towards the ferry ready to begin my new life, ready to finish my first painting again. I don't see John get into the truck, I turn away just before he approaches it, afraid he might be looking at me and if our eyes meet, they will be locked forever—better to never know.

I clear my throat, pull out my phone and flip through all the photos of the lake that I love so much and imagine being in front of a blank canvas again and actually finishing a piece, only I'm not sure if I'm referring to the painting or my life—perhaps both. The painting I started when Henry came to the house, I abandoned right after, so this lake will be my first complete piece in five years; my mind goes to Henry for a moment, and I silently say a prayer for his soul. I find my daughter, sit next to her, and stare out the window, mesmerized by the trees, watching the tips of their branches dancing to the wind once again like they did before the storm, only this time, they dance a little safer, like a waltz on a calm night.

SUMMER
Two Years Later

CHAPTER 37

Soul Searching

Adam

OVER THE COURSE of the last two years, Dad has gone through some deep soul searching; he and Mom speak often on the phone, sometimes they text too, but it's all cordial stuff, and mostly about Mia. Sometimes Dad asks Mom if she is happy, and when he does, she will tell him about her newest painting. That makes Dad smile, he likes to know that she is back to painting regularly—it had once meant a great deal to her and he is glad that she has found love again, even if not with him.

Dad's been living in a tiny one-bedroom rental house just outside of Bridal Veil Falls; he moved in shortly after the storm. The house is so small that the kitchen and living room are one space, separated by the kitchen counter. A small bathroom and tiny bedroom that barely fits a double-size bed are the only other two rooms in the house, but this is fine for Dad, he only needs a place to lay his head when he's not working and planning the rebuild. Shortly after the storm, he had hired a construction company to board up the house—the part that was still intact and not destroyed. A couple months after the storm, he got all the necessary paperwork in process for the insurance settlement and waited throughout the fall and winter of that same year, patiently, to hear back. The following spring, the insurance settlement came through and Dad hired a contractor to rebuild the cottage. Plans were made to begin construction the summer following the storm. The contractor had asked Dad for his plans, his vision, and Dad had reached into his back pocket and pulled out a handwritten list and handed it to the contractor. Dad had searched the debris-filled cottage for this list, hoping, since it had always been kept safe in his room, and when he found it, a bit torn and dirty, he realized it was a sign. The contractor had taken one look at it and said, "You want everything on this list done in phase one?"

"Yeah, every last item," replied Dad.

"Well, we'll most likely get the major structure done, probably even most of the outside, but the inside and finishing touches will have to be done in phase 2 the following year. I'm booked pretty solid and I don't think I'll get everything done in phase 1."

"I'll take what I can get from you. If it takes an entire year, so be it.

That summer, almost one year after the storm, construction started. And Dad bought himself a sailboat, not a big one, but one that he could comfortably live in until the house was ready. Convenient for him since the marina is still where he works. In July, when construction on the new build began, Dad was kept so busy working on his own boat, overseeing the contractors, and his day job, he didn't have much time for anything else. Mia did come up to spend a few weeks with him on the sailboat as well, but Dad didn't take the boat out, she remained docked the entire time Mia was there.

It's the end of June almost two years after the storm and once again the island is back to its full number of inhabitants, boosted by tourists looking to make an escape, to find a new place to explore and make memories. Dad is mainly focused on the finishing touches inside of the house; he's hoping to move in before summer ends.

Dad has not once thought of Henry since that tragedy, and while he certainly didn't wish upon him the fate he received, he is glad that Henry can no longer hurt Mom, and this is comforting—the restraining order wasn't needed in the end to keep him away. Michelle has forgotten about him; she's been spotted around the island with another man, so she hasn't been around to bother Dad lately. Dad has a new spring to his steps this summer that he didn't have before. He skips along on his lunchbreak up to the house one afternoon to check in with the contractors on the progress of the cottage.

"How much longer before the flooring goes in?" Dad asks his contractor.

Cigarette dangling from his lips, the contractor adjusts his toolbelt before answering, "Well, I expect by the end of next week we should be ready." The contractor looks Dad up and down as he pulls on his toolbelt again and asks what he had wanted to ask for a long time now.

"Who are you building this house for anyway? You got yourself a little family hidden down in that sailboat of yours?"

"Nope, it's just me…for the time being at least. Maybe one day, who knows, I might share it with…with someone."

"So, there is someone in your life then? I wondered, but I never see a lady around here, so I wasn't sure."

"Yeah, there most definitely is someone," says Dad, then he lowers his head. "I had a family once, well technically I still do; I have a daughter and she will be here soon—Friday in fact, she's staying with me for the rest of the summer here on the boat again until the house is ready." Dad has a gleam in his eye. He hasn't seen my sister for a couple of months; she had come up to visit back on the Victoria Day long weekend in May, so he is looking forward to spending the summer with her again.

"Well I best be going. I have a delivery I have to check up on," says the contractor, his deep voice hoarse, probably from smoking. Dad waves him off and takes a minute to look around at the construction site, it's the same place where the old cottage was, but after all the work, the house really does look more like a house than a cottage. He's on his lunchbreak so he checks his watch, unsure how much of his hour remains. It's twelve forty-five, so fifteen minutes left.

"I got to head back to work anyway myself. Have a great afternoon." The contractor has already walked away with his safety hat, glasses, and cigarette in hand.

Dear Adam,

The sun is out, there's a light breeze so it's not overly hot and many families gather around their sailboats ready to head out for a day on the water. I might actually take mine out later this evening after work, go for a little sail, barbeque some burgers while the waves crash up against the hull. Your sister is expected here again in a few days and I'm thrilled to go out on the boat with her, it's been years Adam, years. I haven't taken anyone sailing with me since that dreadful day...the afternoon you died. But there comes a time when living in fear and guilt, that the turmoil consumes so much of you that there's nothing left to feed the monster—without fuel, the monster dies, allowing room for new beginnings. I often think about going to visit your mother more often, other than just at Christmas, but I remind myself that I let her go and why—she is painting again, she is happy. Who am I to disrupt the peaceful world she created for herself, who am I to show up and cause instability, confusion—that would be selfish of me, wouldn't it, Son? Kids always have the purest and easiest answer to everything, so if you could answer me, what advice would you give your old man?

Love, Dad

CHAPTER 38

Welcoming it With Open Arms

Clairah

IT'S JULY AGAIN, the end of another school year and I'm back in my empty classroom packing up my belongings for the summer. Only this year, unlike the last seven years, there is a new hope brewing inside me. I'm no longer dreading the summer; instead, I'm welcoming it with open arms. I haven't even needed my therapist for an entire year and a half, those sessions stopped when I finally began living again. I have almost everything packed and I'm ready to switch the light off when Jeremy, the school janitor, peeks his head into the classroom. "Hey, Miss Clairah, just checking in to see who's still around before I lock up the school."

Placing the last piece of tape on the last box, I look up and say, "I won't be a minute Jeremy."

"Do you need a hand carrying that stuff out to your car?"

"That would be helpful, thanks."

We walk out of the classroom, each carrying a box; I have already made two other trips so there are already boxes in my trunk. As we walk side by side, Jeremy says, "You know Miss Clairah, you look good, healthy and happy."

"Really?" I look up at him to see his face.

"Yes, I mean it. I saw a transformation in you this year."

By now we have reached my car, I open the trunk to find it's already full, so I shut it and open the backseat instead. "Thanks, I do feel like a new person," I say, placing my box on the back driver's side seat; Jeremy does the same from the other side.

"I'm glad, truly happy for you," he says as he walks away looking for more teachers that are left in the school, eager to end his day I'm sure.

"Mom, that's so beautiful, the colours you selected work well together. I never would have thought that they would, but they do," says my daughter, as she looks deeply at my new painting. It's a replica of the lake I fell in love with during the drive home from the hospital that last time—after the storm, two years ago now. I don't know why it took me so long to paint this one, I suppose I was waiting for the right time, the perfect moment. I have painted many other things over the course of the last two years, mostly landscapes, images engraved in my mind from the time spent on the island two summers ago: the beaches, the trees, roads. There is one specific painting of the Cup and Saucer Trail, another of the Bridal Veil Falls, some of the cliffs, but this particular one of the lake I saved for now. The first painting that I completed was a replica of the photo that John gave me before I left, the one of when the kids were little, and it now hangs on my living room wall. Looking over the one of the lake, I realize why this particular one is so special, this was the one that would set me free, the one that would allow me to be who I really want to be. I poured everything into this one piece, my feelings, my heart and even a piece of my soul.

I know where this painting will hang, I can even picture the spot on the wall of the cottage, or house; I can call it a house officially as I know that John is fixing it up, expanding even. I did tell him that I didn't think he needed more space, more to clean, but he said if he was going to go through the work he might as well make it more than it was. I plan to send the painting with Ameleiah when she leaves at the end of the week, as a home welcoming gift for her father—I think he will like it, in fact, I'm sure he will love it. He loves that island as we all do, but to him it's always been home, the place where he wants to lay his roots and retire on his sailboat someday. John and I do speak often, we have an open line of communication that we didn't have before. He even came down for Christmas this past year and spent a week with us here at my house. It wasn't awkward at all, it felt rather normal. I miss him when he's not here, or when I don't hear from him for a few days I even begin to worry.

Ameleiah is still standing by the wall looking at the painting, eyebrows knit together. "How exactly am I supposed to transport this monstrosity of a painting to Manitoulin Island?" she asks raising her arms up.

"It's not that big."

"Mom, are you kidding me? Have you looked at it? It's huge."

I consider her words for a minute. It's painted on a canvas so it's not as if she can roll it up, it has to be transported as is. I scratch my chin, thinking. "Wait here." I head out to the garage and open drawers and cabinets searching for the tape measure, surely we have one. "Aha, here it is," I say and carry it back into house where Ameleiah is still standing staring at the painting, most likely still pondering how she will manage this piece and all her luggage by herself. I don't even remember the size of it, so I measure the painting to be sure: thirty by forty inches.

"Wow it's bigger than I thought."

"I can't take this by myself, Mom. It will be difficult for me to manage on my own. Can't you just get it shipped to Dad's? Send it through FedEx or Purolator?"

"I suppose I could, but I worry about it getting damaged in the process."

"Well, you'll have to wait until the next time Dad comes to visit then, he can take it back with him."

"But that won't likely be until Christmas, and that's if he comes this year, we can't expect that he will make the trip each holiday, he might have someone in his life by then." As I say the words, they almost get caught in my throat.

"Well, why don't you just come then?"

I'm not sure if she's serious or not, so I consider her question before answering. "I thought about it, actually."

"Seriously Mom, it'll be the easiest thing to do. Besides, you don't have class anymore."

"That's true."

Ameleiah walks closer to where I am, still looking at the large canvas. "I'm sure Dad won't mind."

It's been half a year since I've seen John, and yes we do communicate often via text and phone calls, but seeing him in person on the island will be different, more difficult, but I also know that after what we went through two years ago, we can face anything—even each other on the island. "You're right, I don't think he will mind."

That night I book a passage for myself on the same ferry ride that Ameleiah is taking, leaving two days from now, and I also book a room at the Queen's Inn for one night, I got lucky as there was a last minute cancellation. I follow up with an email to Kelly asking her not to tell John I'm coming. I don't want to assume that I'll be staying at the sailboat with Ameleiah and John, in fact, I think it's best if I don't stay there. I'll bring the painting, leave it at the house, stay overnight and leave again the next evening. So, knowing that I'll only be gone for one night, I don't bother packing my easel. I consider again if going back is a good idea, but I remind myself of how far our relationship has come over the last two years.

There's a cool breeze this morning blowing in from the north; the tops of the trees shake as if they are holding on for dear life. Ever since that horrible storm that summer, I grow anxious when the wind decides to roar its ugly head.

"Mom, let's go, we'll be late." This time it's Ameleiah telling me to hurry and not the other way around like it used to be. How time changes all things around us, even people.

When we arrive at the house—my old cottage— Ameleiah, unaware of the changes before her, runs down to the marina to see her Dad. They had been texting and so she knows that's where he is. In order to not have John drive to South Baymouth to pick her up, I had told Ameleiah to let her dad know that she had a ride from her friend's parents. After parking the car on the road due to the construction truck being in the driveway, I immediately notice the changes John's made to the outside. There's a white picket fence around the perimeter of the house, a fancy mailbox and next to it a Little Free Library. When my eyes set on the Little Free Library, I hold my breath unable to let the air escape. The old, broken down railing has been replaced with bright white ones, and there's a large bay window in the dining area where the tiny one once was. The only thing missing is the sign with our name—John's name on it; I'm only borrowing it. As I'm admiring the changes to the exterior, a construction worker approaches and startles me.

"Sorry Miss, didn't mean to frighten you," he says looking me up and down. "Can I help you with something?"

I shift from one foot to another. John still doesn't know that I'm here. I made Ameleiah promise not to say anything when she told her dad that small white lie for me—about having a ride from Nena's parents. "I'm looking for John, the owner of the house," I say, pretending that I don't know where he is.

"He's not here, he's at work at the moment, so not available right now. He works over at the marina though if you need to see him, you can find him there."

The painting is still in the back of the car. I could just leave it inside the house with a note and leave and not even see John, but something from inside my heart urges me to go inside.

"He's a busy man, that John." The construction worker hikes up his sagging pants and I pretend that I don't notice the unpleasant sight.

"This is quite a house he's building here, it looks lovely, so different from before."

He raises an eyebrow, "You saw the house before it got destroyed?"

"Yes, I sure did."

"Well, poor guy's been through a lot apparently, I don't know him well myself, but that's what I have heard around here. Got himself a new lady now, he's busy and doing all of this for her." At the sound of his voice mentioning a new lady, my heart stops beating. A sudden feeling of jealousy and hurt plagues me, but I once again look at my pink pearl bracelet and remind myself to be happy for him—he deserves happiness even though he didn't tell me about her.

"He told you that. He said he has a new lady in his life?"

"Nah, but I pieced it all together."

"I don't understand."

He reaches into his back pocket and pulls out a piece of paper, "Here." He hands me a handwritten, dirty, and ripped list; I recognize this list—I wrote part of this list with John many years ago. Some of the items on the list are written in my handwriting; this is our list. I stare at it in wonder.

"Well, gotta get back to it before the boss comes around and sees me standing here talking to a pretty lady. He won't like me slacking off on his watch." He picks up his sagging pants once more and reaches his hand out.

"What?" I ask unsure why he's reaching out.

"Miss, I need that list back," he says nodding towards the piece of paper dangling from my hands, so I hand it back to him and he leaves, heading in the direction of the side of the house, already yelling orders at the other workers.

I get back into my car, the list still first and foremost on my mind. I must not read too much into this, he simply likes my ideas that's all. I must have talked about the white picket fence so much that the thought is his as much as it was once only mine. Oblivious to what I'm doing, I turn the engine on and drive to the liquor store and select a bottle of white wine, head to the inn, the painting still jammed into the back. Once back at the inn, I go to the library on the second floor and select a Jane Austen novel to read, *Pride and Prejudice*, one of my ultimate favourites. I borrow a wine glass from the kitchen, pour myself a drink and carry it back upstairs where I sit out on the veranda overlooking the bay, and that afternoon I read most of the entire book, ignoring calls and texts from Ameleiah. When there's only about sixty pages left of the beloved novel, I set it down on the table next to the chair and head out to the store for a set of paintbrushes and paper; It's a nice evening for a walk and to paint.

Before retiring to bed, I send Ameleiah a text so that she doesn't worry through the night.

Clairah: Hey honey, got busy here doing some reading and painting. I'll come by in the morning

Ameleiah: I thought you left your gear behind?

Clairah: I got inspired and picked up a small set

Ameleiah: Okay Mom

Clairah: You haven't told your Dad I'm here have you?

Ameleiah: You asked me not to say anything, so I haven't

Clairah: Thank you. I'll see you in the morning honey

Ameleiah: Night Mom

I wake up the next morning to the smell of maple bacon sizzling in the frying pan—Kelly must be busy preparing breakfast for the guests; the wonderful scent of bacon works better than any loud alarm clock I've ever had, so I'm instantly up, showered, and dressed. After consuming more food than I can handle and two cups of coffee, I drive to John's house to drop off the painting. When I pull up to the house, there are many trucks parked in the driveway, many men rushing around with tools hard at work. The same construction worker from yesterday is here, he must be the leader as he continues to yell out orders, but his eyes set on mine and he quiets down, walks towards me, shoulders slumped, most likely from years of bending forward hammering. At least today he is wearing a different pair of pants, ones that seem to fall in the right place, avoiding a show like yesterday.

"Hey there Miss, you came back."

"I'm just dropping off something for John," I say pointing to the large painting I carry. "Is it fine if I go in and just leave this there? It's kind of a surprise; he doesn't know I'm here."

"Yeah no problem, go on through the back door, that way you stay clear of the workers installing new flooring," he says pointing to the back of the house as if I don't know where it is, as if I haven't changed both my kids diapers here, cooked many meals here, scrubbed the old walls.

There are more men here today than yesterday. "It's busy here today," I say.

"Sure is," he says, and he adds, "it's a bit busy around here today because we're trying to wrap up this job by the end of the week. John had wanted to be in the house by now, but we got delayed a few days, so I put on some extra men hoping to finish up before the weekend."

"I see, okay, thanks, and I won't be long." I begin walking away, then stop, "By the way, please don't say anything to John about me being here."

The construction worker nods his head and says, "I won't tell John that he missed the visit of a pretty lady, two days in a row, and one who brought him a present no less," he nods again and walks away.

I walk inside through the back door; it's new and no longer a sliding door like we had before, instead the new door is a beautiful, white, double French door that surely will be used to entertain many guests. This entire part of the house was rebuilt due to the damage and when I walk inside, I'm transported into a dream. I set the painting down against the French door, careful not to scratch the newly painted walls; the smell of paint still lingers in the air. I have dreamed about this house for so many years, it's all the items on my list, completed to perfection. The inside renovations are exquisite; the entire kitchen has been gutted and where the old dark oak cabinets used to be are new light coloured cabinets that contain glass on the last two upper cabinets, complete with darker granite marble counter tops, and an oversized island that has a built-in stove in its centre. Off to the other side of the island is an overhang with four stools, waiting for guests to be served and entertained on. Stainless steel appliances fit perfectly like a tailored glove into their designated spots, custom made for its owner. I run my hand along the length of the island and the smoothness of the granite is cool as it touches my skin. The inside walls are painted so the entire interior is so fresh—ocean blue, like my favourite spa, I reach and almost touch it to make sure it's really there and not a product of my imagination, but the smell reminds me how fresh the paint is. I walk down the hall to have a peek at the bathroom and find it, too, has been redone and fitted with an oversized white soaker tub, just like I love, for the nights that I want to sit and read in the bubble bath. Surrounding the tub is a granite ledge that can be used to hold many scent-filled flowers, and vanilla candles—my favourite scent. A full-length mirror hangs on the other side of the door; some lucky woman will use this mirror to check her appearance before heading out on a date night with my husband—ex-husband. The same granite from the kitchen is found here too, with a sink that sits on top—more like a decoration than a functional piece. The old flat dark carpet is no more and has been replaced with maple hardwood—the real stuff not the click engineered stuff they are selling at Home Depot and Lowes. I know I'm not supposed to go to the front of the house where the workers are finishing up, but I can't help myself, so I sneak a peek. Against the wall to the right of the front door is a functional shoe rack, currently empty, and decorative hangers are on the wall above it, waiting for guests to hang their jackets on. I bring both my hands up to my face for temporary obstruction, like a shield blocking my view. If I take a moment to distance myself, I can look at the redecorated space with fresh eyes, unclouded by memories and hope, but when I peel my hands off my face, I find nothing has changed: except it's all different.

There's a voice barking in my ear. "Miss, you're not supposed to be here, it's not safe," says one of the workers aggressively waving his hammer in the air, this isn't the man with the sagging pants.

"I'm sorry, I'm leaving," I say, walking towards the back door. I take one last look at the newly, decorated interior and new designs—my ideas. I pick up the painting and move it from in front of the French doors to the hallway, I look at it for a few moments and I'm content with its outcome, it will look spectacular hanging right here. Again, I almost run my fingers against the wall to feel for a nail that I can use to hang it on, but stop myself just in time, so instead I leave it faced out on the floor leaning up against the wall slightly. From behind me, footsteps approach, one by one; my breathing quickens as I fear it's the construction worker coming to tell me to leave again, but my breath stops completely as I hear my name being called.

I know who's voice it is.

"Clair," whispers John from behind me. He says my name so soft, so low that I can hardly hear him, his voice drowned from the banging sounds of the new flooring being installed. I hesitate, unsure of what to do or say; I wasn't expecting to see him at all, I had made up my mind last night and planned to drop off the painting and head back to South Baymouth to catch the evening ferry, but he's seen me, I'm stuck. Eventually I close my eyes for a few seconds, inhale and turn around, he stands about five feet away from me, quizzical look on his face; when our eyes meet, he tilts his head to one side and brings up his shoulder to it. His stare is soft but intense as he waits for me to respond, to say something, anything.

"John," I whisper back in the same tone he used to say my name only moments ago.

He takes a step closer towards me and I, too, take one step closer towards him; there are only two feet between us, thick air dissipating the closer we get. He shifts his glance to the painting behind me, then back to me, and we both smile at each other, the gap between us closing even more until there's no more space, no more distance between the two of us.

CHAPTER 39

Island Therapy

Adam

THIS ISLAND, MY island, is truly magical in its own mysterious way. It has the energy from deep within its earth to heal physically, the power in the stars to bring on much needed forgiveness, and the vigour in its air to allow new life to grow, blossom, flourish. Island Therapy—that's what this island should be called. If I had that power, I'd rename it to such, because that's what it truly is for my family.

Will there be an island wedding sometime in the future? Wedding number two for my parents? Perhaps, only time will tell. Time, after all, does heal all wounds if you only allow it to.

The universe, you see, is like a jigsaw puzzle, every piece having its designated place—only sometimes the pieces don't fit well together, but only because you have them turned upside down. That doesn't mean that you don't have the right pieces, but instead of forcing them, you should try a little harder to make them fit by flipping them around.

My body was never discovered, and while the cold waters of the north slowed the decomposing process, after all these years, it lies in the head of the sailboat still, but now as a skeleton and no longer human flesh. However, I'll never leave my family's side, I'll never be absent from their lives—I'll forever be a reckoning force, ready and waiting to take on whatever challenges they need me for. I have my eyes on them, always. I have never abandoned them, and I never will. As long as I'm around, they will never be lonely. I'll be here always and forever, watching, loving, and protecting them, only from this day forward it will be from a distance, from far and wide. I'm ready to move on, to leave this Earthly place and go to where I belong—with God. But I am and always will be right here in their hearts; this is, and always will be, my place, my home, my island.

Dear Adam,

Hope. It's only a four-letter word but one so powerful. It's what I see for us as a family. I can honestly say today that for the first time since you were taken from me, there is a hopeful feeling running through me. Sometimes we have to hit rock bottom in order to dig ourselves out of the despair and the misery that we end up in. It's not always easy, but with the right support, with courage and motivation from the people around us, we each can find happiness in the end, we just have to look for it, deep in some places, but it's always there waiting to be unleashed like the eye of a storm—we just have to be willing to take hold of it and embrace it; only then can hope perform its magic and transform itself into true happiness, only then can we find true bliss within ourselves. Sometimes, we search for things we don't truly want to find, only to discover it's what we've been looking for all along.

Love always, and forever,
Your Dad

Telma Rocha

THE ANGOLAN GIRL

CHAPTER 1

Lobito, Angola
October 1, 1975
Present Day

As I STARE out the dusty window across the angry Atlantic Ocean, I ponder what has brought me to this point where I am trapped in my home, fearing for the lives of my whole family. There comes a time in most people's lives when one must decide if they should stay or if they should go. This could be in relation to: a relationship you are unhappy in, a job that is no longer satisfying, or a friendship that brings much pain. For me, this decision is about leaving my home, my country, and all I have known and loved for forty-six years.

Angola is at war. It has been since 1961 when the War of Independence from Portugal first started. Angola is an African coastal colony, the Atlantic Ocean to the west and The Democratic Republic of Congo to the east.

We moved into this house less than one year ago. Eleuterio Carvalho, Leo we call him, is my love, my companion, and my husband. He wanted to provide a better environment for our family. He felt this neighbourhood was safer than the last one we lived in. We do not own this current house, we rent it. We have a house we own, the one we left behind, and it sits on the top of a hill overlooking the bay. Leo built that house with his own hands, and we now rent it out to another family. The income from the rental property helps cover this rental. I thought the house on the hill would be our forever home, until one day it was not. Now, instead of rolling hills and a faraway view of the bay, we live on the Atlantic Ocean and our backyard faces the unpredictable sea. It is a different landscape than what we had for many years.

This neighbourhood is more prestigious and luxurious, but prestige and luxury do not matter when you are in the middle of a war zone. War affects everyone, every nationality, every race.

My biggest concern now is for my family. Telma, my granddaughter, celebrated her first birthday only one month ago on July 29th. She is one year old, but still is, and forever will be, my baby. My oldest daughter, Anabella, Telma's mother, has a good, high paying job, but is often away working for a custom's broker. And so Telma is my responsibility, and I would not have it any other way. She clings to me as if I am her mother, and I am all right with this arrangement.

My youngest daughter, Natércia, is only thirteen years of age. I wonder if she will be haunted for life, or if she will one day forget this memory of war. My other children are older. Carlos, the oldest of my children is now twenty-four years old, and still lives at home. He has a good job and helps us out plenty during times of need. He put me through my paces with his mischievous ways when he was little, and there are many stories I could tell you. João is twenty, and he is the most like Carlos; they are both adventurous. And there is Armando, my youngest boy, who is eighteen. He is quiet, shy, does not make eye contact, and often does not like company much. And so, you can see, it is a full house with many mouths to feed during a war.

Leo and I have been together for twenty-six years, and it was he who picked me up from despair and brought me back to life. My wonderful husband is warm, caring, and forgiving, but he is also spontaneous and has a habit of starting many things but not finishing them. He is a dreamer, always hoping for the best.

But today is a different type of day. Today he takes no chances with his family. As he comes charging through our front door, he is out of breath from running up the driveway, and his eyes are wide open. I know right away something is wrong.

"Rosa, darling, where is everyone?" he asks as he searches each room.

"Quiet, you will wake the baby." I place my finger to my lips to indicate silence before checking the baby's bassinet to make sure she is still asleep, and she is.

"Where are the others?" Leo asks me.

"Bella and Carlos are at work, the others are most likely at the beach."

They love the beach, we all do, and it is a family tradition to spend each Sunday there during the summer months. Even now in August, during our coolest month, it is common for the beach to be full, but rather than swimming, most people would instead be walking, reading, and enjoying the breeze. The kids have always spent a great deal of time walking along the beach, looking for sticks and shells. They have always gone on their own, off on their own adventures, whenever given freedom.

"Why, has something happened?"

"Yes, the town is under open fire not too far from here. There are bullets flying everywhere. We need to get everyone back to the house; it is a war zone out there. Draw the curtains, lock the doors, and stay away from the windows just in case."

Leo begins to do what he instructed me to do.

Only days before this horrific day, I had been listening to our radio and heard of rebel troops moving west toward our town, but there had not been warning signs otherwise. Certainly not anything alluding to what Leo describes now.

"Rosa, get away from the window, it is not safe," says Leo.

Hearing his voice brings me back to reality. It takes me a few minutes to comprehend the severity of a problem and then a minute or so to formulate a solution, or at least a plan. So, it takes me a long time to get over the shock of hearing Leo's words. A ringing in my ears makes me dizzy and I stumble, losing my hearing for a minute. I then back away from the dusty window. Once I get over the initial shock that our city is under attack, I move Telma's bassinet away from the window for safety, before running out the back door.

The beach connects to our backyard, and it is here I search for Natércia, João, and Armando, my three youngest children. I am hoping to find them soon, here on the beach. I remember Leo had said he was going out to get Bella and Carlos from work. Because I was in shock at the time, his voice had sounded muffled, so now I question if, in fact, it's what he said. I search the beach areas I know the kids frequent, but I cannot see them.

The beach that is almost always full is deserted today, which seems strange. Perhaps others heard of the troubles in town and evacuated long before. Why am I not more prepared, more on top of this? I criticize myself. I am a planner, and I am almost always organized, but I am not so organized and in control today. I shake the thought away and focus on looking down the long, sandy beach for my children. Suddenly I remember Telma. If Leo left to get the older children from work, and I am out here, then oh God, oh God, Telma is alone. The thought stops me mid-stride, and I run back, tripping over a log on my way. When I return to the house, the others are already here. I say a silent prayer upon seeing their faces.

"Mother, where were you?" says João. "We came home and found Telma alone."

"I was out searching for the three of you. Your father was here earlier because there is trouble in town. We need to stay inside."

"Yes, we know, we heard people running along the beach telling everyone to get inside, so we came straight home," says Natércia.

With all the commotion and loud voices, Telma wakes up from her peaceful and innocent nap. I pick her up and hold her close to me while the five of us wait for Leo to get home. We huddle together in the middle of the room, and I wish we had a safer place to hide, but we do not. So we remain, waiting, and Leo returns within the hour. Both Bella's and Carlos' places of employment are not too far, so Leo manages the task fast. I now have my entire family here with me, safe. For now.

The radio broadcasts are keeping us informed of what is happening, and soon we receive confirmation of what everyone fears. Two of the main nationalist movement parties fighting for control of Angola are at battle with one another, right here in our own city.

Most of the fighting has happened further east, mainly in the mountains and jungle. This is the closest we have come to the war. Natércia, who is the youngest of the children, other than the baby, of course, is asking many questions. She talks a lot when she is nervous and bites her nails. We are all nervous, but at the young age of thirteen comes an innocence that clouds reality, making it difficult for her to comprehend what is happening. The older two boys, Carlos and João, are trying to appear tough, but I know my sons and I understand they, too, are scared and nervous inside. Anyone would be frightened in this situation, no matter how tough and strong you are, especially if you can hear guns firing in the distance as we can.

The hair on my arms stands tall, and fear crawls deep beneath my skin. I need to go to the bathroom so bad, but I hold it and do not dare go. I am afraid to move for fear I might bring attention from the enemy. I know this is ridiculous, but fear is overpowering my rational thoughts. What to do, oh dear God, I pray and pray today like no other. I have a strong faith and a close relationship with God and so I pray for peace that is long overdue, and I pray for safety. God has been good to me over the years. He has answered many prayers of mine from time to time. He has given me strength and courage to survive many ordeals throughout my lifetime, and I only ask today for the courage and strength to survive one more tragedy.

CHAPTER 2

Present Day

WE REMAIN LOCKED up inside, still listening to horrifying updates coming from the radio. It is now Day Two of hiding. I try to sneak a peek out the window to check if I can see anything, but I cannot see a thing, not from where our house sits. Out the back of the house, the beach is empty, and out front many palm trees block our view for any real distance. "This is probably a good thing," I say, out loud to no one in particular.

Leo does not want me anywhere near the windows, and he reminds me of this. "Rosa, get away from there at once, it is not safe."

Upon hearing his warning, I rush back to the area we designated as our safe zone. We push the furniture into the middle of the front room; this is the room with fewer windows. Since the back part of the house is most exposed, we avoid that area. We barricaded the front window as best as possible with furniture for additional protection, creating a small cave-like space for ourselves.

The second day of hiding in our own home is the most difficult, as the shock has worn off and reality sets in. I fear the unknown, and I also fear the news on the radio. I cannot decide if I am better off knowing or remaining in the dark about the evils brewing outside.

Everyone is antsy and wants to move around. Leo puts an end to this by reminding us of the dangers. On the third day, we try to convince ourselves this is not real, this is a false alarm, and the gunshots are practice runs held by the activists. But this is no practice drill or false alarm; this is real, and more real than we could ever imagine it to be.

To try to help pass the time, we play cards as a family. This is Leo's idea. He says it helps to soothe the nerves and gives us something else to think about other than the fighting outside. I join in some of the card games, but sometimes I excuse myself from the game to read instead, it is my reprieve. I love a good romance book, and reading now provides an escape from this dreadful situation into a new world with no war. An escape is something I desperately need now, even for just a few short minutes.

After the third day we get low on food, and I wonder how much longer this battle will last. I need to get to the market to replenish my stock, and I try to take a mental inventory of what remains in the pantry. In my mind I count the cans as I imagine them on the shelves. I am used to going to the market often to buy fresh vegetables, meat, and milk. Preserving food for a day like today is something I have always done. But as of late, some days even the markets lack food. We wait for hours in long queues only to discover there is no food left. This is an effect of the war. I tiptoe across the room and make my way to the kitchen, to our pantry to get more canned food for us to eat tonight. Everyone is hungry.

On the fourth day of hiding, the radio broadcast announces a story that brings a rush of tears to my eyes. It is about a young woman in her early twenties who had apparently gone out to the balcony of her apartment building to see what was happening, most likely due to curiosity. We are all curious at times, and sometimes we do things without thinking of the repercussions. This woman must not have been thinking straight going outside during a battle in the middle of a conflict. We listen to the radio announcer say the young woman was caught in the crossfire while standing on the balcony of her apartment building. It is a small building, with only five stories. This woman lived on the fifth floor. It is assumed that she was looking out over her steel balcony because she was found bent over the railing. The lower half of her body hangs on the inside of the balcony, and her upper body is slung forward, hanging on the outside. The railing itself is not too high, reaching below her chest. Red blotches stain the light-coloured dress she wore. As I listen, I place my hands over Natércia's ears to try and shield her from the story, from the pain it will cause; because as they announce this dead woman's name, I realize we know her. She is an acquaintance from town, and I often run into her when we are at the market. My attempt to shield Natércia from this news is too late because she has already heard. She looks at me with her big dark eyes, silently asking me if this is happening. She does not speak, but I know her unspoken words. I think back to the time, just a couple of days ago, when I too, due to curiosity, stared out the windows. Shivers run across my dark skin. That woman could have been me. That woman could still be any member of my family.

The Portuguese arrived in Angola in the early 1500s, and its new rulers set about establishing cities, towns, and transport routes, as well as imposing their Western European culture on a country steeped in ancient Angolan traditions. Over the ensuing years, there were also around one million slaves exported from its shores to places like Brazil and North America.

When the Portuguese discovered petroleum in Angola in the 1950s, this once poor country developed rapidly, both economically, and socially. Because of this rapid development, new movement parties became interested in the colony with three of them eventually fighting for control. On April 25, 1974 the Portuguese government granted

Angola independence in what we call the Carnation Revolution. Although Angola gained independence from Portugal, a Declaration of Independence was not declared, and so a new internal fight began. Angola was not yet decolonized, but that day, April 25, marked the start of a deadly war, a struggle for power resulting in the battle we face today.

Leo is now pacing. He does this when he is deep in thought. I remind him to stay away from the windows, as he reminded me. He remains quiet, not saying anything for a long while, before finally speaking. "We need to leave the country."

He found his voice once again.

I do not say a word back, but I look at him and then at the children as we sit in silence on the rug on the floor of our living room, in the little haven we created for ourselves. The only noise now is Natércia's anguished scream.

There is smoke outside our house, and I stare through the crack between the couches and window, watching the smoke rise, taking in the environment around me. This is where I live. This is where my children and my granddaughter live. How did I end up here, in this place, at this moment, in this situation? Has my life always been this unstable? I begin to think back over my life, and I start to remember how I got here.

The last thing I hear before my memories take hold of me is Leo's shaky voice, once again repeating those six words into my ear.

"Precisamos sair do país." *We need to leave the country.*

ACKNOWLEDGEMENTS

As with my first book, this one wouldn't be possible without the help of many people.

To my loyal beta readers and proofreaders: Elsa Daniela Miranda, Tiffany Guerra, and Sarah Graham. I hope you know how much I appreciate your honest and detailed feedback on my original, unedited mess of a draft.

To my editor: Catherine Muss thank you for finding things I never could, and for all the little extras you've done for me. I've learned a lot working with you. Your edits, suggestions and comments have strengthened the story to a point that I couldn't have got to on my own.

To my friend: Rhonda Forrest. Although we've never met in person, I value the friendship we've discovered through Instagram over the love of books and writing. Thank you once again for looking over my work.

To my family: My husband Terry and our two boys: Alex and Jenson. Thank you for always believing in me.

ABOUT THE AUTHOR

Telma Rocha is an avid reader, reviewer, and blogger. She documents and shares her reading and writing journey on Instagram and is an active member of various groups dedicated to promoting local talent.

Telma lives in southern Ontario with her husband and two sons. When she is not reading or writing, she can be found enjoying the outdoors with her family or sharing meals and laughter with good friends.

Born in Angola, Telma immigrated to Canada in 1976 avoiding the turbulent civil war that erupted there in 1974. These events are documented in her first novel, *The Angolan Girl:* The story about her grandmother's life from childhood through the early stages of the war.

Telma is currently working on her third novel. A contemporary family drama that will be sure to pull at your heartstrings.

CPSIA information can be obtained
at www.ICGtesting.com
Printed in the USA
LVHW111725230221
679751LV00007B/1730

9 781999 066741